Toki

MY LIFE, MY LOVE, MY LOSS, MY FAULT

Cover design by LaToya McCoy, H1 Publishing, Inc., and Keith Saunders of Marion Designs

Book design and production by Keith Saunders of Marion Designs (www.mariondesigns.com)

Editing/Typesetting by Carla Dean of U Can Mark My Word Editorial Services (www.ucanmarkmyword.com)

ISBN-10: 0615519717
ISBN-13: 978-0615519715

First Printing© 2012 in the United States of America

1098

This is a work of fiction. Any reference or similarities to actual events, real people living or dead, or to real locals are intended to give the novel a since of reality. Any similarity in other names, characters, places, and incidents is entirely coincidental.

Distributed by H1 Publishing, Inc.

For wholesale orders, please send an email to:
h1publishingorders @gmail.com

Acknowledgements

First and foremost, I would like to give honor to God, the head of my life, for blessing me with this gift that I never knew existed within me.

I would like to thank my husband, my best friend, my hero, and boss for sticking by my side and supporting me like no other. I love you, Hubby. When no one believed in me, you did. When I felt like throwing the towel in, you were always right there to pick me back up, letting me know I got this. You have given me the energy to keep going, and I love you for that. We started off as best friends for eight years strong. Then we fell in love, and now look at us. Husband and wife, and that's for life. I love you, hubby, with my heart and soul. It's us until they bury me, and even in my afterlife, I will always ride for you.

Shout out to my stepson in NC. We love you, LaLa.

I would like to thank my marketing team, the best in the game: Merk Murphy, Peeda Pan and Aja Frazer of Payola Inc. Marketing and Promotions Agency and Glory Boy Entertainment (GBE), our new family. Chicago, they know how we rocking.

Thanks to my parents, Henry and Loretta McCoy, for knowing my worth before I knew myself. While growing up, I could never understand why they were so hard on me, but now I know, and I thank you for raising me and encouraging me to be the strong independent women I am today. Love you, Mommy and Daddy.

I would like to thank my oldest sister for supporting and believing in me and always letting me know I have a little more in me to give to the world. You always had my back whether right or wrong.

I love you, Neq. Shout out to my BoB's, you know who you are. Love y'all like life. To all my nieces and nephews, I love y'all. Sorry, but there are too many of you to name. (LOL!)

I would like to thank my H1 Publishing team and my left and right arms, Octavia Elian and Mariela Lopez, for being there for me through every step of this journey. Thank you for always having my back no matter what. I love y'all like my blood.

I would like to thank my editor, Carla M. Dean of U Can Mark My Word Editorial Services, for having the patience with me during my writing journey and being the best editor in the game.

I would like to thank my book cover designer, Keith from Marion Designs, for making me the perfect cover. Thanks to all my family and friends for believing in me when I didn't even believe in myself. I would like to thank my best friend Emekah Hodge for being herself no matter what. We rode this long twenty years strong. We have a bond that no one or state can break. Thanks for lending me your face...(Innie).

And to anyone that I might have not mentioned, thank you for the support and love.

To all my homies and family in the overpopulated prisons, keep holding it down for the streets and the love of the game. Real niggas doing time without dropping a dime. Free Row. Free Hec.

Last and definitely not least, I would like to thank all my haters for motivating me to go hard. Gold star for all of y'all.

Dedication

"Death leaves a heartache no one can heal; love leaves a memory no one can steal."

This book is dedicated in loving memory of my dear friend, Katrina Hodges.
Love you, Tri. I will forever keep your name alive.

MY LIFE, MY LOVE, MY LOSS, MY FAULT

A NOVEL

LATOYA MCCOY

Prologue

The packed courtroom buzzed as the anticipation grew. The press, spectators, and everyone I knew waited for the verdict for one of New York's most brutal and vicious murders; one of the worst murder cases Brooklyn had ever seen. Although I saw the confident faces of my four defense attorneys, I couldn't ignore the whispers. The onlookers wore wondering expressions on their faces, as if asking, *Is she guilty or innocent?* As I sat next to the best legal team money could buy, I thought, *After this speech I'm about to give, there's no way the jury won't let me walk away from this shit.* I had four of New York's best; each lawyer charged me one hundred and fifty thousand. There is a price to pay when only the best defense team will do.

My first-chair attorney, Pat Goldenblatt, was a short, cocky, Jewish boy. At twenty-nine, he was partner at one of New York's top law firms. Pat's record showed he never took a loss. In the second chair sat crime lab specialist and New York City's best criminal investigator, Joseph Bain. Cheryl Baum, a psychology lawyer, specialized in determining whether a defendant suffers from psychiatric disorders and if the murder was premeditated. Last but not least, there was my favorite lawyer Charles Miller, who specialized in criminal mind analysis. The media went into a frenzy when my trial began. I guess I shocked everyone when I showed up in court with my own dream team, each lawyer solid in their fields and virtually unstoppable.

"All rise! Court is in session. The honorable Judge White presiding," the bailiff said as the crowd fell silent.

The judge sat down and everyone followed suit.

The bailiff continued. "Docket number 4-5-7-4-2, New York State versus Toki Smith on trial for murder in the first degree."

It was day three of my trial, and my hands were soaked from sweating. It was my turn to take the stand and finally tell my side of the story. I was lost in my thoughts and couldn't really concentrate on all that was going on around me.

"You may call your next witness, Mr. Ross," Judge White said.

"I call the defendant, Toki Smith, to the stand."

As I stood, my knees shook. Nervous, I hoped the jury didn't notice how scared I was. Damn! Walking to the witness stand was like walking to the electric chair. *All eyes on me, huh?*

"Ms. Smith, please raise your right hand. Do you promise to tell the truth, the whole truth, and nothing but the truth, so help you God?"

With my right hand raised, I said, "I swear."

The bailiff nodded his head and said, "You may be seated."

Mr. Ross, the district attorney, stared at me for a moment before turning to the jury.

"Ladies and gentlemen of the jury today, I introduce to you the defendant, Ms. Toki Smith. Now, Ms. Smith, can you tell me what happened on the night in question of May 8th, 2008 at 8:45 p.m.?" he asked in his deep Italian accent.

I looked at Mr. Ross and the jury.

*****

"Yo, bitch! Come here! You hear me fucking calling you! Toki! Where you trying to run to? You know what it is, bitch!

You ain't going nowhere! What don't you understand? It's either you and me, or your new home will be six feet deep!"

He grabbed a pot off the countertop and hit me in the back of my head as I tried to escape. He grabbed my hair, which is something he liked to do often because he knew my hair was my weakness. He pulled me close to him as he wrapped my hair around his fist. I tried to run, but he had a tight grip. I was dazed; he had total control of my every move.

"Understand?" he yelled. "If I can't have you, no one will! You won't live in this world without me!"

He slapped me repeatedly, causing the skin of my face to split open. Once he noticed the blood, he loosened up. That's when I snatched my head completely from his grip, ran into the bathroom, and locked the door. Tears flowed as I bit my hands and tried to figure how to escape this man.

I can't fight him no more. I don't have it in me anymore. I'm drained.

I looked in the mirror at my bloody, busted face. He kicked the door and I panicked. I walked over to the bathroom window and tried to pull it up, but just my luck, the window only opened halfway. That didn't stop me. I tried to squeeze through the window, not giving a damn whether or not I ripped some skin. I just wanted to get away from him. Unfortunately, I couldn't fit.

Damn, what the fuck am I going to do?

I panicked because the window was my only hope. He banged on the door. Startled, I jumped and looked around the bathroom for anything I could use as a weapon just in case he broke through the door.

"Open the fucking door!" he yelled while banging on it.

This motherfucker is gonna kill me. This shit is fucking crazy! Why is he doing this to me? I mean, what did I do to him? Shit, I walk on eggshells around him trying not to make him flip.

"Toki, you fucking bitch, open the fucking door! Bitch,

you know I will kick this shit in!"

"Word! Then come on and kick down the fucking door!" I yelled, hoping my invitation checked him at the door.

"Oh, so now you gangster, bitch? Yeah, now that there's a door between us! Don't worry, I will be out here all night long waiting for you to open the door just so I can have the pleasure of beating you to death!"

"That's exactly why I'm not opening the door," I cried. "'Cause you're a liar! All these fucking threats and beat downs I can't do no more!"

He had the nerve to say, "If you open the door, we can just talk. I'm sorry. It's not my fault I love you so much."

He's trying to throw on the little boy charm, trying to convince me to let him in. This nigga thinks I'm some dumb bitch! Like I really trust him. We both know he's not sorry. He's never sorry. He will never stop.

I panicked even more when I saw the door slowly being loosened from its hinges.

Oh my God. Please help me. I feel like any day now my life will be taken from this earth. Oh God, please help me. Is this how I'm going to die, by the hands of this punk-ass nigga?

I looked at my bloody, bruised face in the mirror and tried to fight back the pain. I wiped the blood from my face and sucked up all my tears.

A voice said, *Toki, you have it in you to win this battle. You have too much to live for. You are too strong to have your life taken by a weak man.*

At that very moment, I knew what I needed to do. I made it up in my mind that he would not kill me, that I would not be the one carried away in a body bag from this shit. Shit, I had the right to protect my life by any means and at whatever the cost.

He banged on the door again. "Tokiiiiiii, open the fucking door, bitch!"

I trembled as I stared at the door.

He's a man, and if I'm not holding a weapon, it's my funeral they will be planning. God, please don't let him in. He's crazy! God, I know you hear him. He's fucking nuts. I mean, is there something I did that was so wrong in my life that I deserve this? I'm not supposed to be getting beat down by the man I once loved. I'm not the girl that a nigga is supposed to hit on. This is not me; this is not what my life was planned out to be. I give my all in a relationship, and I'm the one that has to go through this shit. No matter what I do, he will never leave me alone. I will never be free no matter where or how far I go. If he can't find me, he will find someone that can.

I tried to tell myself it will work for me one day, but I can't take this shit anymore. I'm NOT going to take this shit anymore. I know better than to sit around thinking this nigga won't put me in the ground. My brother always told me that when a man only sees the worst in you, it's because he's the worst for you. And when it boils down to you or them, get 'em before they get you. Never put anyone's life before your own. So, before I sit here thinking somebody is going to come save me, I have to save myself. So, fuck it! Fuck the bullshit! I'm going to sit here in this bathroom and wait until he falls asleep. Then, I'ma kill this piece of shit.

He banged on the door again. "That's okay, bitch. You gotta come out sometime," he said.

No one knew about the abuse. I stayed away from my family due to constant bruises and swollen noses. I was in this situation alone. I had to handle it like the woman I am. He told me that if he couldn't have me, no one would. So, it was up to me to show him what that threat did for his life, which was end it.

I sat on the floor and lay my head on the tub as I listened to the sounds of the house. While my ears listened for him to start snoring, I dozed off for about three hours.

Damn! This nigga has to be sleep by now, I thought when I woke up.

I put my hand on the knob and slowly turned it, hoping he was sleep and not standing in front of the door. My hands shook uncontrollably as I cracked it open just enough to peek out into the hallway. I fully opened the door and looked both ways down the hall. I heard the entertainment system playing "Here I Am" by Nicki Minaj. Strangely, it was on repeat.

I carefully crept down the hall towards the bedroom door. While approaching the open door, I heard him breathing heavily; he was asleep. I looked at him from the doorway as he slept in our all-white, European leather, king-size, sleigh bed. Rage grew inside me as he rested. I saw his bitch on the dresser and walked to the left side of the room where my black leather Chanel gloves lay on the chaise lounge. I slid my gloves on and grabbed the glock. I stood for a second just to inhale this new scent called freedom. I smirked at Qwan as he slept unknowingly.

I shook my head while thinking, *Stupid motherfucker never had a clue as to who Toki really was...*

Chapter 1

Welcome to My World - Back In Time

Why niggas feel like a girl has to ride or die with them while they cheat, beat, disrespect, run over, and mistreat her? They kill me. They want you to put up with their shit and take all they have to give. Just keep going nonstop: cheating, sneaking and all that other bullshit. Well, it's not going to happen…not this trip, not this time around.

Oh, I forgot! How rude of me. Hello, my name's Toki. I know it sounds like I could be half black and Philippine, but that's not the case. However, I always understood why a motherfucker would mistake me for a mixed breed, with my butterscotch complexion and exotic beauty. But, now that you got the vision and you can see me clearly, welcome to Toki's world. I'm that female that's seen it all, been through it all, and who feels she knows it all. This is my life, my love, my loss, my faults…

I grew up in the Bronx with both parents in the home, along with four brothers and one sister. We were raised in the projects, but not slumming and barely eating. Both of my parents worked hard and made sure our three-bedroom apartment was laced. If it weren't for the fact that we were really in the projects, one would think my parents owned a condo in the city with a doorman and shit.

My parents kept us dressed fresh in all the latest designer clothes. My mother was a shopaholic. I guess that's where I got it. My mother was also the lady in the projects that tried to help everyone she could. I always said my mother was a walking angel.

My dad and I were tight like that. I was definitely a daddy's girl; whatever I wanted, my father got it. My father was originally from Harlem. He still thought he was young, sporting his Air Force Ones and fitted Yankee hats. He had a few old crows chasing him, but my mother was the baddest bitch. And if she had to, she would pop off real quick, with my sister and I right with her.

We lived in the projects until I was sixteen. Then my parents bought a ten-bedroom house in Mt. Vernon, the town of the black upper class. I never really adapted to the town. It was suburbia, and there was nothing really to do. But, don't get it twisted. Mt. Vernon had its strong points, like the well-known strip club, Sue's Rendezvous, located about five blocks from my house. Sue's is known worldwide by any nigga getting money, whether in your hood or on the B-ball court. If you were a part of the who's who worldwide, then you've been there. If not, more than likely, you will never make it there.

I attended Campus High School in Harlem on 135th Street and Convent Avenue for my junior and senior years. I graduated and went to college in Sullivan County, New York. College was more like a party resort. About eighty-five percent of the students were from Brooklyn; the rest were from the Bronx and Harlem.

College was a party sun up to sun down. My crib was the hangout spot. All the niggas and bitches wanted to be around us. The niggas named our townhouse Bad Bitch Central. I mean, what eals were they gonna call a house full of bad bitches.

I was kicked out of college in the middle of my first year

for fighting in the student lounge. I have low tolerance for an out-of-line bitch, so the chick got that ass whipped in the same spot she talked shit in. Truth be told, school was boring me. I was tired of playing the “good girl” role. Besides, my patience ran thin. The right path to success was about four years too long, and that didn’t work for me. Shit, I wanted this and that. Well, all of this and that cost a few stacks, and college wasn’t giving out fast cash. So, I had to put my education on the back burner.

I wanted to live like a basketball wife: gifts, gifts, and more gifts. But, Toki doesn’t like kissing ass. So, me being the groupie only lasted for a short minute due to my independence and boss chick demeanor. I decided I liked being the chick that would take a flight, cop some shit, come back, and move it versus me sucking mad dick to get gifts. I concentrated on my own fast moneymaking career. Once I got a taste of the hood fame, I found out my dream job was street money. Corporate career checks would never add up in one year to what I made in a day, so that’s the route I decided to take. I tried a few scams; some worked and some didn’t. For the times that it didn’t work, I always had a sponsor standing by ready to foot the bill.

Rules and I never agreed. I’ve never been a “yes” bitch. I’ve always been in some shit because bitches tried me and found out I’m not to be tried. Bitches disgust me. They see a fly-ass chick with a pretty face and banging shape, and think I’m on some weak bitch shit. They couldn’t handle my presence. I made all the bitches sick. It didn’t matter where I was: in the streets, schools, wherever. They always looked me up and down. Sometimes I posed a little for their mental camera. “Bitch, take a picture,” I would say.

I was very experienced in the streets, and I don’t mean I was a fast-ass, hoe bitch. I was raised to make something out of myself, so I gained street wisdom. I trained my mind that money was first after God and family. My motto: money first.

I chased it; I demanded it; and it showed in my presence.

I grew up fast, and I understood my worth early. I always told myself that when I got older and a nigga wanted to holla, it would cost them. I knew what type of niggas I wanted.

If he couldn't meet my demands, I didn't give up the skins. Always at the A-list events, I was determined to snatch me up a boss. I lived life on a wave. The highlight of it all was the day I went to a Brooklyn event. It was a party worth remembering, because in Brooklyn parties, there's an icy nigga everywhere you turn. I'm not talking about the ones that had on them crystal chains. Nah. I'm talking about the real niggas that spent money the long way after that one event. The Borough of Brooklyn was where I liked to be. The borough was something like my first love. Brooklyn was just a city I couldn't get enough of. I was addicted to the fast life.

But, living in the fast lane, we replace our value and our morals with dollars. Some forget to pay attention to the consequences that comes behind the money chase. And we can't forget the hood fame we yearn for. Yeah, being the hustler's wife and the bitch all the chicks call the baddest is like a high. To most, it gives us pleasure to know your man is first pick on every chick's list. More importantly, they know you're the first pick on his list. While chicks are out working a nine-to-five, you're out tearing up the mall buying new shit and just living hood rich.

But, when you're fucking with a boss man, there are certain things to be expected. Yeah, down the line you might find out he has another bitch on the side with his possible kids living another life. And yeah, we accept it because they blind us with money and gifts. But, let's not confuse that for giving a nigga the green light to disrespect. It's so easy to get caught up in the street life and ignore the real-life struggles and consequences of being a hustler's wife, the Jacker's main bitch, or The Credit Card King's Queen B; you know the Boss Bitch terminology.

Fast money replaces self-priorities. Most chicks search and fight to get on the VIP list at all the events, chasing rappers and athletes, thinking they have the key to the American dream. *If I can just get him alone for just one night, maybe he might make me his wife,* is what they liked to believe. Thinking as long as we riding with our hood-rich nigga, we're warranted at least a car, and if we're lucky, a house, too. It's the only way we see the wealth so much quicker. While that's living for the moment to some, to us, it made sense.

Yet and still, I always seemed to find myself drawn to the connects. They make for better business than pleasure. I rather them throw me bricks than pay for my living. I had a secret weapon named Nice that moved shit like a jet, so I talked my way into their business.

I can talk a nigga out of anything. I've been known to have the gift of gab, and my mother always told me that my mouth was going to write a check my ass can't cash. So far, I've cashed every check with no problem. But, in the back of my mind, I prepared for that day. I stayed true to myself. If I feel it, I'm saying what I want to say. If a nigga could deal with my demands, we could kick it. And if not, the exit is the same door they walked in.

Beating around the bush is not something I'm into. Biting my tongue? I never learned how to. I've been known to put niggas on blast. I mean, I call it how I see it, and that's real talk. Never been known to be a weak bitch, especially when a nigga is trying to holla. I make them work for it, because in this world, ain't shit free. That's what my brother always told me.

He would say, "You see, Toki, a nigga only do what chicks allow them to. So, if you're showing a nigga that your expectations are very few, then that's how he will treat you. It's like saying you're happy with a Happy Meal. Meanwhile, the next bitch is going on shopping sprees and taking trips to

Milan. If you know your self-worth is priceless, make sure you make a nigga work for it."

I lived by that. I know I have the total package, and I could talk a nigga right out the pockets without giving up any of my pretty ass, and if he wasn't giving up the cash, he had to keep it moving; I saw no reason for us to keep in touch.

Anything a nigga gives me is extras. They call them gifts. I call them overs. I mean, I told those dump motherfuckers all the time to figure out what they could get me that I didn't already have. But, they never seemed to get it. They still knocked on my door with almost the same shit, like bags, shoes, cars, and keys to condos. I already have furs and don't need anymore.

Now diamonds? A girl could never have enough of those. Buy me a motherfucking business. Send your motherfucking lawyer and accountant over here to go over the contents in the white envelope with all my stock contracts, my figures, and the total amount you invested in that business. That's shit I don't have. Shit, I'm even open to discuss franchise. But, they never got it. They still kept those bags and shoes coming. I would tell them dump motherfuckers to save it, put it on eBay, or sell it in the hood for half. I mean, how many of the same bags and shoes can a girl really have? But, that's how I give it up. That's me, Toki.

Chapter 2

"Damn, I think I need to go shopping," I said, while standing in the middle of my walk-in closet. I pressed the button on the wall that made my clothes rack turn. "Shit, I have nothing to wear. Let me call Morgan and see what she's putting on. Tonight is movie night."

Whenever we go out, we show up, show off, and show out on the club scene.

"Hello," Morgan said.

"Morgan, what you doing?"

"Nothing. Why, what's up?"

"You going to the mall, or do you already know what you're wearing tonight?" I asked.

"Bitch, you know me. I got shit for days. I already have something to wear," she replied.

"Okay, so do you want to go with me to find something to wear?"

Morgan replied, "Damn, Toki, you got it bad. Shopping is your thing. You never miss a beat."

I laughed. "Shut up, bitch. You know Black Friday at Spirit Nightclub is the best party in the NYC. Everybody comes out for this major affair."

"You telling me," Morgan agreed. "Damn, Toki, why didn't you go this morning when the big sale was going on?"

"Sale?" I said like it was a fungus. "Bitch, you know I don't do sales. I can't deal with all them people pushing, running, and willing to die for a pair of McQueen shoes 'cause they wouldn't be able to afford them at the regular price. That's why I have a personal shopper, to avoid that kind of shit!"

Morgan laughed. "Then why didn't you call her instead and have her bring the shit to you?"

I replied, "I did. She's booked up all day, and I wanted some ribs and wine from Houston's. Come on, Morgan."

"Damn, Toki, why you never like to drive your cars? What you got them for?

"Damn, bitch, what's up with the third degree? Just come on so we can get something to eat. I'm treating," I told her.

"Okay, and I'm ordering the most expensive shit on the menu."

We laughed before I hung up. I took my shower and got dressed. A short while later, Morgan was out front. I set the alarm before I walked out the door. *Never leave your home unarmed.*

I jumped in the car with Morgan, and we drove to Short Hills Mall in Bergen County, New Jersey, to do what we did best—shop till we dropped.

Chapter 3

Young Jeezy's "Gangster Party" blasted from the ten-foot speakers as my crew and I switched through the crowd of Spirit Nightclub. We made our way to our VIP booth, passing everyone and anyone we knew. As usual, the club was rocking, packed wall-to-wall with niggas and bitches fronting in their Sunday's best. Spirit Nightclub was located in lower Manhattan in the area that never sleeps, Chelsea. There were two clubs on every block. But, Spirit stood alone, taking up the whole block. Spirit is the club that popped the most. If you've never been to Spirit, you will never understand why it is number one on everyone's list.

The décor was white with splashes of red. Spirit had two levels. The low-budget VIP was located on the second floor and overlooked the dance floor. That's where all the bums who thought they were doing something partied. Niggas bought two bottles for twenty niggas and passed them around like a forty.

Now, the A-list VIP booths stood alone in each corner of the club. Only niggas buying twenty bottles and better get to party in the sky. We always have our usual VIP booth right next to the DJ. The booths at Spirit were taller than the ten-foot speakers, and when we up there, we see everything. We called them skyscrapers. Our booth was always on reserve, and VIP is where you could always find me and my crew. If we ain't red carpeting it, we don't fuck with it.

"Damn, it's popping in this bitch tonight," I said with excitement in my voice, but always calm in my actions.

As we made our way to our booth, I stopped in my tracks when I felt someone tap me lightly on my shoulder. I turned to see who touched me. It was my homegirl, Shaunie.

I said, "Hey, girl! What's it doing?" I was surprised to see her.

"Hey, Toki. Long time no see."

"I know. How have you been, and how's little man? I haven't seen you since Nice went to jail and Sin disappeared."

She paused like I had hit a soft spot. Maybe it was guilt, maybe not.

She replied, "I know, girl, but I had to get away from that crazy-ass nigga. I heard he's back in town, and knowing Sin, he's up to something."

I was shocked. "Hmmm, word! When you hear this?" I asked her.

"Last week. I been here for two months, but I been on my grind. I had to get my shit together, so no one knew I was back but my mother. I didn't even take Sincere to see Sin's mother, and you know how much she loves her grandson. She was destroyed when I just up and ran away. When I heard he was back in Brooklyn, I isolated myself even more."

"Damn, girl," I said.

Shaunie nodded. "I'm pretty much scared to go out and scared that he would come there. Toki, you know Sin. He don't give a fuck about nobody when it comes to his son and me. I didn't want to put my mom through no bullshit with Sin, so I've just been laying low. The only reason I'm out right now is because my little cousin graduated from high school today and made me come out to celebrate with her before she goes off to college. I won't hold you up, but we must get up."

"Yeah, girl, we must. Give me your number. I'll call you,

and we can set the date."

After I put her number in my cell phone, we kissed each other on the cheek and I walked off. My crew stood guard, always on some overprotective shit. But, I am, too. I mean, that's my crew.

We made our way through the crowd and up the spiral stairs to our VIP booth.

"A lot of Rosé is what we will need tonight," I told the hostess.

Morgan added, "Yes, and a bottle of Patrón and a few bottles of that Spade."

The hostess looked at me. "How many bottles of Rosé and Spade would you like?" she asked.

"You be the judge," I replied.

She smiled as she heard the ATM cash out in her head. She knew the more bottles I bought, the bigger the tip.

We enjoyed the music, while swag surfing and making it rain in the club. We felt out the scene, seeing who's who and what's what. I laid my eyes on the waitress and a few of her coworkers carrying our bottles of Spade, five bottles of PJ Rosé, two bottles of Patrón, some Red Bulls, and a few cold waters. They came through the crowd with our bottles in the air and the sparkling sticks, letting the club know we had money to blow.

"Toki and her girls are in the building!" Kodee, the promoter, shouted into the microphone, while standing by the deejay booth. He always showed love to my crew and me.

"Okay, Toki. I see you and your crew giving it up like you always do. Waitresses, take a few gold bottles to Toki's section. We got the baddest bitches in the building! The ballers and ballettes are showing up tonight!"

The deejay played "Got Money" by DJ Kahled. We got it rocking and made a blockbuster movie that night. Morgan's extra ass pulled out a small paper bag full of nothing but twenties and threw that shit over the crowd. Of course, I had to follow suit, and so did the rest of my crew. We gave about forty racks to charity.

I threw back mad shots of Patrón, sipped champagne, and partied like a rock star with my crew. We had everybody's attention, but they knew how we always gave it up. We made it rain with a few extra ones we had left over from the day. But, I couldn't avoid or even ignore the VIP booth across from us. They were balling like we were. I saw a lot of wealth.

I tapped Sweets on her shoulder to focus her attention to the niggas on the other side.

"Wow! Who the fuck is that?" she asked.

"Don't know. Never seen them before," I said.

"Damn, that whole shit is lit up like an all-white Christmas tree."

I nudged Morgan with my elbow and nodded my head in the direction of the next booth.

"Who the fuck is them niggas? They balling out of control over there," she said with her eyes open wide like a deer in headlights.

At that moment, I noticed Morgan's attention was still focus of the mysterious rich niggas. Her radars went up, alerting her to the ballers in the building.

I need to know who the fuck is this new mob of flossing-ass niggas? I thought. *I've never seen them around anywhere. I can't even pick one familiar face out the bunch. I know damn near everybody in the game, but them I've never seen before. Looks like some fresh meat landed in NYC, and from the looks of how they're partying like rich niggas, it tells me they eating heavy, and I want in.*

Morgan turned to us and said, "Bathroom break. Gotta pee and make sure the MAC is on straight. I think I see a Big Daddy on the other side, and uh, I ain't leaving him for the next bitch to profit off of. Naw, I got first dibs."

"Damn, Morgan, you go hard in the paint. You not even

trying to peep these niggas out, and you already spending their money. You too much, but I fucks with you 'cause you know your worth," I told her.

As we made our way up the stairs coming from the restroom, we decided to walk around the club before returning to our section. We spotted Lucy, the fucking groupie. Although I didn't see her since we walked in together, she always liked doing shit like that. She liked walking around the club by herself, peeping the scene, seeing who's who, who's spending what, and who's creeping with who. So, it didn't surprise me when I saw her mingling by the new niggas' VIP section. She peeped me, but we always on our cool shit. We head nod and keep it moving. While passing the crowd of niggas, we didn't let them see us looking. I never wanted to make a nigga think I'm some whack-ass chicken running around a club watching a nigga spending. So, whenever we went sneak peeking, we always did it from a distance.

We peeped the niggas partying first-class. I made eye contact with one shorty. He wasn't all that icy, but he had gangster swag about him, a drug dealer aura, something like a boss. He wasn't acting all crazy and drunk; he wasn't even playing with the bitches. He was just chilling with his hat pulled down over his eyes, cool and laid back, not trying to attract too much attention. Or was it that he wasn't trying to attract the wrong attention? He appeared to be screaming on something, and I liked it.

After we locked eyes for a second, me and my crew made it back to our booth. It was just too crazy over there. Bitches were hungry. I didn't want to drag a bitch through the club for stepping on my red-bottom shoes 'cause she was bugging, going crazy, and trying to get to those dudes.

"Let's keep it moving before I'm forced to drag one of these bum bitches," I said.

"You know how we do," Morgan and Sweets both said as

we walked up the staircase to our booth.

On the flip side of shit, those niggas showed up, showed out and showed off. Shit, they bought out the bar. It was definitely a movie night. From a real bitch's point of view, they definitely showed me that they were about this life. If I saw potential profit, I wanted in. While the other bitches got drunk and looked for a dick to suck, money stayed on my mind.

Before the party ended, we made our way towards the exit. The drunken crowd always equaled confusion, and when you are worth something, you can't afford to catch another nigga's bullet. Sweets slid off with her shorty, so her party was over early. As usual, we had to look for Lucy's groupie ass.

"So you mean to tell me we can't leave because of this bitch? Morgan, you see her?" I asked.

"Naw, Tee. She always do this shit, and if we leave her ass and something happens to her, then it will be my fault," Morgan replied.

"She be bugging," I said. "She's always walking off! That shit is getting old fast. My tolerance level for this bird-head shit is wearing off. I hate having to keep looking for this bitch whenever we go out."

Morgan tapped me on my shoulder. "Toki, there that dumb bitch go right there. Figures. All up in some nigga's face."

As we walked up on her, I noticed this bitch had snatched her a nigga up from the crew of niggas that was blowing money fast in the other VIP section.

"Yo, bitch," I said with an attitude. "Yo, why the fuck you always have to be the one that gets lost? Every time we go out with you, we end up walking around the club for an extra thirty minutes looking for you 'cause you don't answer your phone or text back when we texting you asking where you at. It's like once you get caught up with a nigga, you forget you came with us. It's cool, though. I'm never a hater, but next time, bitch, BYOC."

Lucy looked at me, confused. "Huh? What's BYOC, Tee?"

"It means bring your own car, bitch," I said.

I felt a tug at the sleeve of my navy blue Marc Jacob puffer with the light brown mink collar. I snatched my hand back. I was not in the mood for chickenhead bullshit.

The shorty I made eye contact with earlier walked from behind his man with a little smirk on his face. He looked all sneaky and shit, but it was sexy. I liked it, but I played it cool.

I snatched my hand away from him while giving him my bad bitch look. The dude who Lucy had been talking to then took the opportunity to make a complete ass out of them both. His broke ass put his arm around shorty, pulled his chain out from underneath his shirt, and posed like they were taking a picture.

"What?" he said. "Don't act like that with my man, ma. My nigga gets money."

I knew the nigga was a clown. I could tell he didn't have any money by doing fronting-ass shit like that. He was naked. His neck, ears, and wrists were missing ice. I knew he was just a spectator, a pretender, balling with a crew of wealthy niggas.

Ashy-face motherfucker. So this is what Lucy disappeared in the club for? She went and found the brokest nigga out the bunch. We gonna have to have the Toki talk at a later date, because she can't be partying with me chasing niggas like this.

I looked at Morgan with a smirk, then looked at him and said, "Listen, honey. We don't give a fuck about all that. Please, we're not looking for your money. Are you blind, nigga? A nigga that got money can always tell if a bitch is holding just by how she carries herself. So, yeah, your man probably does have money, but I doubt he got enough for us."

Morgan laughed and added, "Fuck out of here! We've never been known to be the needy bitch type. Don't no man take care of us. We do us on our own."

"And on that note, Morgan and I are taking flight. What you doing? You leavin' with this clown or you following us?"

Lucy hesitated, so I took that as her opting to stay with the broke nigga. Morgan and I walked toward the exit, leaving her behind. Before we walked out, I stopped, turned slightly to the side, looked back over my shoulder, and put my hand on my hip.

Shifting my weight to one leg, I said, "Don't no nigga father this ass. But, extra gifts are always accepted. So, in the near future, don't ever mistake me for being a needy bitch. Nigga, I got my own shit."

He looked at me and said, "I like that. I like that, lil' lady." His thug grabbed a hold of me, as he walked in my direction. "Shit, I love a chick that has her own. How about you ladies let me walk you to your car?"

"Cool," I told him, "but I have two questions. One, is that dry-ass nigga your man? 'Cause he's a clown, and if so, we can walk ourselves. Question number two, why walk? Why not drop us to our car? What, you walkin'?"

He laughed. "As for homie, we cool. Wouldn't say he's my right hand, but he's definitely a fan. You know there's always a nigga around for so many different reasons."

"What you mean by that?" I asked.

He gave me a blank expression as if he had no worries at all, just real laid back, like his life was straight and he was just living.

"Homie is a human holster, and, lil' lady, as for my ride, it's around. I'm no regular nigga, ma. I can't move around in these streets like a regular dude. I have to move smart, make sure niggas don't know where I'm parked."

Morgan looked at him. "What? You got some type of beef or something, because my cousin and me can't be victims of being at the wrong place at the wrong time? Or in your case, being around the wrong nigga at the wrong time."

"One thing for sure, ma, and two things for certain, I get respect in these streets. You all the way good when you're with me, you dig? I got the dilly in my boot, and niggas know I'm loose. So, walking with me will never be a problem for you ladies."

I never could understand why my bugged-out ass loved fucking with bad guys. Even if he said he was on the FBI's most wanted list, I probably would have still talked to dude.

"Okay, walk us to our car," I said.

He talked about some other shit as we walked around the corner to the parking lot, but I wasn't listening. Morgan handed the parking attendant the claim ticket, and a short time later, Morgan's all-white BMW 650 pulled in front of us.

"Damn, ladies, y'all riding clean," he commented.

"Yup, and that's not even half. But, thanks for making sure we got to our car safely. It was nice kicking it with you." I paused and looked at him before asking, "What's your name?"

"Qwan, but my friends call me Que. Don't think you're getting away from me that easy. So what? You're not gonna give me your number?"

I smiled. "Should I?"

Morgan cleared her throat.

Qwan replied, "Awww, come on. Don't do me like that, lil' lady."

I tilted my head and asked, "So before we even discuss exchanging numbers, where are you from?"

"Brooklyn. And from the smile my response just put on your face, I take it you like Brooklyn niggas. Where you from?"

"The Bronx, but I live in Jersey now."

"A'ight, lil' lady, now that we've gotten over that bump,

how about giving me your number?"

"Uh, not for nothing. It wouldn't make sense for me to give you my number if you got problems at home, such as a girlfriend, ex-girlfriend, or an out-of-control baby mama. Toki don't do those. If you do, then this is where we must say goodbye and save some memory in our phones for someone who can afford to use it."

He laughed. "Nah, ma. I have none of the above."

"Okay, then gimme your number."

After he gave me his number, I got in the car. He closed my door, and we drove off.

As soon as Morgan pulled off, my phone rang.

"Uh uh, who is that?" Morgan asked.

"Girl, Tommy's tired ass."

Tommy and I dealt with each other for quite some time. He had a family at home. Although he wasn't married, he'd been with his baby's mother for almost fifteen years. And then he had me. It was all fun in the beginning, sneaking around and shit. But, once my feelings overwhelmed with love for him, playing the second women role got old to me. I'm too selfish to play second to no bitch. So, Tommy had a choice: leave home for me or I would leave him with home. He was dragging his choice, so I gave him a hand and kept it moving on him.

We met through Morgan. She used to fuck with his man. Tommy was more like a ladies' man. He wasn't the violent type, and he didn't have gangster in him. What he did know how to do was break that bread off whenever I wanted him to.

Tommy lived on 126th Street and Lenox Avenue. He was well known throughout Harlem. He pushed a supercharged Range Rover in champagne gold, while his baby's mother pushed a 500 SLK. Tommy wasn't a drop-dead gorgeous nigga, but he had a lot of swag. His baby's mother was cute, but she couldn't stand next to me on a bad day. My favorite part of the relationship was that he had lots of cash and didn't mind blowing it on me, so he was right up my alley.

However, that all changed when I got tired of playing the second woman role. I put my all into our relationship, thinking he would see I was for him and be willing to take that chance and leave ol' girl. But, in all reality, he never had any plans to leave. He wanted to have his cake and eat it, too. Toki may be the side bitch for a spell, but that shit got old really quick.

I ignored his call.

"That's Tommy?" Morgan asked.

"Yes, girl. He's taking this 'Toki's fed-up attitude' kind of hard. He just doesn't want to let me go, but I'm tired of this fake-ass relationship. I'm tired of faking like I'm happy and trying to ignore the fact that I go to bed alone most nights. This bitch right here wants her own man. I mean, what did he expect me to do? Sit around and wait forever for him to possibly leave? Nope. Fuck out of here, Morgan. I mean, don't get me wrong. We were good for what we were, but now, it's time that I move on. You know me. I lack patience. I'm not in the business of keeping no nigga if he don't want to be kept by me. So, for tonight, Morgan, we riding home drama free," I said, before turning up my nigga Jeezy.

Chapter 4

I relaxed as I sat in the oversized white leather chair getting pampered. I was long overdue for a pedicure. But, my phone vibrating in my bag quickly interrupted that mood. It was Tommy, just as I assumed. He blew my phone up, and I ignored his old ass. Finally, I decided to take him out of his misery and pick up.

"Hello."

"Yo, Toki. What the fuck is wrong with you? I've been calling you since last night. You can't pick up the phone for me anymore? It's like that between us now?" Tommy said.

I rolled my eyes.

"Yup, that's how it is right now, Tommy. Why you acting like you give a fuck? I'm the side girl, not your main bitch, remember?"

"I never treated you like the side bitch," he replied.

"I never made you feel like you did. I had my guard down with you, Tommy," I said. "You almost had me. I will admit you got the womanizer game down pat, because it takes a lot to get inside my heart. You manipulated me into thinking you was having all these fake-ass problems at home, like you were unhappy and shit. Lying and saying if it wasn't for the bond you have with your son, you would've been gone. Acting like I might just be the one to take you from her. But, that was all a bunch of bullshit. You had me going for a minute, but then, I woke up. Ultimatums and chances didn't work. So, I decided to open the market up."

"Open the market up!" he repeated. "So what, bitch, you working the track?"

"Working the track? Nah, that's your mother giving happy endings for a hundred pennies. Don't get fucked up living in your subsidized building. Acting like you drop twenty-five hundred dollars on a mortgage every month, knowing you living almost for free. Low-income ass. Forgetful motherfucker, you must have forgot how you eat. Watch your mouth before I clog your pipeline up."

"Wow. I guess the jokes on me, huh, Toki?" he asked. "But, that's my fault. I should've treated you like you turn tricks."

"What! Tommy don't play with me, you pussy, and you know I have no problem with letting my peter speak, you feel me? Yeah, I think you know I will be brief with your ass. Don't push my buttons, before I have my brothers waiting for you in front of your pissy-ass building. You Cinnabon-ass niggas kill me. You know you soft as shit, but always popping shit.

"And since when has it been open season on Toki? Don't temp me, old man. Just accept that it is what it is. We were good while it lasted, but it's dead. Tommy threw it in the casket. Shit, Toki's dick-sharing days are done."

"Fuck you, Toki. Real talk. Coming at me like you the baddest bitch on the planet? I got mad bitches. You just did me a favor, 'cause I was planning on leaving you anyway. I got a new shorty, a bad bitch! I been fucking her and still coming over to beat that pussy up. So, joke's on you, Toki." He laughed. "Oh yeah, and I think she's pregnant."

"A round of applause for Tommy. He just added another bastard child to his list of Cunningham kids. Please, nigga," I shot back.

"Fuck you, bitch," he said.

I laughed. "I know you fucking that bum-ass bitch Summer. Good luck with that."

"Why would I do that when I can have any bitch I want?"

"Maybe when your money was long, but don't forget who you cop from, with your one-hundred-grams-once-a-month buying ass," I said. "You don't cop heavy no more, Tommy. Your run is up. That lil' shit you cop I use as toilet paper. It's really unimportant. I could do without it."

"Wow, so this is what it has come to, Toki? You talking crazy to me, and now you letting our personal interfere with our business?"

"Yeah, that's because you let it."

"So you never loved me, Toki? I knew you were a gold-digging bitch. You used me, and now that hard times have come upon me, you want to act like you don't know me. You knew when I got with you that I had some issues, but you acted like you could handle it. You knew I was a nigga that love bitches, and now you got a problem with it. Fuck you, bitch!" he yelled.

"Use you for what? Please, nigga, you got me cracking up. Let me make myself clear being that you talking phone gangster language I don't understand. I'm gonna slow it up for you a bit. I'm tired of being faithful to a motherfucker who's attached. Time to start my life. You know, start living for me. Like who the fuck do you think you is? Like Toki is supposed to obey your every command while you share your baby dick with any and every chick. Tommy, get it together with your big, grown ass. The back lashing and calling me out of my name is getting a bit redundant, don't you think?" I laughed.

Before he could utter an answer, I said, "Oh, I forgot. In order for you to know the definition of redundant, you would have to learn how to read, write, and spell. So, I'm gonna tell you like this. Tommy, beat it. Get off my line, because this phone call ain't bringing me in a dime."

With that, I hung up on his old ass. *Tommy got me fucked up,* I thought, while exhaling and laying my head back against the vibrating massage chair. I went into deep thought while getting my feet massaged and my toes polished.

I guess this is what you call going through that gangster love. That's what I get. When you mess with a nigga that got another home, he will never give all his love to you because he belongs to someone else. No matter what he tells you, no matter how much he claims to be in love with you, and no matter how much is says he's unhappy, he's not going to leave home. I know most men, if not all, cheat. Just like he got you, he probably got another two in his life other than his wife.

For a while, they lead us to believe they are going to leave. But, when reality sets in, and it hit us that he's just playing games with our feelings, we realize it was all just a waste of our time. We then realize our worth. That green light comes on in our head, telling us it's time to let go and move on. Before doing so, though, we give them one last chance to choose, giving them that ultimatum of either choosing us or their wife. If a nigga didn't choose me, I cop my first-class seat and take that trip to It's All About Toki. Lift off!

Chapter 5

As I walked out the nail shop, my phone rang again.

"Yeah, Morgan," I answered.

"Bitch, OMG! You will not believe what I found out today while shopping in Barney's."

"What? And bitch you went to Barney's without me?"

"Shut up, Toki," Morgan said. "Listen! Remember the other night in Spirit?"

"Yeah, I remember."

"Well, my homegirl was telling me that lil' nigga you met the other night just came home. I think she said like a week ago. He is caked up. He was locked up for three years, and as soon as dude came home, he was on the come up. From my understanding, his older cousin is supposed to be the man in Atlanta and DC. She said word on the streets is dude's cousin was pulling in a cool three hundred thousand every other week in the A alone. Not to mention what he gets in DC."

"DC? Now that's dope capitol. I would love to own a nice piece of prime real estate there."

"He was hustling with the EMF crew, and you know them niggas is caked up, Toki. They got that oil money."

"I think you overdoing it, bitch. Go ahead with that stupid, 'gas me up' talk, Morgan. So who's this bird that was feeding you all this bird food?"

What the fuck is wrong with this bitch bringing back this chicken head news? I wondered, figuring it was probably some pretender-ass bitch feeding her this bullshit. *Morgan knows better than to be calling my phone with that "my friend said this, and my friend said that" shit. Probably some whack chick running around in Barney's fronting with empty pockets and trying to pick up two-thousand-dollar shoes, acting like that price won't land her ass in the shelter. Bitch, please.*

I continued questioning Morgan. "What's his older cousin's name? Did your friend tell you where he's from in Brooklyn? Besides, how old is dude? Did you tell her that I'm not the one to believe everything I hear on the streets? People lie so much."

More than likely, this story had been switched up ten times before it got to Morgan, who was all out of breath and overexcited like she was telling me about a billionaire. I had my own million, so why the fuck would I need his change? I wondered how Morgan could be so smart when it came to her job, but when it came to niggas, she was dumb as a doorknob.

"Toki, let me finish," she said. "His cousin's name is Caki. He's from Brooklyn in Crown Heights. Do you know him?"

"Caki? Hmmm. Yeah, I know of that nigga. He and Nice were cool. I haven't seen him in a minute, though."

"Yeah, 'cause he moved to Atlanta and took over. I mean, they saying homie got mansions as stash houses and big-ass estates as his living quarters."

I sensed the gold-digging bitch was all smiles on the other end of the phone like she had just won the Mega Million.

"That's what's up, but get to the point," I said impatiently.

"Whatever, bitch, with your cocky ass, acting like you're not impressed," she responded.

"I mean, come on, Morgan. Why would I be, when Nice has been doing him since he was fifteen? That shit doesn't faze me. You forget how we living?"

"Nah, I don't forget shit. I just know more is better. I

never limit myself as to what I can get out of this game. So, if a nigga busting up on me while I stack my chips, then yes, I'd rather spend his ends than fuck up my shit."

"And why you calling me about the help? A bad bitch is a boss' bitch. Call me when you get next to the boss."

"Damn, Toki! Can I just finish?"

"Go 'head."

"Dude just got out of jail."

"Why do I want a motherfucker that's in and out of jail? I'm looking for in-house dick, not a damn pen pal. I can't even Skype a nigga in jail. I'm good. I'll pass."

"EMF hit him off, Toki. Homie's eating heavy. You need to snatch his ass up. Don't leave him for the next bitch. He's only been home for a month, and in less than two weeks, he's standing tall on his feet."

"And you're telling me this with so much excitement why?"

She laughed. "What, bitch? You know you was feeling lil' man's swag."

We both laughed.

"Shut up, Morgan," I said.

"You should holla for real, Toki. He might just be your Prince Charming. Lord knows that fucking punk-ass Tommy wasn't, and I'm glad you kicked his ass to the left. Maybe God sent him to bring you peace and happiness in your life."

"Go 'head, Morgan, with all that Prince Charming shit. There's no such thing in the hood. It's either you fuck with me or you don't, or maybe from time to time we can just beat. All that white horse and carriage bullshit is not going on where we come from. Stop forgetting we're in these streets playing a chess game for our life. Get your head out the fucking clouds, Morgan."

"Did you call him yet?" Morgan asked, ignoring what I just said.

"Do I look like a thirsty bitch?" I responded. "I'll call him when I get a chance."

"Yeah, well, you need to call him, Toki. I'm telling you, I like him for you."

"You like him for me? Bitch, you don't even know him."

"And neither will you if you don't call him, Toki."

You know what, bitch? You're irking me. I'll call him later."

"You better, Toki. I'll get with you later," Morgan said, then hung up.

*****

I walked in my door and turned on Meek Millz song "Tony Story". I put it on repeat and poured myself a glass of wine, and rolled a blunt.

Maybe I will call him just to say what's up. What could it hurt? I thought.

I lit my blunt, sat back, and put my feet up on the footstool. While thinking about the conversation Morgan and I had, I picked up my cell phone and scrolled down to Qwan's number. Without a second thought, I pressed call. I had butterflies in my stomach.

What the fuck is wrong with me? Damn, just saying his name got me feeling all weak and shit.

He had me all hot and bothered. The thought of him was already tickling my clit, and we hadn't even had a conversation yet. At that point, I knew I had to play it smart and safe. Get to know him before he knew me, in case he wanted to get stupid. He wouldn't be hard to track down.

He didn't answer, so I went to my bedroom for a nap.

I woke up to my phone ringing.

"Hello?"

"Yo, who this?"

"Who's this?" I stated with an attitude. "Nigga, you called my phone."

Qwan chuckled.

"Is that how you talk to ladies when you return calls?" I

asked him.

"Nah, I'm not a rude-ass nigga. I have respect for ladies that act like ladies. And from the sound of your soft voice, I can tell this is the lil' lady from the other night."

"So you remember me?" I said.

"How could I forget you? I peeped how you and your girls made a movie that night. Besides, how could I ever forget your pretty face, Ms. Toki?"

I smiled. "You sure have a way with words. So what, you some type of professional con nigga?"

"Con nigga? Nah, ma. You got me fucked up. I'm too gangster for all that."

He didn't know how much I loved that gangster shit. I lived for it.

"So you consider yourself a gangster?" I asked, while lying in my bed playing with my hair and staring up at the ceiling.

Qwan replied, "Yup, that's what I am, not what I consider myself to be. I mean that from the heart, baby. When you're from where I'm from, you have to get it how you live. You fucking with a real street nigga, Ma."

"And what you think, I'm some uptight med school chick? Nah, I respect a nigga's hustle, I got love for all the trap stars. We're all out here trying to survive."

"Now that you got the rundown on me, Ms. Toki, what's your history?" Qwan asked. "Let a nigga know who Ms. Toki is."

"In due time, honey, in due time. You will know all you need to know as long as you play your cards right."

He laughed. "Play my cards right? Well how about I try my hand and ask you to dinner tomorrow…say around eight o'clock?"

"We can do dinner. That's cool. Where we going?"

"Lil' lady, I got a nice spot where I want to take you. Text me with your address so I can come pick you up. Okay?"

I smiled. "Okay."
"Until tomorrow, take care and make sure you behave."
No, he didn't! Make sure I behave? Hmm, he just met me.

Chapter 6

"Hola, Toki," my beautician, Maria, said as I entered her salon on 135th Street and Lenox.

"Hola, Maria."

We gave each other a kiss on the cheek.

"I hope you know you're sitting under the dryer today, missy."

"I know. Why you think I'm here so early? I have a date, so I need to look perfect, and no one knows how to do it better than you. You're the best, Maria!"

"Okay, Toki, sientate," Maria said, pointing to the washing chair.

After Maria rinsed the last bit of shampoo out my hair, she asked, "Deep conditioner, right, Toki?"

"Sí. I told you that I want the works."

Maria wasn't just my beautician. She was like my older sister. I had been going to her for years to get my hair done. Plus, we did a lot of business together.

Maria had so many clients that she had to open other shops after her one-year anniversary. She had a chain, one salon in every borough.

Her Harlem salon was closer to my home, so I preferred going there. That shop was her first, and she would never leave it. In my opinion, Maria was the best Dominican hairdresser. Her service was on point, and my hair was always flawless. She loved doing hair; making money was just a bonus. She was born into money. Her father was the most feared drug lord in Columbia. He was well respected in his country by all, even the authority figures. The entire country had to answer to him. The country needed him to survive.

Maria and her mother moved to the United States to build a fortune here. The plan was that her dad would give up drugs, money, and murder, and move here to join them. However, his addiction to the game kept him in Columbia. He still took care of them, though. Maria turned the dirty money into a bottomless pot of gold. She was a whiz at making her money work for her and her family.

After she deep conditioned my hair, she rinsed it, clipped my ends, and roller set it. I then sat under the dryer for almost two hours because my hair is mad thick.

"Okay, Maria, I know I'm dry by now. You know I hate sitting under here."

"Okay, Toki, you big cry baby," she said in her Columbian accent. "Come on. Get in the chair. Let me do what I do best."

I moved to the chair and sat down.

"So, Toki, you finally kicked Tommy's old ass to the curb. Good, I'm glad. I was tired of hearing his name coming out of bitches' mouths."

"You and me both. Maria, you know when niggas are getting money and they got a bad bitch riding with them, they tend to over think their position, thinking they can do better. As for Tommy, I was the one who made him somebody. Now he remembers. He keeps calling me tripping, but I'm done with that."

"Yeah, I've seen him drive by my shop a few times looking like his world is over. So, Ms. Toki, when am I going to see this dude that's taking you out?"

When I didn't reply right away, Maria paused and looked at me through the mirror.

"You ignoring me?" she asked.

"No."

Not pressing the issue, she continued doing my hair, making individual pin curls so my curls stayed in place.

Once she finished, she spun me around to face the mirror. "Okay, Toki, all done. Make sure you keep a hair net on until you're ready to walk out the door."

"Will do," I said, while putting on my shades.

"And make sure you call me when you get home. No matter what the time."

I gave her a hug. "Okay, Maria. Just put this on my tab, and I promise to call you."

Just before exiting the shop, I stopped and looked back at Maria. "If he's worth me introducing him to my loved ones, then I will. If not, then I won't. I love you," I told her, then walked out the door and went shopping.

I ended up purchasing three pairs of Christian Louboutins, one pair of grey YSL Tributes, and a black Hervé Léger dress. As an added touch, I made my way to Victoria's Secret, my favorite place to shop. I usually went to buy one thing, but came out with some of everything.

Once home, I oiled my skin after exiting the shower. Morgan called just as I was applying my makeup. I knew her nosy ass would be on my phone.

"Yes, Morgan. What can I do for you?"

"You ready, bitch?" she asked, almost like she was going, too.

"Damn, bitch, you in my window?" I laughed. "I'm almost ready."

"Did you go to the closet, or did you get brand new on this nigga?"

"Girl, you know me," I said.

"Brand new, fresh out the box, huh? Although, you didn't need to since your closet is full of shit with tags on it."

"Yeah, I know, but I need to be brand new tonight. Even

though shit got tags on it, it's not new to me because I've already seen it."

While Morgan laughed, Qwan beeped in.

"Okay, girl, this is him. I'll call you back." I clicked over. "Hello?"

"What it do?"

Immediately, I started blushing. *Damn, this little motherfucker is making me weak in the knees. He's just so fucking calm and laid back. Damn, that shit is sexy,* I thought, biting on my bottom lip. *I love the low tone of his voice. Makes me want to jump on his dick and ride it for however long he can hold his nut. Wow! Let me find out I'm feeling him.*

"What's it doing, Qwan? It's not seven yet. So what, you canceling on me?"

"Nah," he said. "Canceling on you? Never. Now, did I cancel all my meetings for today just to spend some time with you? Yeah, I did that. But, Miss Lady, it is past seven. I was calling 'cause I didn't get your text. I was making sure you're not flaking on me."

"Oh my God, I forgot. I have my clocks set an hour ahead for business purposes. Sorry, babe. I'm going to text you now. I'm ready anyway."

Forty minutes later, he called to say he was outside. When I stepped out, no one was there.

Is this nigga on some 'set me up' shit? I trust nobody but my family. A nigga will try me just because I'm a female.

I walked back in and sat on my couch for a few minutes before my phone rang again.

"Yeah," I answered.

"Yo."

"Yo? Why did you have me waiting outside like you was here, but you wasn't? What the fuck is up with that, homie?"

I never wanted a nigga to think I'm stupid. I always thought the worst before I thought the best. So, when a nigga called and said he was somewhere I knew he wasn't, alarms automatically went off in my head.

"Damn, honey, you get feisty quick. I have a lot of learning to do, but the feisty shit you got going on I like it," Qwan replied with laughter, like my attitude amused him.

"I don't find shit funny," I told him.

"My fault, Miss. Lady. I was sitting on the wrong block in front of the wrong house. Sorry. Don't shoot my head off. I'm outside now. You can look out your window if you don't trust me."

"Nah, I don't need to do that."

As I walked towards his truck, I noticed the window on the passenger's side lower slowly. Qwan's sneaky, sexy grin and the horny look he had in his eyes massaged my clit in a good way. I smiled, experiencing chills. Something about him made my pussy wet.

Damn, shorty makes me want to jump his bones. He's just staring at me in a lustful daze.

I love that I got the type of beauty that will make a nigga bust on himself. I was told I had the sexiest bedroom eyes a motherfucker had ever seen. I guess because my eyelashes are extra-long with a curl. And no, I don't go to the Koreans to enhance shit. I mean, if you're a bad bitch, you were born a bad bitch. There's no faking it.

I opened the door to his navy blue Cadillac truck. Before hopping in, I checked the tires. He had rims on it, so I knew it wasn't rented.

"Well, hello, Mr. Qwan. Nice to see you," I said. Then I blushed, squinted my eyes, and leaned in to kiss him on his cheek. I leaned back and smiled.

Qwan stared at me as I reached for my seatbelt.

"You look very pretty, Miss Lady. I love the smell. What are you wearing?"

"Island Creed, one of my favorites," I giggled.

"I never heard of that. How much does a bottle of Creed

cost?"

I laughed. He joined in, but he was confused.

"What's so funny?" he asked.

"How one minute, you're a diehard gangster, but right now, it's like I'm talking to a shy little boy?"

He grinned.

"As for the price of a bottle of Creed, the smallest bottle is ninety dollars. Let me find out your ex was a chicken head. I mean, you shining. So, I can't say it's something you couldn't afford. Why don't you know how much a bullshit bottle of Creed cost, when I know you can go and buyout the store?"

"You got jokes, lil' lady?" he replied.

I can tell he's used to dealing with chickens. C'mon, honey, get with it. And I don't want to hear nothing about him knowing Gucci and Loui. Who wouldn't? That's common hood shit. I see I'ma have to upgrade him. Get him a few belts with the H on the buckle.

"Don't worry, hun. I'll help you catch up on what's in. I mean, you're definitely good, but I can do a few adjustments," I said.

We both laughed.

"Okay, Miss Toki. I see you got a lot of swag, so let's just say we can enhance each other. And as for the perfume, I thought I made it perfectly clear I'm a gangster, not a perfume shopper. My life is the streets. It's been that way for me since the day I was born. I really can't recall a time in my life when I was taught the perfume lesson."

I laughed. "You funny. That was a good one. Okay, *gangster*. By the way, how old are you?"

He looked at me like I had asked him for a million dollars.

"I'm twenty-five, honey. Why?" he asked.

"Just making sure I cover my ground. Don't need a statutory case."

"Nah, ma. I'm all the way legal."

"Okay, Mr. Legal. So are we going to sit here all day, or are we going to eat? A bitch is hungry. I've been running all day, so I barely ate."

As Qwan pulled off real smooth, he leaned back a little.

"So is the little boy act just an act, or do you have different personalities?"

He chuckled at my question. "Nah, honey, it's just me."

When we pulled up to Houston's, the valet opened my door. I smiled while thinking to myself, *Qwan must not get out much. This is me and my girlfriends' hangout spot. It's cute that he thinks this is exclusive.*

We walked inside to the hostess.

"I have a reservation for two," he told her.

The hostess smiled at me and said, "Hello, Ms. Toki. Party of two. Follow me."

Qwan looked confused.

"Baby, how does she know your name?" he asked.

"Well, I'm a regular. I know all the waiters and waitresses, as well as the chef. I tip well. So, of course, they know me by name," I said with a wink.

Once we reached the table, he pulled out my chair.

Who the fuck does he think he's fooling? This straight-up street nigga is pulling out chairs? Cute gesture. I guess he'll get a brownie point.

I blushed. "Thank you for trying to be a gentleman."

We laughed. The difference is he thought he was laughing *with* me. While in all actuality, I was laughing at him.

The hostess handed us menus and said, "Your waitress will be right with you."

As soon as the hostess walked away, our waitress appeared. Houston's doesn't believe in making customers wait to order.

"Hello, my name is Rachel, and I will be your waitress for this evening." She smiled at me and said, "Hello, Ms. Toki."

I nodded my head and winked at her.

"Can I get you some appetizers and drinks before you order?"

"Yes. I'll have the usual," I replied.

"Half or full spinach dip?" she asked.

"Full."

"Moscato?"

"You got it," I said with a smile.

She turned to Qwan. "Sir?"

"Yes, let me get a bottle of your best champagne."

"Our best we have today is the Moet et Chandon, Dom Perignon."

"Okay, I'll take that with two glasses," he told her.

As the waitress walked off, I looked at him and said, "Toki gets the diamond treatment, huh? Keep this shit up, and you may be able to hang around a little longer."

I laughed. He chuckled.

"Oh, so you don't plan on keeping me?"

"I don't just jump into relationships. I have to understand what type of motherfucker I'm dealing with. Been hurt a few times before, but I always told myself after the hurt, I will never let my head hit the floor. You want in? You gotta earn that shit."

"I see," he responded.

"Be right back," I said, standing up. "Nature calls."

As I walked toward the bathroom, I knew his eyes were glued to my fatty. So, just for an ego trip, I paused and looked back at him. I thought his tongue was going to fall out of his head. I knew he was fantasizing about laying some good dick to me. I got that shit that makes a nigga want to call my pussy home.

When I made it back to the table, I noticed Qwan's expression was different.

"You okay?" I asked.

"Business on the brain. Ain't nothing. I'm good."

The waitress returned, opened the champagne, and poured until our glasses were half full.

Qwan raised his glass. "A toast to new love."

"To new love, maybe," I said as we clinked glasses and sipped.

He winked at me, and I thought about sucking his dick.

After dinner, it was VIP at another nightspot. We got the rooftop booth so I could smoke my sour. Me without my weed was a situation for disaster. Plus, my super freak comes out when I'm full of sour.

We smoked, drank, chatted, kissed, and enjoyed the night relaxing. Qwan had a glow on the ride home, kind of like an expectant wife.

"So, lil' lady, will I be able to get a second date?" Qwan asked as we entered New Jersey.

"I think we can work out a second date. Let's have your people call my people to see what days we both are free."

He looked at me confused until I laughed. Then he joined in.

"Yo, you're a funny girl. You had me going for a minute. Toki is full of surprises," he said with a joker grin across his face, showing his pearly white teeth.

Once we pulled in front of my house, he walked me to my door.

"Miss Toki, are you going to invite me in for some coffee?"

"Get the fuck out of here, nigga. You know you don't drink no fucking coffee," I said.

We both laughed.

"Well," he said, "you gotta give me credit. It was worth a try."

I smirked. "Very clever, Mr. Qwan. Too bad I'm no dumb bitch."

"True that. So, it's goodnight for now, Miss Toki," he said, then kissed me on the cheek and walked to his truck.

Chapter 7

Qwan and I were together almost every night since the first date. This particular night, we decided to bring our friends to party with us. I told him that I hoped his friends came correct, because my bitches were wild and would front on a clown.

Qwan was cool. He was holding it down, and he liked to share. At that rate, he may become my nigga. Maybe Morgan was on to something. One thing was for sure, Toki was feeling her some Qwan.

I called up my girls, Morgan, Sweets, and Lucy, to let them know it was going down and for them to bring their "A" game.

We had to be in the best of the best, so we got the Porsche limo to take us to the club. As the driver turned onto 6th Avenue, we saw how packed the street was with niggas, bitches, and luxury cars.

"I love when we book the driver," Morgan expressed. "I like the scene already. I'm glad we decided to do it big."

"Of course," Sweets said. "This is Toki's first time partying with Qwan's people, so we have to let lil' man peep how we are first class."

"Y'all bitches ready to do this? I plan to get white girl wasted," I told them.

Sweets said, "And you're the only one who believes that. You can't hold your liquor, Toki."

We all laughed as we pulled up in front of the club.

When the driver opened the door, Qwan's face was the first I saw. He looked good in his Gucci navy blue sweater, Yankee fitted, True Religion jeans, and high-top Gucci sneakers. To top it off, he was icy as hell: ears, neck, hands, and wrist.

He approached me with that sneaky, sexy, yet grimy grin. He kissed me and grabbed me into a hug. I inhaled the mesmerizing scent of his Jean Paul Guiltier cologne. The smell immediately soaked my panties.

Club Ruby Falls had thirty-five spacious VIP sections, a state-of-the-art sound and lighting system, and seven thousand square feet of party space. Ruby Falls was only open to the who's who in New York. My crew and I walked through the crowd like we owned shit.

I watched the respect Qwan received. Everybody stood in line to shake his hand, and they respected his presence. I had to admit I was impressed, because some of the gangsters he shook hands with were ones I had crossed paths with due to my affiliations. They gave Qwan props. The crowd admired Qwan's new showpiece: me. Brooklyn definitely showed me that they had mad love and respect for Qwan. From the time we walked in until the time we left, Qwan had unlimited attention.

I liked the feeling. I thought it was something I could get used to. I knew being a hustler's wife had great perks, and yeah, he would probably cheat. If he did, he had better come home with something nice wrapped in a big red bow.

That night, Rick Ross performed, and the New York Giants were in the building. The party rocked, and Qwan got just as much love in the club as the celebrities. He was shouted out on the microphone several times, and the bottles kept coming all night. My panties were ready to come off after seeing all that.

After we leave here, I'm gonna fuck the shit out of this

nigga, I thought to myself.

"Damn, it's a jungle in this bitch," Lucy stated. "I might just find a man that my dad approves of. All I see is money. There are so many sponsors in this bitch that a girl don't know who to pick."

"Bitch, please. You know you a hoe. Choose the one you know you're gonna choose, and that's the one spending the most. Stop acting like a goodie two-shoes. You know gifts brighten up your day," Morgan said, laughing.

"Shit, Toki, you might have just hit the jackpot with him," Lucy said.

I noticed two chicks walking toward our section. Qwan stood and greeted them.

"Toki, this is my sister, Tammy, and her friend, Cookie."

I shook their hands. "Nice to meet you." I then turned to my crew. "Tammy, that's Morgan, Sweets, and Lucy."

Everyone waved.

Cookie was icy. I knew she had a man spending chips from the looks of her big-ass Royal Oak Audemars Piguet watch. She seemed a bit older, but I could tell she was either a ball player's wife or a baller's wife. I classified her as a bad bitch. Tammy, on the other hand, was average. It was obvious she kept with name brands, but looking at her, she liked to be common. Her whole outfit, including the shoes, was covered in little Gucci logos. I've never been into the free advertisement, so logos and I never meshed.

Her outfit was cute, though. She wore a cream, oversized cashmere sweater that hung off the shoulder, with some cream leather leggings. She had a cute shape. However, when it came to giving credit, Cookie owned that. She could have easily been a part of my crew. Our bling ran neck and neck, and she wasn't no ugly bitch.

As the time wound down, everybody was as drunk as they could be. I peeped Tammy having words with a fat, greasy-looking bitch. It was heated. The fat girl looked a hot mess with a homemade lumpy weave. From where I stood, I could see her tracks. Then I saw Tammy pick up her glass of Patrón and throw it on the girl. The shit got totally out of control.

Qwan jumped over the table and got in front of Tammy because fat girl's crew looked ready to pounce on Tammy, and it was a gang of them. They looked ready to fuck some shit up.

I would have helped Tammy, but I didn't know his so-called sister like that. For all I knew, they could have been fucking. But, Cookie definitely held her down right on the front line. Her loyalty to Tammy was evident.

Morgan grabbed my arm. "Toki, let's go."

I stood in a state of shock as I watched Qwan transform from a charming little boy to a deranged, insane lunatic.

Morgan pulled me again, this time a little harder than before. Snapping out of my trance, I followed her to the door. I stopped in my tracks because I felt like something was missing. So, I turned and looked back. Just then, shots rang out and people scattered.

"Oh shit! Where's Sweets?" I asked, jerking my arm from Morgan.

"Toki, what the fuck are you doing? C'mon!"

"Sweets isn't behind me! What the fuck you mean c'mon? We can't leave without her!"

I looked around for Sweets after hearing five more shots.

"What was she doing? Why wasn't she behind you, Toki?" Morgan asked.

"Hell, I don't know. But, she's probably the only girl in here with a cropped True Religion jean jacket on. Sweets loves everything jean. Look for the jean."

"Now is not the time for jokes, Toki," Morgan said as tears filled her eyes.

"Shut the fuck up with that scared shit! Please, bitch. You done seen worst shit, and knowing Sweets like I do, she's good. Stop crying, crybaby! Just look for a jean jacket with crystals on it," I replied still laughing.

Damn, I hope she's alright. Sweets is smooth on the streets; her eyes open even when she sleeps. I know her fucking ass. If she's missing, she's probably playing with her pussy, cumming from the action. Sweets feeds off violence.

"Where the fuck is she?" I said. "Now I'm getting pissed. Fuck all that being scared shit. That's our bitch. Shit, we family."

Morgan started to panic even more. "Where is she, Toki? Why wasn't she behind you?"

"She was and then she wasn't," I told her. "Just keep looking, Morgan."

Morgan was known for being the scared one out of the crew, but just because she was scary Mary, it didn't mean she wouldn't take your head clean off your shoulders.

We pushed through the crowd with no fear, elbowing whoever was in our way. When we made it back to our section, I noticed Sweets standing on the chair watching the aftermath of the commotion. The expression on her face looked as if she were thinking, *What the fuck just happened?*

"Sweets!" I yelled.

As she looked in my direction, we walked up on her.

"What the fuck you doing, Sweets? You bugging. Since when do we start breaking rules? That's not how we move."

"I had to, Toki," Sweets said, stepping off the couch. "Trust me, I have my reasons. I needed to watch this shit go down. Your new friend Tammy and your boy Qwan are foul. I peeped the screaming between those two. At first, I thought he was fucking her and they were just pretending to be siblings. But, to stand there and watch the grimy shit with my own eyes tuned my mind into the setup situation."

"What if you got hit, bitch?" Morgan yelled.

"Then I would have to take a few down with me," Sweets replied sarcastically.

"What you talking about, Sweets? You bugging," I

repeated. "I think you had a little bit too much to drink."

"Naw, I'm not drunk, bitch. This shit seems like a badly-written script," Sweets commented.

Morgan agreed. "Yeah, Toki. I wasn't really comfortable with this whole scene."

"Lucy, you feel that way, too?" I asked angrily.

Just as Lucy opened her mouth to reply, we heard someone yell, "It's in my back! It's in my back!"

We looked in the direction of where the screams were coming from, and I spotted Qwan in the commotion.

Should I just take my girls, go ahead home, and forget I ever met Qwan? Or should I be the real bitch I'm known to be and make sure he's good at least? It's not in my character to walk off and not see if Qwan and his peoples are cool.

Going with my thoughts to do what I think is the right thing, I headed in the direction of the screams, but before I could get far, Sweets grabbed me by my shirt.

"Where you going, Toki? You just told me not to walk off. C'mon, let's go."

"I'm going to see who got hit and make sure Qwan is okay," I said, yanking myself from her grip.

"Really, Toki?" Morgan said.

"Yeah. I mean, what does that say about my character if I don't show some concern?"

"Toki," Sweets said, "I don't mean to let you down, but, honey, just as you was barking on us, homie was walking out the back door. He saw you, Toki, and he didn't even slow down. So, that says a lot about his character. That little gesture proved he doesn't give a fuck about you, and that's a good thing. Let him loose. He is off the chain, Toki. You and I know you have a hell of a lot to lose. So, just void him out like a bad check. Shit, act like you two never met."

I looked at Sweets with a "What the fuck?" expression.

"That's crazy. On the real, he just made it easier for me to delete him from my list of potential boyfriends. He left, and my phone isn't ringing?!"

"He didn't even have the decency to call you to make sure you was okay, Toki," Morgan said.

"Come on, y'all, before this night gets any worse."

Just then, I heard Tammy scream, "Oh no, God! Please, Cookie, don't die!"

We stopped in our tracks and looked in their direction.

"Damn, y'all, that's Tammy's friend, Cookie," I told them.

"From the looks of it, all that ice she had on is gone," Morgan commented. "She had on shit you can't miss."

"This was a straight robbery," Lucy and Sweets said in unison, as if they were twins on the same brain wavelength.

"I knew something wasn't right about that whole altercation," Sweets continued. "That's why I had to get a clear view. I could have sworn I heard Qwan tell the big, black bitch to pop off. I told you something's not right, Toki. I'm telling you, that girl came here to get robbed and killed. We were just celebrating her departure."

The ambulance arrived only to find out they had to call the coroner.

As we finally tried to make our exit, I paused when I spotted them pink-faced pigs waddling their fat asses through the door.

The head dick, who had on a tight, white, captains button-up shirt, said, "I need everyone to stay where you are. Please don't attempt to leave until one of my officers speaks with you."

Just my fucking luck, I thought.

The last thing I needed was a cop snooping in my shit. I hate cops, I despise precincts, and the government and me ain't never been friends. So, talking to the cops I don't do.

Tammy slowly crept her black ass in our direction. I guess because her so-called family left her ass.

"That bitch better not bring her hot ass over here acting

like we all together," Sweets said.

"Here she comes," Morgan said.

I didn't give a fuck that she was coming our way. She was a non–factor. Fuck if she heard us talking. Shit, if she got froggy, they were gonna need two body bags instead of one.

"This night has been complete hell," Tammy said as she walked up.

The paramedic pointed the cops in our direction because she brought her ugly ass over to us.

"Shit," I said, glaring at Tammy. "Here come the pigs."

My crew and I stood still with our attitudes on full blast. My arms were folded, and my killer stare was on point. I simply was not in the mood.

"Excuse me, ladies, may I have a word with you?" the rookie officer asked.

We simply stared at him. If looks could kill, that pig would have been straight barbeque.

He raised his voice a little. "Ladies, what are your names?"

We stood there like his white ass hadn't said shit.

"Okay. I see we have some stubborn ladies. If you don't cooperate here, then maybe you will at the precinct."

"Naw, we not doing that," Morgan responded. "We're allergic to precincts and shit. If it's that serious, then let me get our beast of an attorney to speak for us. I got him on speed dial, and trust, he has no problem with waking up in the middle of the night. But, we hear you. So, shoot. Ask your questions. We're not running. We're not hiding, 'cause we haven't done anything."

The rookie sized me up like he wanted to pop off. I guess that's because I gave him the screwface and made no attempt to answer any of his snitch questions. His eyes then focused on Tammy.

"Excuse me, miss. Aren't you a friend of the victim?"

Tammy walked out from behind us. "Yes, that's my

friend," she replied.

"Well, may we have a few words with you?"

The rookie's partner looked at Tammy like he was puzzled.

They walked off with Tammy to question her.

"I love that I know how to read lips, just in case this bitch acts like she knew us prior to tonight," Sweets commented. "I mean, look at her. She's over there performing for them pigs. One minute, she's crying, and the next, she's hiding. I swear, these fake-ass, in-the-street bitches are so confused, they don't even know themselves." She turned to me. "I don't know, Toki. This whole night seems shady, and your new friend Tammy is a foul-ass bitch. I think she lined her friend. Word, that's what I'm seeing."

The rookie cop came back over with the head dick.

"Well, the tape shows that you all weren't involved," the head dick said. "So, I'm gonna allow y'all to leave. But, you must give my officer your full name, address, and phone number just in case we need to contact you if something comes up."

"Naw, we not worried about shit coming up," Morgan told him.

Sweets looked at Morgan and said, "Get Pat on the line, 'cause this right here is a waste of our time."

Morgan handed the head dick the card. "Here is all the info you need, and if we happen to bump heads in the near future, this is who you contact. He will answer any questions you may have. And just to be sure, here he is on the phone." She handed over her phone to him.

After the police captain talked to Pat for a few seconds, he hung up, and with an attitude, he said, "You ladies are free to go, but trust me, I will be in touch."

"That's why I gave you my lawyer's card, just in case your nose draws you toward our way," Morgan replied. "No worries, he will pick up when you call."

As we walked off, I felt them watching us. I guess he figured because we partied hard and fucked with street niggas, we didn't know our rights, like we were some low-budget chickens. Hell, he was lucky we weren't pulled over on the side of the turnpike. I would have told Sweets to let that peter speak.

We laughed as we walked to the car. Qwan must have been watching, because as soon as we stepped out, my phone rang. I didn't look at it, though.

The driver opened the door, and we climbed inside. My phone rang again. I was too upset at the fact that he basically left me to deal with the fucking cops and his fake-ass sister.

He can keep calling, but all he's gonna get is the recording for him to leave a message after the beep. I'm writing his ass off like a voided check. Clown!

Chapter 8

It was damn near ninety degrees, the beginning of summer. The Kingdome Tournament was upon us. Of course, the crew and I were going. I hadn't seen or spoken to Qwan since the incident.

I met Sweets at the NYC WOW Hair Clinic to get our hair done. It's the best black-owned salon in Manhattan when it comes to weaves, clip-ons, and wig caps. NYC WOW boasts the top ten black hairstylists in New York.

Now, Maria was my girl, but she wasn't cutting my hair unless it's just my ends. I wanted some layers and about two inches taken off. Plus, WOW was like a secret society for elite chicks. You always found out who was doing who.

That day, though, I left my phone at home, which completely threw me off. I knew I missed mad calls.

"Toki, you have a call," the receptionist called out to me.

"Hello."

"Toki," Sweets yelled through the phone all crazy. "I was calling you. Why you not picking up?"

"Why you think? I left my fucking phone at home, and you know I'm on the edge right now. If Carla wasn't charging five hundred in advance, I would have left already. Where you at, because you know she likes to keep your five-hundred when you don't show?"

"Naw, I'm on my way. You know I had to stop and get me a burger real quick."

"Where you at? In Jimbo's in Harlem?" I asked.

Sweets laughed because she knew I knew her ass was sneaking and buying turkey burgers and shit. Her laugh was interrupted when I heard a familiar female voice in the background say, "Hi Sweets!"

"Hold on a second," Sweets told the person. Then she busted out laughing and said to me, "Girl, you will never guess who's standing here thinking she can speak to me!" Sweets laughed again. "Hey, Toki, why the fuck is Summer's old, dry ass standing in front of me looking real ratchet."

I laughed a little.

Sweets continued. "Toki, she must be slobbing Tommy's knob right, because I see she managed to suck a pair of chicken-head luxury Prada footwear out that lil' dick nigger. Like really, patent leather hot pink? And Tommy wonders why you're not giving a fuck about him and his new mutt."

Sweets gave Summer hell, assassinating her character. She always said if a bitch spoke to her when she knew she shouldn't, then the bitch should be prepared for the "You can't be serious" speech.

"Just because you see me by myself and not with my girls, don't mean you can fake like I like you. If you're a non-factor, then be that. Don't set yourself up for a moment of embarrassment."

"I was just saying what's up," Summer stated sarcastically.

Since I could hear Summer's response so clearly, I figured Sweets must have been up in her face.

"For what, to get dissed? You should really consider thinking before you talk or walk when it comes to my crew and me. What, you don't get it? We don't fuck with you…"

"Number twenty-three!" the cook yelled.

"Hey, that's me," Sweets said. "Gimme a half lemonade, half iced tea."

Sweets is crazy! I shook my head and chuckled. I love my

crew. They always ride for me whether I'm present or not.

"Summer, you should only speak when spoken to. Remember that, so next time, you won't make an ass out of yourself. Tell Tommy I said to stop giving you the leftover ones he usually spends throughout the day in the corner stores. Fucking for chump change. Thinking you can speak to me just because you manage to suck the dick of one of Toki's dudes. Don't think you move her. As you can see, pretty Tommy is washed up. So instead of being cocky over your lil' dick nigga, you should question your position. 'Cause last I checked, Toki left him. You was only good enough for him to fuck with when his chips were down. I don't know, but to me, that just made Tommy look weak and makes you look like a bottom bitch. You bum bitch, walking around all proud, wanting the streets to know Tommy's fucking you now."

Sweets laughed before continuing her verbal assault. "That's so funny! His chips are down, so he downgraded to a free hoe. I don't know how you think, but in my eyes, we look at you like a prostitute. So, please don't think you gained extra points in the streets when you fucking and sucking for free. All you did was brand yourself as a low-level street walker."

I heard the door chime as Sweets exited the restaurant.

"Girl, that bitch is a hot-ass mess. Anyway, Toki, I'm jumping in the town car now. I'll see you when I get there."

"Who's driving, Trav?" I asked Sweets before she hung up.

"Yeah, why? What's up?"

After pausing and thinking for a moment, I told her, "Never mind. I was going to send him to my house to get my phone after dropping you off, but fuck it."

Trav is our limo driver. He's been driving Nice since he was a little kid, and from then on, it's been that way.

Sweets was the only one out of the crew who didn't know how to drive. She always said it was much better to get picked up and dropped off by a personal driver than to be paying for parking or filling up a gas tank. When you have a driver, you don't have to worry about none of that.

Sweets walked into the salon and spotted me immediately.

"Bitch, you late," Will's gay ass stated out loud, putting Sweets' tardiness on blast. "You almost lost your five-hundred dollars with Carla."

Sweets replied, "Naw, I wasn't losing that. Carla and me would have to have a debate about that." Then she turned to me. "I can't believe that trick thought we cool enough to speak to me."

"Yeah, but I'm not surprised," I said. "She be thirsty for attention, no matter what kind."

"The bitch must have lost her marbles to think you're losing sleep over her and Tommy."

"Please. Tommy was last year's news. He is dead in my book, and Summer who? The bitch is a bird. Tommy got with the chick he knew would suck him with pride without getting a dime. Money is funny for Tommy right now. My niggas got him scrambling just to keep up.

"He would have gotten left somewhere on the side of the road for disrespecting me. You know Row wouldn't mind catching one just for wreck. But, Tommy is pussy, and there's nothing to gain by leaving his pussy ass in a ditch. Tommy is mush. He's not built for what my niggas would do to him.

"I hear he's promoting his new bum bitch, which I don't have a problem with it. I have a problem when Toki's name gets brought up in the bird talk. So, he's fucked. And he must have forgotten I'm the one who stopped his rush and slowed his pipeline up. If he keep playing with me, I'm gonna clog it. Now that would put a hurting on his pockets, especially with Tiny at home and all the kids he got. There's not enough money to keep a bad bitch like me on lock, so what did he do? Promote the free hoe."

Sweets nodded. "I mean, what the fuck you expect him to do? He's hurting over you. He only knows one way to try and get your attention," she added.

"If so, he picked the wrong bitch, 'cause how can I get mad at a chick that don't exists."

"Hey, Toki…Sweets," Carla said, greeting us. "Can I get you ladies anything?"

"No, thank you," we responded simultaneously.

"Okay," Carla said. "Well, my assistant will be with you in a minute."

Carla was Sweets' hairstylist. They were really close, and Sweets wouldn't go to anyone but her, even for a doobie.

Carla was nasty with the scissors, and so was her first-chair stylist, Will. Let's not forget the weave queen Shanequa. When I watch her fingers go to work, she makes me want to braid up my twenty-inch mane just to rock one of her killer weaves for one day. That's how sick she is with it. Will ran the shop when Carla traveled to do celebrity styling. Most of the time, Shanequa accompanied her.

"Where's Shanequa?" Sweets asked Carla.

"She's on vacation," Carla replied.

"Oh okay. Well, I'ma let Will do my hair, Carla. Go on and start on Toki," Sweets said.

"So y'all going to the Kingdome?" Will asked.

"Yes," Sweets replied. "You know the first and the last day are the best days. Are you going?" she asked him.

"Girl, you see all these bitches in here? I got too many customers. I would never make it," Will replied. Then he looked at me and said with sass, "So, Toki, I heard what happened between you and Tommy."

I looked up from my magazine so fast that I almost caught whiplash. I guess nobody told the fag I don't play that beauty shop gossip about my personal business. But, I didn't want to snap at Will's gossiping ass without hearing what he heard. The gays know everybody's business.

"Mmm, word. And what you hear?" I asked sarcastically.

"Nothing really bad. Just that you cut Tommy's ass off," he said.

Will liked to start gossip. He was a regular male version of Wendy Williams. It was okay for beauty shop entertainment, but I wasn't in that mode. Business was on my mind. My nerves were on edge. Without my phone, I felt like my business was totally out of control.

"Well, Toki, at least Tiny will be looked at like wifey number one again, being that you gave her baby's daddy back," he said.

"You mean wifey, the dumb one," Sweets said as she walked back from the wash area.

I knew Sweets peeped my attitude. Sensing I was not in the mood, she filled in the blanks.

"I mean, the way he do her, I would have killed Tommy," Sweets continued. "Two to the back of his dome. And as far as him and Toki goes, she left him alone. He just played himself by thinking that hood rat would ever make my girl jealous. He knows Summer don't hold no weight. Tommy is washed up, and Summer is the bottom of the barrel, a Jane Doe bitch."

"He's not even on the baller charts anymore since Toki took away his worth. I mean, that's the word on the streets," Will added.

I got a little agitated being the subject of this conversation.

"Please! Tommy knows better. Why would I care if he spent fifty dollars on the bum's hair? He knows him and Summer will never move me. She's washed all the way up, and she's only twenty-three. Tommy's eating slowly now, so he can't afford me," I commented. "Shit, he's two seconds from eating his full-course meal on a garbage can lid. Losing sleep over him and Summer? I'm definitely not."

"Toki, you okay, honey?" Will asked. "You want

something to drink?"

"As a matter of fact, let me get a mimosa."

Will told his assistant to go fix me a mimosa.

Sweets yelled, "Make that two. Damn, Will, I'm your client, and you didn't ask me if I was thirsty."

"Please, Sweets, you're not a guest in the shop. Toki pops in once in a blue moon. You're here every weekend. Besides, bitch, I heard you asked for Shanequa first, so don't even try and front like I was your first option," Will stated in his sassy way. "Shit, you know how to make it yourself."

"Whatever," Sweets said, taking a seat in his chair.

Will's assistant brought me the drink.

"Toki, do you want anything else?" Will asked.

"Naw, I'm good. Just not in the mood."

After Will roller set her hair, Sweets sat next to me under the dryer.

"So, Toki, have you spoken to your friend?"

"No, girl, but trust, he has definitely been blowing up my phone. I know when I get home, I'm going to have a bundle of missed calls. Most will be from him."

With a serious tone, Sweets said, "Toki, you better not call him."

"I'm not."

She looked at me sideways. "Yeah, okay. I know you and your curious ass. Toki, if homie keeps calling you, eventually you're going to pick up for him."

"Sweets, please, it's not that serious. He really turned me off, with all that out-of-control bullshit. I can imagine what his days are like. I'm good on that note," I assured her. "He got too much going on for me."

She looked at me with a smirk. I smiled in return.

Just then, Carla called me to her chair. By the time I was finished, Sweets was standing at the front of the salon paying her tab. I took an extra look in the mirror as I stood up from the chair.

"Thanks, Carla. I love it." I paid my tab and tipped her.

As Sweets and I were about to walk out the door, the TV hanging on the wall over the front desk caught my full attention. I was frozen in shock at what I saw. My mouth fell wide open, and my bottom lip hit the floor.

"Girl, what is it?" Sweets asked.

I pointed to the TV.

"Hey, can you turn that up?" I asked the girl at the front desk.

The entire shop paused. Cookie's face was plastered on the screen.

"This is Loretta McCoy, reporting to you live from Channel Twelve News. A night out with the stars turned into a bloodbath a week ago. Five New York Giants were partying with other sports celebrities at Ruby Falls Nightclub. The star-studded guests list included other current NFL and NBA players, along with a few big names in the hip-hop industry, including the victim Cookie Carter, wife of one of Atlanta's biggest recording artist. It did not come out until today that this mother of two was the victim.

"We learned that Cookie was visiting New York to celebrate and support her longtime friend, Tammy Hooks. Ms. Hooks launched her new promotional company, Dime Piece Promotions. Apparently, a few of the Giants were her first celebrity clients. Our sources tell us that Ms. Hooks got into an altercation with a group of women, and that altercation turned deadly. Gunmen fired five shots, two of which struck Ms. Carter in the back. She was pronounced dead at the scene. She leaves her husband, Lou Carter, and their two children. So far, no arrests have been made, but the club's management is cooperating with the ongoing investigation. Police are asking anyone with information to contact them. Back to you, Troy."

"I told you something wasn't right about that night, Toki. Damn, I wonder who the suspects are. I hope it ain't us,"

Sweets said.

"You know we're not on their radar. At least not for no robbery," I told her.

We left the shop still in shock, not because of what happened or because I was there, but more or less as to who robbed her.

"Damn, nowadays, partying in the city is like taking a risk with your life, especially if you're going out all icy. That night of fun might be the last night of your life," Sweets said.

We hopped in my car and went to my house to get dressed for the day. We had about three hours before the games started, and I had to get my phone. I knew I missed a lot of calls.

I pulled inside the garage. As soon as we got out the car and made it into the house, I heard my cell phone ringing. By the time I made it to the living room where I had left it, it stopped ringing. Then it started again. I looked at the screen; it was Qwan. I had to admit, I was curious about him. For some reason, I couldn't shake him. He stayed on my mind, even after the incident.

"Toki, you gonna answer your phone?" Sweets asked.

I hit the end button to send Qwan to voicemail. "I got a lot on my brain. Today is not the day."

"Oh yeah, Toki, have you spoken to Nice lately? His trial starts soon, right? You know the streets is missing him."

"Yeah, I know. That's because when he's home, everybody eats. I'm not fucking with everybody. Nice said if it ain't family, don't trust it. Besides, I can't afford to pass shit out on the arm. As for the ones that tried to walk before they crawled, they're hurting. Probably sending 'Help Me' kites to Nice while he's fighting for the whole Brooklyn. So, yeah, they're missing him. That's what they get for being grown, thinking they could do it on their own."

"Yeah, they found out if you can't swim, you drown. Nice is like a lifejacket. The streets need him to survive."

"Brooklyn owes my brother. They better show him when his date comes. He should be calling soon. Pat said his trial will start in a few months. That whole motherfucker better be packed, real talk. I'm talking young ones to oldies," I said.

Sweets replied, "Yeah, I know Brooklyn is definitely going to stand up for him. Nice is a real nigga. Of course, Harlem is going to come out."

"Yeah, Morgan's bringing a truckload in. You know how she do."

We both laughed.

"Yeah, I know," I replied. "Especially the Puerto Ricans. You can't tell Nice he isn't a dark-skinned Puerto Rican."

"So is this snitch really on the run, or is he in protective custody?" Sweets asked. "You know how the fucking government do. When they're protecting a rat, they make up shit to make you look in another direction while they head in the opposite."

"Either way, before this trail gets here, whoever their key rat is will never make it on the stand," I replied.

"Word," Sweets said. "Did he tell you who the rat was?"

"I'm sure he knows, but Nice ain't telling, especially not over the phone. Nice always told me if you want to take a nigga out and be able to go to sleep at night without keeping one eye open, you must always do it by your lonesome. You know Nice already paid for the rat's termination, so why would he discuss it at all unless he wants to raise the government's eyebrow?" A tear fell from my eye. "I miss him."

"So when you do speak to him, are you going to ask him about that nigga Qwan just to see what he's really about?"

"No. Nice knows not a lot of shit impresses me, so if I start asking about a nigga, he's gonna think I'm interested in that person. Getting advice from him about the next nigga, when I know he'd rather me not date at all, will not be a good response. I mean, Sweets, you know Nice. He don't think any nigga is ever good enough for me."

"Well, that's how Nice has always been. You know that, Toki. I don't know why you just don't stop looking for what's been in front of you all along and give Nice some skins," Sweets said, laughing.

I giggled a little and replied, "You and Morgan with y'all 'Toki and Nice, husband and wife' comments."

"Well, I think you should just stay clear of Mr. Qwan until you speak to Nice again, because something is telling me he's bad news. Besides, your brother has a lot on his plate. The last thing he needs to be worrying about is you, Tee, while he's fighting for his life, right?" Sweets asked.

"The whole world knows when it comes to my brother, I don't need nobody checking me about him. Don't give me words of advice about how not to stress my brother. I will die before I give him anything more to worry about. Shit, I'm a big girl, Sweets. Stop talking to me like I'm a child. You got me fucked up. I fuck with Nice from the heart, so why are you even going there with me?" I said.

"I'm not going anywhere with you, but Tee..." She paused for a moment. "Maybe you should take a look in the mirror and see what Qwan and I see—a beauty with a heart as big as the moon. You're not the normal rider. You got hella picks. You're the total package, all in one. And on top of that, you're the sister to Brooklyn's youngest and richest dope kingpin. Some niggas might see you as a dollar sign that they treat like a trophy. I'm just telling you to be smart with Qwan. That's it, Tee."

"Like damn, Sweets. You act like I'm getting married to homie tomorrow. We just kicking it, and I would be a fake bitch to lie to you and say I'm not feeling him, because I am. But, understand this. I know what's good for me and what's not. I know what stress my brother doesn't need, and I know he's number one to me. So, stop coming at me sideways when it comes to him. He's good; he don't want for shit. His lawyer is paid up for the trial, and in case he blows, he's paid up for all Nice's appeals. What I do for Nice and what I do for Qwan doesn't need to be approved by nobody. You don't like Qwan? Cool. But, don't treat me funny and act like I've changed, Sweets. This bitch right here is still the same ol' G. You got me?"

She simply stared at me without responding.

"So what you wearing?" I asked, while grabbing my shower kit.

"Denim. You know me," Sweets said. "Doesn't Bishop come home any day now?"

I smiled, while thinking, *That's my girl. We disagree? We speak on it and move on.*

"Yes, girl. I've been counting down the days. I miss that little motherfucker. I'm glad he beat the case and all the government could do was hold him on a nine-month violation."

"And he maxed out?" Sweets stated.

"Yep. No more back and forth for Bishop. With both him and Nice being away for a long period of time, it definitely would have put a hole in my heart."

After we got dressed, we jumped in my candy-apple red Range Rover. I backed out of the garage and drove towards the George Washington Bridge going into New York. My Bluetooth in my truck rang. I pressed the talk button on my steering wheel.

"Who's that?" Sweets asked.

"Bitch, you asking like my name didn't pop up on the screen," Morgan said.

We all laughed.

"Shut up," Sweets said.

"Uh, bitch, you better have me a parking spot. If I can't park in front, I'll be making a U-turn back home and park in my garage," I told her.

"Shut up, Toki, with your extra ass," Morgan replied,

giggling. “You know I got you. That’s why I’m calling. I paid a dope head to hold two spots for us. Are you close?” she asked.

“Yeah, we’re actually driving down Lenox Avenue now. Where you at?”

“Just pulled up in front of the projects, and, bitch, it’s packed,” Morgan said.

“I’m there in sixty seconds.”

Sweets and I bobbed our heads to “Live Fast, Die Young” by Rick Ross. My custom speakers blasted the beat as we cruised through Harlem, the borough that never sleeps. People were on every corner, drinking and chilling. People also chilled on the stoops or sat in front of their buildings with folding chairs.

When we pulled up on 115th and Lenox Avenue, Morgan stood next to the dope fiendd she rented to hold down the parking spots. She looked like Lisa Raye, wearing all-white linen pants and a white tank top. She rocked her white with some blue YSL Tribute sandals and a navy blue, patent leather Louis Vuitton Vernis Alma bag. Her hair was wet and curly all the way down her back, with a blue and pink Louis Vuitton headband tied in a perfect bow on the top of her head.

I was rocking my red Christian Louboutin spike pumps, white J Brand jeggings, and an oversized red sheer button-up blouse. My fatty looked extra good. I decided to give the unfortunate a sneak peak at my newest arm candy caviar, a jumbo red Chanel Classic flap bag with the silver hardware. I turned heads in Harlem.

Sweets wore all denim everything, as usual. She had on some True Religion ripped and bleached skinny jeans with the vest to match and a black YSL belt with the big YSL buckle in gold. Her abs and breasts were in perfect shape, so she rocked the vest like a tank top, with just a little stomach showing.

I slid the fiendd a bundle of my famous dog food.

"Here's an extra tip for you," I said. "Now go home and share with your friends. Trust me, this is going to be the best you ever had. Remember, today was your luckiest day because you did a job for me that deserved a nice tip. When you get home, you will know I got the best shit on the streets. To get a hit of that good shit again, go to 118th Street and 7th Avenue. Ask for Tommy. Tell him Toki sent you."

While approaching the courts, we heard the crowd roar. The place was electric as the music boomed from the speakers and the crowd cheered for their favorite team. It was the hottest day of summer, and people came out early to watch the sneakers scrape the pavement and soar through the air. It was the Kingdome Classic. No introduction needed, no ticket required, but an invitation or connection is your only chances of getting anywhere near the action. Everybody comes out for the first day of the Kingdome Tournament.

The teams are put together by some of New York's favorite rappers, hustlers, and bosses. The players polished their games on the gritty court at 115th Street, located in the heart of the projects. Kingdome is a big deal in Harlem, almost like a Harlem reunion.

It was a festival, equipped with food vendors like the nut-cracker man, old ladies frying chicken, and the Italian Icy lady with her cart. Kids ran around and grandmothers enjoyed the festivities. The first day of the tournament also meant the biggest barbeque put on by the team owners and coaches. The police even barricaded off the streets.

It didn't matter what time me and my crew arrived, we were always guaranteed a seat. Morgan's juice card was accepted all over Harlem. As the security guard escorted us to our courtside seats, all eyes were on us, but that's how it always was whenever we went out. My crew rocked the best shit, so people always stared. Harlem had a lot of amateurs with some bad bitch potentials, but their juice card didn't compare to mine; they stood in line waiting for an empty nosebleed seat.

As soon as I sat down, I checked out my surroundings. It's a force of habit. When my vision landed on the other side of the court, I locked eyes with Tommy. I looked towards the scoreboard and saw Tiny. I smirked and saw her mood change when she peeped my presence. She looked like she needed to take a shit. It's probably because my presence made her sick. She knew that when I was around, she didn't exist to Tommy.

I always made her nervous, especially since she knew I'm unapproachable. She rolled her eyes at me like she always did, and again, I smirked right back at her.

Shit, she can sit back, relax, and take off that girdle, 'cause Toki is no longer a threat.

"Damn, Tee, baby mama is grilling you kind of hard," Morgan commented.

"I know. I see her with her looking ass. Looks like my presence just turned her stomach. Looking like she needs to pass some gas."

Morgan laughed as loud as she could. With the stare-off boring me, I turned my attention to the game. Basketball is my sport. Nice is more of a fan of it than I am, but by being around him, my love of the sport grew.

We got there in the fourth quarter. DipSet was losing by one point, with twenty seconds left on the clock. RocAFella was styling on the court. Skippy was showing off new moves, faking out the whole DipSet team. He lived for showing off on the court, while everyone watched him in his glory, popping street ball shit as always and trying to wind down the time. DJ Brushy B kept shouting out Skippy like he was the only player on the court. Tommy, who was DipSet's coach, called a timeout.

When the timeout was over, the buzzer sounded.

"Oh shit! DipSet got a few tricks up their sleeves," Brushy B said. "RocAFella, you might have a problem in these last ten seconds. DipSet just unleashed the dragon! They put Little in the game. I guess they saved the best for last, Harlem! It looks like we're in for a ride!"

Everyone's eyes were glued to the court, waiting to see if Little would pull out a win in less than ten seconds.

Little got the ball and moved on them niggas like a snake on the loose. They couldn't stop him. He made it down the court with five seconds left. He stopped, pulled up, and made his shot. The crowd went silent as the ball soared in the air. It went in the hoop just as the buzzer sounded. The crowd cheered, and Harlem's anthem "Fool's Paradise" blared through the speakers. It was time to celebrate.

"I know Tommy is happy his team won the first game," Morgan yelled as we exited the basketball court.

Everybody was out. Fat Joe and Diddy paid us a visit, even though neither of their teams played that day. If you were somebody, then showing your face on the first day was a must.

We decided to stick around for a little while. Morgan had to make her rounds, mingling and talking extra loud. That's because she was the friendly one.

The Dirt Bike Boys got busy on their KLR's and four-wheelers. The pigs usually chased them off the streets, but on these types of days, they let them live. The Dirt Bike Boys were a part of Harlem's entertainment – popping willies and 360's, doing dirt bike stunts, and burning rubber.

Tommy broke his neck trying to keep an eye on me as people walked up to congratulate him on his win.

Sweets tapped me on my shoulder. "Tee, there go Summer in all her glory, wearing them big-ass pink Prada's, acting like she runs Harlem. I should go over there and smack the cheese off her teeth."

Sweets said the statement in a joking manner, but if I had given her the go, she would have popped on Summer.

Confused, I looked at Sweets. "Now why would I do that?

I keep telling you I don't know no Summer or whatever y'all call her. So, please, stop informing me of this non-descript bitch that Tommy went to the Section-8 building to get. Please, Sweets, enough with my name in the same phrases as that bird."

Sweets laughed.

I felt someone grab me by my waist. I turned around and looked right in Tommy's face.

"If you don't get your no-frills, hood-rat ass off my back, nigga. Go find your baby momma," I said.

Disgusted, I frowned up my face and walked off with Sweets, while Summer stared hard. I knew he followed me, not giving a fuck if his bitch saw him, but that was nothing new.

"Yo, Toki, you just gonna walk away from me like that?" he said.

I put one finger in the air and said, "Exactly."

From behind, he sped up and grabbed me like he owned me.

"Okay, I see you want to make a scene," I said. "Cool. I have no problem with it, because you're the one with a wife that you go home to most nights. I'm single; I have no one to answer to. So, what's up, Tommy? Speak your peace."

"Oh word! You single now, Toki?"

Does he not remember our last conversation?

"How quickly we forget, Tommy," I replied.

"Word! You coming at me sideways, Toki? Okay, I got you. You're feeling yourself. You think you're that bitch."

"The difference is, you think I'm that bitch, while I *know* I'm that bitch. I don't know why you fronting like this cold shoulder you getting is a shock. I told you, bad bitches like me ain't second to nobody. Shit, you know the games. You know the rules, right? Then you need to act like you do. I mean, you went from a porterhouse steak to a can of sardines," I said, then laughed and nodded my head in

Summer's direction. "So there's no way you can think you hold any weight when it comes to me."

He turned to see Summer stabbing holes in his back with her eyes.

"What?" he yelled and frowned up his face. "I don't fuck with that bitch, Toki. You know better than that. Why would I fuck her when I got picks? So is that why you're flipping on me like this, because you think I fuck with that bitch? You bugging, Toki. You know I fuck with you. The whole Harlem knows you're my bitch."

"That's true, but now they know I'm not," I said and laughed again.

He looked defeated and shocked that he really had been canceled. He didn't care about hurting me, so why should I care about hurting him?

"What happened, Tommy?" I asked. "You need a little help picking your face up off the floor?"

Sweets laughed and said, "Toki, come on."

I guess she was trying to spare the old man's feelings.

I looked at Sweets and giggled, then noticed Morgan looking in our direction. She stopped her conversation when she peeped the scene between Tommy and me. Summer stared from the left side, and Tiny walked up from behind. I knew I made his blood boil.

"I knew you were a foul bitch, running around here fucking another nigga. That's why I never left home, because I knew you was a sneaky bitch, you fucking hoe!" he yelled.

I stopped and turned around laughing. "Really, Tommy? I'm a hoe? Your baby momma gets fucked in the Cherry Lounge parking lot, but I'm a hoe? You mad 'cause I left you, but who's acting like a hoe? Better yet, nigga, you're a pussy. Don't get tough and forget who you talking to. You don't want this heat. I can't believe you call me a hoe, but you're fucking a call girl raw. Fuck out of here, Tommy, with your small dick. That shit don't even stand tall on its own. Nigga, you must have bumped your motherfucking head, because you pussy. You're not built for this. Don't bark loud if you don't got no teeth to bite, and don't get fucked up trying to disrespect me. You punk-ass nigga, no one fears you in these streets. If anything, they keep your pussy ass paying and running. I can name a few occasions when a motherfucker chased you and made you shit your pants. So, all that tough-talking gangster shit you're doing, you should nip it in the bud. Because you know I will fuck your old ass up.

Not stopping to take a breath, I continued going on him.

"You're talking crazy old man," I chuckled. "I swear you old dudes are always trying to keep up with us new schools. Why ain't nobody telling you that you're washed up, Tommy? Slow down. You're trying too hard to keep up. You look tired and worn out. I don't know, maybe you need a nap or something. Because you hallucinating coming out your face. You asked for it, so I'm dishing. Now you're trying to play Mr. Innocent. What happened? You can't take it. I know, Tommy. Toki's a little too much for you, so slow down and chill out, because you're a few years too late. This is a new day and age.

"That bullshit you got in your pants that you call a dick, you should have spared it for some years, but instead, you just went outside with that shit. Hanging out and offering it to any chick willing. Fuck out of here. Go get that prescription for Viagra so you can give your little shit a boost. You should watch who you're talking to, because you know I will slaughter you."

Sweets and Morgan stood by me just in case his bitch-ass felt froggy. I wasn't even mad, but that nigga had me fucked up. I was glad his dumb bitch was right there to witness the whole shit. She knew who wanted who.

"And on that note, you need to go fuck your trash. She looks like she could use a new garbage bag," I said, pointing to Summer and shaking my head. "Go fuck yourself, Tommy.

Better yet, kill yourself." I turned to my girls and said, "Y'all ready? Come on. Let's blow this borough. My time in Harlem is done."

"Yeah, this ain't Brooklyn, hoe," he said.

"Yeah, Tommy, you right. But, the hoe just crept up behind you," I said over my shoulder and then switched my ass extra hard while walking to my car.

When we got to the cars, Morgan said, "I'm hungry, y'all. Let's go to Taste of Seafood on 125th."

"Naw, bitch. I got a taste for Ruth Chris. I need a nice, big, juicy steak on my plate right now, 'cause all day I've been chewing up chickens."

We all laughed.

"You're crazy, Toki," Morgan said. "You always got a slick way of coming for a motherfucker's head."

"You know I call it like I see it," I told them. "And Tommy, Tiny, and Summer are all the chickens I needed for the day."

"Then Ruth Chris it is," Sweets said.

I followed Morgan to her garage so she could drop her car off just in case I got drunk. Morgan then jumped in the back, and I jumped on the FDR South heading to Midtown.

"My homeboy I went to school with works there, so he'll definitely hook us up," Sweets yelled over my music.

"Bet. I'm always down for nice, juicy lobster tails. Mmmm, make it happen, Sweets."

"I'm going to call him now so he can have a private room set up for us. You know we get loud as fuck when we get drunk. So, a private room is perfect."

We pulled up in front of Ruth Chris, and the valet opened my door. After scanning my tags, he handed me a ticket. Since I'm always losing shit, I passed it to Morgan. We walked in, approached the hostess, and Sweets gave her name.

The hostess grabbed our menus and said, "Follow me,

please."

Couples ate; families laughed and enjoyed their meals. Some pale faces stared, but we held our heads up high. They probably thought we were a rap crew. It wasn't the first time heads turned when we ate there. We made it upstairs and noticed all the rooms were full except ours. Ruth Chris was popping that night.

"I've never seen all four rooms full at the same time. It's definitely a packed house," the waitress said as she opened the glass door.

Our room was set-up with a table for three. The linen was white with plush, all-white suede chairs. Our water and breadbasket was already on our table. Just before I entered the room, I looked back because the VIP room across from us was full of icy niggas. I quickly glanced at them, not wanting them to catch me looking.

"Damn, I see the ballers got Ruth Chris on lock," I commented.

Morgan said, "Niggas all around me. I'm loving my view."

"Yeah, I bet you do. But, I'll take the seat facing the door," I said.

"Whatever, bitch," Morgan replied.

She switched to the seat next to Sweets with her back to the door.

"Bitch, please, you not saying nothing."

"Niggas usually like the view from behind anyway," Morgan shot back.

We laughed.

"I know," I told her. "I just did you a favor."

Nice always told me when you're in the game to never sit with your back to the door whenever you go out to eat.

After we were seated, our waitress asked, "Can I get you ladies something to drink? Any appetizers while you decide what you would like for your main course?"

"Yes, I would like a bottle of Moscato. Matter of fact, make that three bottles," I demanded.

Morgan said, "Can you add on some salt and pepper jumbo shrimp to start with? A full size, please."

A few minutes later, our waitress returned with our wine and shrimp. She placed our glasses down in front of each of us, popped the cork, and poured my glass first. Just as she finished filling Sweets' glass, another waitress entered our room with a bottle of Ace of Spade on ice and three champagne flutes.

"Where you going with that?" Morgan asked her. "We didn't order it."

Ignoring Morgan, the waitress placed the ice bucket in the middle of the table along with the three champagne glasses. She popped the cork and was just about to serve it, when I placed my hand on top of the glass to stop her from pouring the Spade.

"Miss, do you speak English? We said we didn't order that," I said.

She bent over and smiled. "I know. This is sent from the gentlemen in the room across from you."

When I removed my hand from over my glass, she continued to pour. From where I sat, I had a good view of those eating dinner in the room across from us without looking like a thirsty bitch. I lay my eyes on Qwan's grimy smile. He held up his glass. I smiled broadly, raised my glass, and nodded my head, toasting from a distance.

Morgan and Sweets turned their heads to see who our secret admirer was. Morgan smiled when she recognized Qwan, but Sweets' attitude went south.

"Damn, Toki, homie all on you," Morgan said, while sipping her champagne and all smiles.

"Whatever. Homie knows it's going to take more than a gold bottle to even peek at me again."

"Homie definitely be all up in your mix, Toki," Morgan

continued. "I don't know how you don't know him. You know everybody."

"She doesn't need to know him, Morgan," Sweets interrupted with an attitude. "Why should she even give a fuck? Personally, I don't like the little motherfucker, and I always felt he was grimy and sneaky. You can look in his eyes and see his intentions with Toki are not all good. Then again, Morgan, I know how you do. If a nigga tricking, those are things you overlook. You're blinded by the money, but that's nothing new."

Ugh, I hate when these bitches argue, I thought, while sitting there listening to the two of them. *Shit, don't they know I make up my own mind and move in my own time?*

The waitress delivered our food.

"Shut the fuck up, Sweets," Morgan said. "Toki is a grown-ass woman. She makes her own decisions, and you know me. I'm gonna say whatever the fuck I want to say, whether I'm joking or not. So, you just shut the fuck up, Sweets."

"Whatever, Morgan, with your gold-digging ass. Just fall back on this one when it comes to Toki and dude. Let me handle the worries. I'm looking out for her health, while you're looking out for her pockets. I'm telling her what's real. You're telling her to go shopping."

Morgan and Sweets got in each other's faces across the table. Them bitches went at it like a pair of Rottweilers.

"Listen, Toki," Sweets said, while looking me in my face. "I'm not trying to tell you what to do or who to screw. I'm just telling you what I see in dude. He is no good for you. I know you, and I know you're going to do what you want. Just do me a favor and keep your guard up if you're going to fuck with this dude."

"Please, Sweets, you act like you know him or something. And since when have you been the relationship expert?" Morgan yelled.

"Shut the fuck up, Morgan," Sweets shot back.

"A'ight, y'all, this junior high shit is getting out of hand. Y'all know I'm not checking for him, so what are y'all beefing for? He knows he turned me off with that shit the other night, and he's trying to make it up. I guess this is his way of apologizing. Calm the fuck down, both of you. Shit. Let's just drink this bottle of Ace of Spade on him."

After the two nuts settled down, we ate and drank. When we finished, I told the waitress to bring the bill. When she returned, it had the words "PAID IN FULL" stamped on it. I was confused.

"Excuse me, but this is not our bill. It says paid."

The waitress smiled. "Yes, I know. The gentleman that was across from you paid it."

When I looked across the hall, I noticed Qwan and his crew were gone. I never realized he had left. I gave the waitress a hundred-dollar tip. She smiled so hard I could tell I made her night. I loved it. I got that joy of giving to others from Nice.

"Well, at least we didn't have to pay for our five-hundred-dollar dinner, thanks to Qwan," Morgan said.

We walked to the valet, and Morgan handed the valet the ticket for my car.

"How was your meal, lil' lady?" a voice asked from behind me.

I turned around to the familiar voice. Who else would have been calling me lil' lady?

All smiles, I replied, "What's up? Where you come from? I hope you're not stalking me."

"Nah, ma, I'm no freak. I don't stalk. I get stalked."

I laughed. "Well, Mr. Qwan, I think you have just met your match, because stalking has been something that's been going on with me since my mother pushed me out."

He laughed. I did, too.

"I see you got jokes."

At that moment, the valet pulled up in my car.

"Yo, Toki! C'mon, the car is here," Morgan said.

She smiled when she saw Qwan, while Sweets folded her arms and stood in a defensive stance.

"Give me a minute. I'm coming," I told her.

Morgan jumped in the driver's seat.

"I'm gonna wait until you're done talking," Sweets said.

She gave Qwan a serious screw face. She was not playing that night, and Qwan sensed it. I knew she was itching for him to blink wrong. With Sweets, squeezing her hammer was like having an orgasm. She got off on it.

"Damn, lil' lady, looks like your crew don't like me anymore," Qwan stated.

I giggled a little. "Naw, it's not that. Sweets is a tough cookie, very cold hearted. So, it may take her some time to get over the celebrity night from hell."

"I understand," he responded. "Don't get me wrong. I'm a man who recognizes my faults."

"I mean, to keep it all real, I haven't fully gotten over it," I said.

"Lil' lady, I'm so sorry. The night was not supposed to go down that way. It definitely was not my intention to put you and your crew through that bullshit," he said.

But you left me, I thought.

"Yeah, okay. Anyway, how's your sister holding up since she lost her friend?"

"She good. I mean, that's what is expected where I come from. Every day that we wake up, we prepare ourselves for a blind date in these streets, looking over our shoulder and hoping a nigga won't creep. Death don't faze us; it just prepares us," he responded.

Sweets yelled, "Toki, come on!"

"Okay, well, I don't want to hold you up. I just felt the need to speak my peace being that you tough loving a nigga."

"Huh? Tough loving?"

"Meaning you feeling me. I know you are, but instead of listening to your heart, you ignore my calls. That's what I call tough loving."

I smiled. "So that's what you call it? I call it knowing my worth, honey. You feel me?"

"Yeah, I feel you, and I want you. As of now, lil' lady, I'm not going to make your girl madder than she already is at me. So, let me leave you with. If you let me, it will be worth it. I can give you whatever your heart desires, but only if you let me."

I smirked, nodded my head, and walked to my car while Sweets watched. We climbed in the car and Morgan drove off.

Chapter 9

I had just finished my workout around noon, when my doorbell rang. No one called to tell me that they were coming over, so I grabbed my piece and peeked through the blinds. A deliveryman stood outside with an armful of packages.

This dumb motherfucker is probably at the wrong house, I thought. *They be killing me. Always ringing my bell with someone else's shit.*

I opened the door.

"I have a delivery for Toki," he said, struggling to hold all the packages.

"Um, I'm Toki, but this must be some kind of mistake. I didn't order any of this."

I looked at the packages. There were three big-ass Louis Vuitton gift boxes, a few extra-large Saks and Barney's shopping bags, mad shoeboxes, a few dozen roses, and other trinkets.

"This is forty-five Milford Road, right?" he asked.

I nodded.

"Then I have the right place and the right person."

"Damn, so all this is for me?" I asked.

He handed me a card and said, "Yes, ma'am."

I read the card. Apparently, Qwan wanted to make up, for real. The last line of the card read, *Have a good weekend on me, Lil' Lady.*

When the deliveryman handed me a bank envelope, I sat

on the front steps and counted twenty grand in crisp hundred dollar bills.

I was stuck on stupid. *O-M-motherfucking-G! I love this man. OMG! What do I do first?*

I tipped the delivery guy a hundred, and once he took off, I grabbed my phone off the kitchen counter. Morgan was the only person I could trust to be happy for me and keep my good mood going.

I called Morgan and told her to get her big ass over to my house ASAP. She was there in ten minutes flat, with a scarf on, greased up, and the hammer on her hip.

"Bitch, you dressed for war. You joining the army or something when you leave here, 'cause you looking extra crazy?" I laughed.

"No, bitch. You called me like it was about to go down, like you was surrounded by a bunch of snakes," she responded.

"No, hoe. I called 'cause look." I pointed to my delivery.

She opened her eyes wide and said, "Yeah, bitch, I was just about to ask you who died. Why you got all these flowers?"

"Fuck the flowers, bitch. Look!" I showed her the money.

She grabbed my hand and said, "Where you get this bank bread from? It's so crisp! You went to the bank and got all this?"

I laughed.

"What's so funny?" she asked.

"No, I didn't go to the bank. Qwan sent this to me."

"Qwan?"

"Yeah, the one who paid for our food last night," I reminded her.

She looked at me in disbelief. "He sent all this?"

"Yes, bitch. The deliveryman just left like ten minutes before you got here."

"Damn, bitch, you must have put it on that nigga the night

he took you out."

"I know, right? But, we barely kissed. We just had a nice time, and yeah, he tried to come in. But, come on, Morgan, you know me. That was not happening after a dinner date. So, of course, I had to let him know who the fuck I be, and hit him with the deuces for the night. We kicked it a couple times after that. The last night I saw him was that night of the shooting."

"Toki, I'm really liking him for you," Morgan said.

"I know. You like any nigga getting money that don't mind blowing it."

We laughed.

"I'm getting dressed, bitch. We're going shopping."

"Word," Morgan said.

"I think he knew if he didn't come at me right after last night, there was no way I was giving him a second try. I think he earned it. What you think, Morgan?"

"Yeah, I think twenty grand is a good price to pay for a second chance."

We both laughed.

After I got dressed, we took our asses to the mall.

As we left the mall, I called Sweets to see where she was. Figured she might as well join us.

"Yo, Sweets, what's up?"

"What's up, Tee?"

"Shit. Where you at and what you doing?" I asked.

"About to go to the shop for a wash and set," she replied.

"To who? Carla?" I asked.

"Nah, I'm gonna go right downtown to Maria's."

"Oh shit, it's raining pigs. You're going to Maria's? Bring out the Ace of Spade."

We all laughed.

"We gonna meet you there," I told her. "I'm with Morgan. How far are you?"

"I'm pulling up in front right now, and it's packed like a

Mexican sweat shop."

"That shit doesn't apply to us. I'm on my way." I turned to Morgan after disconnecting the call. "We're going to Maria's."

*****

Maria washed and deep conditioned my hair. Then she sat me next to Sweets and Morgan. The summertime made bitches want wash and sets, so it was one of Maria's exceptionally busy days. Her line was out the door and almost around the corner. All the dryers, chairs, and sinks were occupied. As soon as my dryer stopped, Maria's assistant was right there to wash out my deep conditioner.

My crew and me wait all day? Nah, that doesn't even sound right. Maria makes sure we're tended to right away. Me waiting for a bitch to be done is not up for any type of discussion. Fuck being my beautician; Maria's my sister.

As I made my way to Maria's booth, I heard my name spoken too clearly. I looked around for the mutt that barked my name. I mean, if anybody's speaking Toki, they better fucking do their homework on me, because they must not know me. Or either they have some type of mental condition to think they can talk Toki in my sister's shop.

"Toki is not all that. I don't know what the big deal is. That's why I snatched Tommy up from her ass. Yeah, she knew better than to bring that shit my way. That's why when she was beefing with Tommy at Kingdome, she knew not to put my name in her mouth."

I looked around to see who was talking about Toki. My eyes landed on Summer, talking loud like she was bad.

This bitch done lost her damn mind thinking she can talk about me in my sister's shop.

I punched that bitch right in her nose. From the way the blood ran from it like a water fountain, I knew I broke it. She stumbled, but she didn't fall because her chicken-head friend was right there to catch her. Bitch should have known better.

I spit on her and her friend.

"What, bitch? Do something," I taunted.

Maria grabbed me before I charged them nothing-ass bitches.

"Next time, bitch, watch your mouth. Now get the fuck out of my shop," Maria said, while pulling me back.

"When you talk Toki in my city, be prepared to get your shit rocked," I added.

When she finally realized it was me who gave her that lashing, her and her ratchet-ass friend made a U-turn and took their raggedy asses right back out the front door.

"Fucking bum bitch!"

Morgan and Sweets ran up to the front with Jenny, Maria's assistant. Maria's shop was so big that all the dryers were in the far back. If you were underneath them, and especially if you were listening to an IPod, you couldn't hear anything, let alone an unexpected knockout.

"Toki, what the fuck happened?" Morgan asked, as she and Sweets ran from the back of the shop with rollers falling out of their hair.

As usual, Sweets had the hammer ready for whatever.

"I just had to pop on this bitch because she needs to know my name should never be in her mouth."

"Who?" Morgan asked.

"Summer. That bitch must have lost her marbles."

"What happened? She said something to you, Toki?"

I looked at Sweets with an expression that said, *Yeah, right. The bitch knows better.*

"Did she know you was here or some shit?" Morgan asked.

"No. She's never been inside here to be able to know anything about me being here."

"But Tommy knows you're always at the shop, Toki," Maria stated. "What did she say to make you break her nose?"

"As I was walking to your chair, I heard my name being spoken. You know there's only one Toki, so I'm looking around to see who it was talking shit. When I realized this bitch Summer was talking freely like she really knows me, it sent me straight to twenty. Out of nowhere, I slapped that bitch right back out the front door. Summer must feel like she got one up on me because she's fucking Tommy. I canceled his ass already. She can have him. Hell, he's fucking the help."

"Yeah," Morgan interjected, "that bitch ain't on your level, Toki. She's a dirty bitch. Niggas is always gangbanging and running trains on Summer's stank ass."

"Yeah, and as soon as she let your name depart from her lips, she got blood slapped out of her," Sweets said.

We all laughed.

"I think Tommy sent her ass in here," Maria stated. "She's never stepped foot in my shop. For one, she can't afford the services I offer, and two, I don't like the hoe. Before I even noticed her ass was in here, Toki had already fucked that bitch up. Yeah, she had to have known this is my salon, because for the life of me, I can't understand why she would even test me. Yeah, Tommy put her on."

"I know this nigga didn't send that bitch in here to get a reaction from me. All he did was get him an extra hospital bill, because I'm pretty sure I broke her nose. Either way, he knows me too well. Summer was a desperate move for him."

"The only reaction he was going to get was Summer running out leaking or in a body bag," Sweets said. "It was good I wasn't up here, because Toki has more of a forgiving heart than I do. I been trying to snatch that ass up after Kingdome, but she played her position and didn't give me a reason."

"Well, today, I had my reason," I interjected.

"She gonna learn today," Morgan said, mocking Kevin Hart and making us laugh.

Chapter 10

Qwan and I talked the entire weekend. It was a breezy Sunday, so I rocked my all-black, low-cut Bad Bitch Central t-shirt. The letters BBC were written across it with a bad bitch wearing red crystal lipstick and aiming two .45mm handguns at whoever stood in front of me.

I threw on a black leather jacket by French Connection and a pair of red True Religion jeggings that complemented my perfect, round fatty. My finishing touches included a pair of black leather Bianca Jazz platform red bottoms and my red Louis Vuitton Epi Alma MM, one of the gifts Qwan sent me to buy him a second date. So, I figured why not show him that I appreciated the "I'm sorry" gesture. The way I looked at it, Qwan had the whole day to convince me that he was worth a second thought. If not, it is what it is.

As I ripped down Route 4 toward the George Washington Bridge, my Bluetooth rang, interrupting my Lil Wayne flow.

"Hello, Morgan."

"What's up, Toki?"

"Nothing much. What you doing?"

"Nothing. Going to get me some pain meds for my cramps. You know how I am when it comes to that bitch Mother Nature. I lock myself in and drug myself up."

"Yes, I do know how you get the first few days of your period. I try to stay away from you 'cause you turn into the bitch from hell. So, on that note, hit me when you're feeling better."

I love Morgan, and I know I can trust her, but I needed to keep this second date a secret until I figured out what Qwan was really about.

I drove on the FDR heading for the Brooklyn Bridge. Needing to do more homework on Qwan, I decided to pick him up so I could see how he lived. Qwan didn't know how I loved Brooklyn, and I wanted to keep it that way. I prayed I didn't see anybody I knew. I wasn't ready to let Qwan know what I did.

I called Qwan as I crossed the bridge. When I pulled to the light on Myrtle and North Portland, I saw Nice's cousin, Goodie, standing in front of Kum Kau, BK's famous Chinese restaurant.

"What the fuck!" I said out loud, while slouching down in my seat. *Oh shit, I hope he don't see me. He knows all of our cars, and if he see me, I'm gonna have to pull over and explain where I'm going without some muscle.*

My family didn't believe in letting me roam free if I wasn't going to kick it with family. I can handle myself, so I tend to be rebel to that rule and roam on my own.

Just as the light turned green, Summer's musty ass came out of Kum Kau and handed Goodie his food. I laughed and shook my head.

They do say strays roam everywhere, I thought to myself. *And Tommy's old ass thinks he's the only one fucking her. Yeah, okay. But, she's in Brooklyn sucking my cousin's dick. I love Goodie. He smashes all the bitches, even the ones that think they're exclusive.*

I turned on Qwan's street to see him standing in the middle of the block. He didn't realize it was me who pulled up on him. I decided to watch him for a second before rolling down the window.

He had on a white t-shirt that read "Horse Nigga Shit". The picture was of a red horse eating piles of money with a syringe sticking the horse in the ass. Only niggas pushing dope can relate to that shirt. In addition to the shirt, Qwan had on his white-on-white Uptowns and a blue Yankee fitted.

I wonder what Qwan is into. If it is what I think it is, then maybe Qwan and me might have to do some business. I know my brother said keep business and personal separate, but if this is what Qwan does, then the extra income would cool my brother's worries.

"Excuse me, are you waiting for me?" I said, as I rolled down my window.

"Damn, lil' lady, you riding clean. First, your girl got the 650. Then y'all pull up to my party in a Porsche limo. Now you picking me up in a red Range Rover."

I smiled.

"So are you going to let me in, or did you just stop by to break my heart?" he asked.

"You crazy, boy," I said, laughing at his remark.

I unlocked the door and Qwan hopped in. After rolling up the window, I drove off.

"So, Miss Toki, where are we going?"

"Well, Mr. Qwan, I thought I would hang out with you today, so you decide where we're going. I'm team Qwan today."

"Okay, pretty. Let me show you what a day is like in the life of Qwan."

"So where we headed?" I asked him.

"We can swing by my hood. Today is Brevoort Day."

"I heard of those projects. A friend I went to school with lived there. Is that where you grew up?"

"Nah, I grew up in Albany projects, but I run both."

"You run both. You are too cute."

"I'm not trying to be. That's the truth about me."

I laughed and asked, "What's up with wanting me to see you as a gangster? Whether you are or you're not, if I like you, then I like you."

"So, Toki," he said, "do you like me with the baby boy charm?"

I smiled. "You cool. Don't know you yet. But, I think after you show me who you run with, I can tell you who you are. Feel me?"

"I like that slick tongue talk you got going on," he replied. "That shit is sexy as hell. A bad, feisty chick that got her own shit is what I'm addicted to. Make a right at the light."

I did as told.

"Pull up in front of them niggas over there."

When I pulled up, he opened the door and hopped out.

Before he closed the door, he said, "Give me one minute, lil' lady. I need to handle some business."

He then closed the door and slapped fives with a few niggas.

I saw a few familiar faces, like a nigga named Neck and two of his goons, Prince and Flea. Neck was a straight dick rider, constantly on my brother's dick, trying to copy his style. He was a fat, swaggerless dude. The only pussy he got is that which he bought. I met him two years ago at Fort Green Day. I knew he and Nice did a lot of business together, but it wasn't until Fort Green Day that Neck learned I existed. Overprotective, Nice always tried to keep me out of sight. If a nigga found it in his heart to cross me, then Nice found it in his heart to smoke the nigga.

Neck liked to talk loud about his money to make himself look good. He also thought all that loud talk would get my attention. He didn't realize it wouldn't impress me. I've always thought that loud men were bitchy. I despised loud men.

I was glad my tint was black as shit, 'cause Neck would have blown my cover. I know Qwan had heard about Nice, but he didn't know everything. My family stood a lot to lose, so I sat in the car and hoped Qwan didn't bring any of them to meet me.

A short while later, Qwan opened the door and introduced me to some bug-eyed, big-lipped nigga.

"Toki, this is my brother, Numbers. Numbers, this is the girl I was telling you about."

He reached over Qwan, extended his hand, and said, "Nice to meet you. I've heard a lot about you."

"Oh, you have? That's funny. In order to hear a lot about me, you would have to have been talking to someone that knows me," I responded, without extending my hand back to him.

"Damn, shorty, you no joke, huh? Can't nothing get past you."

"Naw, I'm just not that easy to gas. You feel me?"

"Damn, son!" Numbers said to Qwan. "She's quick on her toes. Not too much can fly past her. Well, Miss Toki, nice to have met you. Enjoy your night."

I smiled back at him and replied, "You do the same."

"So, Miss Toki, are you hungry?" Qwan asked.

"Yes, I'm starving."

"So where you want to go, Miss Lady?"

"Let me take you to my spot in Harlem called Amy Ruth's. Do you like soul food, Mr. Qwan?"

"I'm black, ain't I?"

We both laughed.

"I love soul food," he continued.

"Then Amy Ruth's it is," I replied.

As we pulled up in front of Amy Ruth's, Qwan noticed the look on my face.

"What's up, baby girl? Are you okay? You look like something is bothering you."

"Yeah, I'm okay. I just be wandering off in my mind sometimes with thoughts of business."

"Business, eh? Do you mind me asking what you do?"

"Let's just say I have my money invested in a few different areas."

"So what's up? Tell me what's bothering you. Do I need to put a hot one in somebody?"

"Naw, nothing like that."

"You sure, lil' lady? I got you. I will never let anything happen to you. Let me do your worrying for now on. If you trust me, you'll see my word is all I own. If I say I got you, then trust that I got you." He kissed me softly on my forehead and then glided his hand down my face with loving resolve. "That means it's okay. You can sleep. No need to worry. I got you. I'll handle all your worries as long as you can promise me that you'll always trust me."

We parked and walked inside the restaurant.

"Excuse, me, miss. Can we get on the top floor?"

"I'm sorry, Miss Toki, but the top floor is booked for a private party this evening."

"Okay. Can we get a quiet corner then?" I asked, just wanting to eat in peace.

Once we were seated, Qwan asked, "So what, are you gonna make me work for your background info, lil' lady? Seems like you are well known in the NYC. I'm a little confused because I don't know you."

"I mean, yeah, we know a lot of the same faces, and yes, my name perks ears. I think the reason why we never met is based on your background check. From what I heard, you've been in and out of jail. I think that's why."

"Then there it goes. The reason we never bumped into each other was on my part. Don't worry, lil' lady. I'm here to stay, if you let me."

"Why are you always in and out of jail?" I inquired, curious to know.

"I was locked up when I was younger. I got hit with a three to four. When I came home, all my re-arrests were violations. I've been smoking since I was twelve, so that's part of my downfall. So where you from?"

I smiled. "The Bronx. I grew up in Edenwald projects."

"Edenwald? The projects that crack built."

"Tell me about it. I lived right across the street from the ramp. Buildings 1141 and 1135 is where it all took place. I had a front row seat of the movie, even though I was too young to jump in the game back then. It always fascinated me to want to be a drug lord's wifey."

"So you know money then, lil' lady."

"I know it. I live it. I love it. I am it. Money is my middle name."

"Okay, okay. I see you opening up a little more to me."

The waitress interrupted our conversation to take our orders. After writing them down, she walked off.

"Mr. Qwan, how can you order something if you don't know what it is?" I asked him.

"I mean, the last date, I followed your lead, and I was pleased. Tonight will determine if we like all of the same things," he responded.

"Well, I can't lie. Almost everything here is good, but the honey-fried chicken is very tasty. So, Qwan, do you have any kids?"

"Yeah, I got a little boy by this bird in Brownsville, but fuck her. She don't matter."

"I never worry about another bitch, because bitches don't help me eat. All that baby mama drama I'm not for. I'm quick with it. I don't like hair pulling. So, most times, I'll just cut a bitch. So, make sure you keep her out of my way." I smiled, but looked him dead in the eyes to let him know I was serious.

He took a sip of my wine and just stared at me.

When the waitress returned with our food, I ordered another glass of wine. Qwan ordered a Pepsi. I told the waitress to make that two.

"So far so good," he said.

When we finished eating, the waitress came back and asked if we wanted dessert.

"Nah, I'm good. How about you, lil' lady?"

"Nah, I'm straight. I'm not the dessert type of chick," I told him.

We both laughed.

Qwan paid the bill and left her a good tip.

On our way out, we bumped into Tommy and Tiny. The fat bitch instantly went screw face until she saw me with some new dick. Then the bitch beamed. Tommy's hoe ass carried a bitter-ass face.

"What's wrong with your face, Tommy?" Tiny asked.

He didn't answer.

"What's wrong with your face, Tommy?" she asked again, louder this time. "Huh? Why you mad, Tommy? You look upset."

"Bitch, shut the fuck up!" he yelled back, then pulled her inside the restaurant by her arm.

She got a kick out of it. If I were him, I would have been mad, too, because reality hit him that I was totally over him.

When we got in the car, Qwan asked, "So that was your ex, huh?"

"Yeah, that's him and his baby mother."

"So what's the story with him?"

"There is no story. He's history."

"Good. I didn't want to have to dismember homie."

"Nah, he's harmless. He not on no gangster shit. He get money, and he fuck with bitches. All Tommy knows is drugs, money, cars, and hoes. He wouldn't even bark back if you two was to bump heads. Besides, he's not a worry of yours. He got his baby mother. She is always going to be there. I was just around for a short while, just passing time, letting life ride by until I found what I wanted in a man."

"So you was wifey number two when you was with dude?"

I laughed. "Naw, not number two. Number one was my position. She was and will always be second when it comes to me. That's why she was so extra when she saw me with you, because now she knows the only bitch that had his heart over her is playing wifey to a nigga she's never seen before. Tonight is a night she will love to remember."

"Yeah, well, as long as he knows you are no longer his worry. You're mine now."

Qwan leaned in and kissed me. Grabbing the back of my head, he tongued me down. We lip locked so passionately that I almost forgot where I was.

Chapter 11

Just as I was about to leave and start my day, my house phone rang. I looked on my television screen and noticed a blocked call. There was only one person who called me from a blocked number. I was glad I caught it. I would have been pissed if I had missed my brother's call.

"Hello."

"Tee, what's poppin'?" Nice said in a very low, calm voice.

I was overexcited to speak to him. We hadn't talked in a month. Although he had a cell phone in jail, he blocked his number so he wouldn't receive any calls. That way, he only called when he wanted to talk.

Nice had never been a phone person nor was he a writer for that matter. He denied his visiting rights, so we couldn't go see him. If we tried, he refused the visit. He said it was easier for him to bid when he blocked out his love for those that mattered the most. It was best he did his bid alone. So, when he called, it was for business talk.

I needed to check Qwan's credit anyway, so I was glad Nice called. Qwan and Nice knew the same niggas, and only a few were getting money in Brooklyn.

If Qwan is who he claims to be, then Nice has to know him, I thought.

"What's it doing, Nice? Damn, I miss you. I hate the rules you set when you bid. You really won't accept no visits.

You're going to have to break your stubborn shit and let me come see you. I miss you, nigga. I just want to look you in your face just once," I rambled. "It's bad enough they took you away, but all that 'I bid alone' is some real bullshit. I don't want to pressure you because you have enough on your plate, so I'll just leave that alone. How have you been? I can't see you, so can you at least try and call a little bit more?"

Once I paused to breathe, he took the opportunity to speak. "Bidding is what I'm doing. You know that, Tee. You know I would give my right arm to see you and the family. But, a nigga can't stomach seeing the fam for an hour, and then y'all walking out the door to leave me here. That shit fucks me up, so I gotta block that shit. But, I'm good, Tee. You know a nigga gotta kill me to ruin me. All the shit I went through in my life, I'm straight. This shit I'm going through is just another one of life's lessons. It's not how long you know a person that makes them loyal, because it would be that childhood friend to cross you easier than the one you just met."

"I know you good, and I know how you bid. I get it, Nice. Just missing you, that's all."

"I'm good as long as my family is okay. You know me, Tee. As long as y'all good, I'm Gucci. How's the world treating you?"

"Good. The world is showing us mad love," I replied.

"Good to know," he responded confidently.

Nice was a laidback, humble dude. He never had much to say outside of money, sports, and which trick sucked the best dick.

"I'm on my A. Everything is straight. You know the little niggas in Bushwick is doing their thing on Decatur Street."

"So I've been hearing," Nice said.

"Yeah, Bishop raised them little motherfuckers up right. The feins be bugging over the new shit Papito sent us. When the yougings sell out, the feins sit around sick and waiting until the eagle lands. They would rather get sick waiting for your shit than going somewhere else and copping garbage."

I could sense Nice smiling on the other end of the phone. He loved talking that dope fein talk. He would get game whenever I told him how some of the feins would hit their veins before leaving the trap, not waiting to get home. When the dope had them craving that bad, we called it "pain".

"A'ight. You know Bishop comes home tomorrow, right?"

"Yeah, I know. I spoke to Row and Matrix. They went to get him for me because I have too much to do today, and now that I got your new list of things to do, I have to push the pedal to the metal and squeeze all of this into my day. So what's up, Nice?"

"I need you to go get next to Row and Matrix. They got some change for you. Hit them with the fresh shipment and give the leftovers to the little niggas holding down the trap in Bushwick. Send Morgan to handle my niggas on the inside. One hundred dollar money orders. You got the names, right, Tee?"

"Yup, I got them."

"A'ight then. Go see Ofia. Give him twenty-five stacks for Bishop's Audimar Puget watch so he can wear it to his welcome home party. You got everything all set up for his arrival?"

"Of course," I responded. "I've been anticipating his arrival for some time now. We straight. I got him set up on stage. He's good, Nice. Ain't nothing changed."

"Good. You know I have to make sure the ones I love are straight. So, Toki, besides that, what's good? How is everything? Meet any new friends lately?"

The streets must be talking if Nice is asking me that.

"You know your sister is chilling. Come on, Nice. I'm too much of a busy woman. I don't have time for friends. I have too much going on. I don't need no one else's problems in my life. That's why I parked Tommy's ass; too much was going on with us."

"Yeah, homie is a soft-ass nigga. But, he was who I'd rather you stick it out with until I get home. Reason being, he not in the streets toting his hammer. He making money and chasing bitches. That's that nigga's thing."

"Yeah, well, that thing wasn't working for me. It's just best I avoid Tommy and any other nigga for that matter. I have too much to lose."

"As long as you know," Nice stated.

"Trust me, Nice. My guards stay up. Besides, who will ever treat me better than you?" I said sarcastically.

The conversation was getting a little uncomfortable because I never lied to my brother. It felt weird, but I knew it was for the best.

He replied, "I'm glad you know, Tee. But, if you are kicking it with a nigga, keep business separate from personal. Guards up at all times. I taught you how to judge character. You are one of the smartest and wittiest girls I know. Got the ability to point out bullshit. I know how faithful you are, and any nigga on the streets would give an arm and leg to have you on his team."

"I know, brother. Trust me, I know what to do and what not to."

"True, but I know your brain always manages to convince you to do the 'what not to'. And before you tell me the truth, you'll be acting like shit is all good. While in reality, that clown you chasing will slowly be cleaning you out right underneath your nose."

"Please, Nice," I said. "Stop coming at me like I'm a blondie. Come on, my head stays on straight. You know that."

"I know that, Toki, and I'm not coming at you. I'm telling you."

"What's the difference in you telling me and the sound in

your voice like you're doubting my word. I should ask who's this new person I'm talking to, 'cause my brother would never doubt me."

"Not doubting you, Tee. I just know how you get when you get in these bullshit situations you like to call relationships. It's like you lose sight of Toki and your drive to stay on top. You use your heart as your thinking tool, and that shit isn't cool when I'm in here and you're out there. You tend to forget about your own, and you start losing sight of our goals. Then there goes Toki back in the hood chasing these nothing-ass niggas. If you slip and fall, we fall together. I already made the agreement with my heart that no matter what I got you forever, Tee. You been there with me from the day I came home from my first bid, and you held me down from then on. I promised myself when I got on, you would never fall. So, hold shit down out there, keep your bag closed, and hold your pockets. Don't have these clown-ass niggas digging in your Chanel pick pocketing what you got. Remember, I am the streets. I know shit before you know shit. Keep your head on straight. I will know if you don't. You hear me? Son is good for now. Don't fucking let me down."

With those parting words, he hung up.

He be bugging. I don't know what he wants from me.

I felt like Nice would be happy as hell if I became a motherfucking nun. That nigga fucked all day when he was home. I had needs, too. If he had it his way, I would have been a virgin all over again. We were extremely overprotective of each other.

Who I'm fucking should not be what concerns him right now, because he has more important shit to stress over.

Chapter 12

"What up, Matrix? What's popping, nigga? Just letting you know I'm on my way to you."

"A'ight, we out here," Matrix said.

Matrix was a gangster for real. His name meant something in the streets. He was one of the most dangerous, well-respected niggas with lots of cash. Matrix earned every point. That nigga got love in Brooklyn and Harlem, but Brooklyn is what he repped. Matrix was serious at times, but he had a good sense of humor. He liked to crack jokes on niggas just as much as he liked slapping pretenders back to reality. Bitches blamed kids on him, when they knew he was 99.9 percent not the father. Matrix's name is in the dictionary as the definition of a real street nigga. No matter how much money he got, he was that nigga you would see sitting on his stoop repping his city.

Now, Row was his brother, a little charming motherfucker. Crossing him was a no-no because Row held no understanding. When it came to family, he never played around. He knew Nice was fair to the hood, so a motherfucker crossing him would be a goner, by any means necessary. Row was like a nuclear bomb with a little man complex. Testing him assured death.

I met Row and Matrix through Nice. From that point on, we were family.

After pulling up on Marcus Garvey, I stepped out my red M6 BMW and bumped straight into a dice game.

"What's bank, motherfuckers? The clean-up man is on a roll. Who got this bet? Who's fucking with me?" Row asked with a satisfying grin.

As I approached the dice game, I noticed Matrix standing by holding his Blood down. He always had his hammer where a nigga could see, with his long dreads looking like a little Wayne Perry. Matrix knew that Row had about fifty thousand on him, besides the thirty thousand Matrix had in his True Religion jeans.

"What's popping, Mel Matrix?" I said, as we slapped five.

I gave the head nod to a few add on niggas standing nearby. You know, the niggas that are just there. Immediately, I took my stance just to watch Row in his glory, popping shit like always. After shaking the dice in his hand, Row swiftly let the dice roll. The crowd was stuck waiting to see if Row had luck.

"Come on, wifey. You know what time it is. Roll a six or better for daddy. Yeah, baby! That's what the fuck I'm talking about!" Row shouted, while riding that wave called a winning streak. "Walk that track for daddy. Bring my money back. Head crack! Jackpot, motherfuckers! Pay up!"

"Yo, Matrix!" Row yelled out as his gathered his winnings. "Looks like niggas might have to go to the crib and dig in their stash," he said jokingly, counting his money and teasing the broke ones. "Because today is the day I will be taking niggas' last," he stated in a cocky way, as he proceeded to roll again.

"Got them! Head crack! Triple six, baby," he yelled out before rolling the dice. "I'm on a roll today. Shit, today just might be one of my lucky days," he added, as he slid the dice across the floor, watching as they bounced off the wall and landed on another head crack.

Row laughed as he picked up the cash.

"Okay, baby boy, I think they had enough of losing for one day," I said, as me and Matrix walked up on him.

"Oh shit! What's popping, Tee?" Row said, then embraced me and planted a kiss on my cheek.

"What's popping is we got some business," I replied, snatching him by the arm and pulling him inside the bar along with Matrix.

"How much you win gambling?"

Row laughed. "Come on, Tee," he said. "You know me."

"And don't you forget it," I said with a wink. "So, niggas, here are your orders. You know how we do. Supply and demand; your wish is Toki's command."

Row handed me the duffle bag.

"Okay, fellas, you know Toki don't sit around to count no dough," I told them. "I'll point it out if we come up short," I said and we shared a laugh.

There was no need for me to sit around counting money. Shit, my team was built on loyalty.

Just before I was out of sight, Row called out to me, "Yo, Tee, you going to Morgan's house?"

"Nah, I have to go to Bushwick and hit Killer and them off."

"A'ight then," Row replied before I walked out the door.

Hmmm, he loves him some Morgan. They not fooling nobody, I thought to myself.

Bushwick Brooklyn is the city that breeds the best dope boys in the game. Bushwick is where my brother was raised, which is a second home for me. Once I got a taste of Bushwick, I was hooked. Not because of the niggas, but because of the rush you get when you see how fast money comes when you bubbling on a dope block, like Decatur street better known as D Street, and you moving that "pain". The feins would go insane. My trap pulled in an easy sixty to seventy thousand a day, and that's only if we ran out. Most of the winners coming out of Bushwick were mostly Spanish.

So, if you were black and winning, you must be a star. Nice had been winning since a younging. Fuck starring in the dope game, he was producing it. He always said he was born with a needle in his vein.

When pure dope, rated ten being the best hits the streets of Bushwick, the fiends come out in packs, as if GBE and MMG were giving a free concert on Decatur Street. And that's what Nice lives for. It gives him this energy that most trappers chase.

"What's popping, lil' niggas," I said as I rolled up on Killer and Hands.

"What's cracking, Toki?" they said in unison.

Hands gave me the duffle bag. I unzipped it and peaked inside.

Satisfied with what I saw, I smiled and said, "A'ight. The ride is around the corner. That should hold y'all lil' niggas over until tomorrow night. It's about three hundred in there. That should be enough without y'all running out. A'ight, lil' niggas, I'ma holla," I told them, while pulling off.

Just before I got to the corner, I checked my rearview mirror and saw crazy-ass Killer putting a gun in the mule's face. I guess the mule was giving back lip, and back lip is what Killer hated. If he was feeding you, he demanded you do what he said. Despite him being only fourteen years old, Killer was cold as fuck, and I loved him.

Chapter 13

In our family, when you come out the can from doing a bid, you get rewarded. Period. Taking one in the name of the game is rough, and appreciation is warranted.

I made sure Bishop arrived home with something decent. Well, a little bit more than decent. Not only did I send Row and Matrix to pick him up in his new all-black S550. Matrix and Row also saw to it that he received the customized chain. And more than likely, Lucy got a bitch to give him some brain. We iced him out in a flawless jumbo Jesus head that hung on the biggest Franco Cuban link chain money could buy.

I sent April, my personal shopper, to make sure his clothes were extra, just like me. She picked him up a fresh True Religion jean suit, a Dolce & Gabbana t-shirt with a picture of Scarface on the front, and some high-top red spike red bottoms.

He pulled up to the spot smiling. He then got out the car, walked up to me, and pulled me in for a hug.

"Thanks, sis."

"Welcome home, baby."

"Good to be home." He smiled, showing all his pearly white teeth.

Matrix and Row got out the car.

"Sis, look, we drove him over to holla at you real quick.

You know the nigga's day wouldn't go straight until he saw your face, but we gotta get our dude's back broke in," Row said.

"Yeah, time to bust this nigga's head," Matrix followed.

I laughed. "A'ight, y'all. Make sure he's on time."

Just before they walked off to get in the car, I called Bishop back just to give him one more hug. I raised him like he was my own son, so my love for him was all the way different. He looked to at Nice and me as the parents he never had. Nice had taken care of Bishop since before he was seventeen.

As soon as they pulled off, Qwan pulled up in the driveway. He jumped out his truck without a piece of a smile on his face. He walked up on me like he wanted to kiss, but he just wanted to make sure I heard him.

"Yo, who the fuck was that?"

"What?" I snapped, moving back to look him up and down, wondering who the fuck was the nigga in front of me. "What you mean who the fuck is that? That was my family. My little brother just came home, and they brought him to see me. Why?"

I was confused as shit. I mean we had just got together and already he was snapping on me. *Well, he got the right one. If he snaps, I'm snapping back.*

"What the fuck you mean why? I live here, and as long as I live here, I don't want them niggas here."

"What?! You bugging. That's not happening. That's my family. They bought me this house, Qwan. I mean, I'm all into you, but what you won't do is come in between me and my crew. That's not going down."

I walked off on his ass and left him on my porch stuck.

He got me fucked up. He's not in a position to say who can come to my house. Mr. Que needs to slow his roll.

Chapter 14

Since I flipped on Qwan yesterday, I felt kind of bad, especially since he always made it his business to spoil me. So, the next day, I decided to open up a little and show Mr. Que the housewife in me. I figured a little soul food, a lot of pussy, and some good head should do the trick. Momma taught me to be a lady in the streets, a cook in the kitchen, and a freak in the sheets. He needed to see I was more than a pretty street girl.

"Damn, bitch. You been cooped up in this house, all in love," Morgan stated as she walked in my front door. "By the way, where is Mr. Prince Charming?"

I laughed. "Morgan, you crazy. He's in Brooklyn."

"I had to come by. I haven't seen you in over three weeks! Bitch, you glowing. Toki, you look so pretty, so happy. What the fuck is going on?"

"Please, Morgan. You act like I've never been happy before."

Morgan followed me down the hall into the kitchen. "Damn, the nigga got you cooking in this bitch. What's that? It smells good. Toki's playing the housewife role well. I can see you married with a kid!"

"Don't you think you jumping the gun, Morgan? This is the first time Qwan will be eating my cooking. We've been eating out since we've been kicking it. I think we done been to every restaurant in New York City. I'm tired of that shit.

So, I thought I would surprise him with a little bit of Toki's soul food cooking, thanks to my mother."

"I smell yams and the whole nine. What you making him, a thanksgiving feast?" Morgan asked, taking a seat at the glass dining room table.

"I made turkey wings, cabbage, macaroni and cheese, yams, fried chicken, white rice, and corn bread muffins. I know you want a plate."

"Sure do." Morgan smiled.

She loved my cooking. Without a doubt, I could throw down.

I prepared Morgan's plate and set it in front of her with a glass of ice cold Pepsi. I watched her take her first bite.

"Mmmm," she said as the food marinated in her mouth. "Toki, this shit is good as fuck. I swear you can cook your ass off."

"That's what I like to hear. So you think Qwan will be impressed?"

"Damn, Toki. I never seen you go so hard to try and please a nigga before. Usually, they have to do all the pleasing to get you. I think Mr. Qwan hit a soft spot."

I smiled and checked my chicken that was still frying.

"What's up with Nice?" Morgan asked.

"He good. You know Nice. He pop in and out with the phone calls. I haven't spoken to him in a while. You know me. I call Pat every week just to make sure he's good and to send him a message. I miss him so much, Morgan. It felt like they took half my heart away when he got locked up."

"And now you're trying to fill the void with Que?" Morgan stated.

"What you talking about fill the void? Nice and Qwan hold two different positions in my life. Nice is my brother for life; Qwan is my lover for now. I could never put a nigga in his shoes. There is no comparison. No man can ever take the place of Nice."

"I know, bitch. Don't bite my head off. I know Nice is your world. I was just playing," Morgan said as she dug into her plate.

I laughed at her. "Damn, bitch. Slow down. You're gonna choke."

She took a sip of her soda to wash the mouth full of food down.

"Remember how you meet Nice?" she asked.

"Yes, bitch. How could I forget? You pissed me off that day."

I met Nice over the phone a few years ago. When I meet him, I was eighteen. At the time, Morgan and I used to hit up the Cherry Lounge in Harlem. One night, we were out having a good time, when Morgan met this nigga from Bushwick, Brooklyn. They were kicking it for a few days, and one day, he asked her to come see him. So, she asked me to go with her. I did, of course. He lived on Decatur Street off Wilson Avenue.

When we got to the dude's crib, him and Morgan went straight in the room, while I sat in the living room with his roommate who was thirsty as shit. I guess Morgan's shorty misled homie. *If he thinks I came to kick it with him, he's in for a nice surprise,* I thought. Once he tried his hand a few times and saw that I wasn't receptive, he gave up and decided to go take a shower. While he was in the shower, his house phone started ringing.

"Hey, shorty! Can you get the phone for me? Tell whoever it is I'll call them back after I get out the shower!" he yelled from the bathroom.

"A'ight." I picked up the phone and said, "Hello."

"You have a call from Nice, an inmate at New York State Correctional Facility."

Now, I knew it was a jail call, but the voice on the other end of the phone sounded like a little boy, so my curiosity made me accept the call. I wanted to know who the little boy was, why he was in jail, and what he did to get there.

"Hello, who this?" he asked, sounding no older than fourteen.

He must not be used to girls answering his friends' phone.

"Hello," I said. "My name is Toki."

"Hi, Toki. Are you my homie Splinter's girlfriend?"

"Nah," I said. "I just met him."

"Yo, shorty, who's that?" Splinter asked, coming out the bathroom and entering the living room with a towel around his waist and his body still wet.

I would be impressed, but ever since I walked in the door with my cousin, he's been trying too hard to get my attention, all aggressive and shit. I mean, he looks good. Maybe if he was more laid back, I might have given him some small talk instead of giving him the cold shoulder.

Instead, to pass the time, I sat on his couch, smoked my weed, and waited for my hoe-ass cousin to finish getting fucked in the next room.

"It's a jail call," I said. "He said his name was Nice."

The look he gave me almost scared me a little. He quickly turned from being a sweatbox to looking like he was ready to hurt me for accepting the call. *Hell, if it's the money he's worried about, I'll pay for the call.* I just always thought when a friend or family member goes to jail, you suppose to always be there for them, but he was acting like I just answered the phone for a nigga who was trying to get at him or some shit. I mean, from the sounds of the Nice's voice, he had to be no more than fourteen.

What could he possibly have to say that this clown doesn't want to hear?

I watched him switch to Mr. Nice Guy, fronting like he was happy to speak to the nigga.

Niggas ain't shit. Word, Morgan needs to hurry up so we can get the fuck up out of here.

After I heard him kiss ass on the phone, my stomach

started doing flips.

To me, a nigga that's fake is a nigga that's a snake. A fake nigga is a weak nigga. I overheard him say the boy Nice was coming home. It came to me that whoever the kid Nice was he was definitely a problem.

He's probably the hot boy of the hood, and him being locked up gave this clown some light. Now he's coming home, so homie's show is over and he's bitter as fuck.

"If that nigga calls back, tell him I'm not here," he said after hanging up.

I couldn't help but ask, "Why? Ain't that your friend?"

"Yeah, that's my man, but I got shit going on. I don't have time to reminisce with him. It's a new day and age. And fifteen minutes talking to him about a movie that he made four years ago is fifteen minutes I can't afford to waste when it's money on the block to make."

"And what block is that?" I asked, sitting back on the couch with my arms folded.

"Decatur Street. That's my block. What? Morgan didn't tell you? I run Wilson. This is my hood."

"Word," I responded sarcastically, yawning to let him know his fictional story was starting to bore me.

"Can you knock on your man's door and tell Morgan to come on before I fucking leave her ass?" I asked, changing the subject.

I didn't want to give him any more conversation or make him think I wanted him to go on telling me about his fantasy. He walked out the living room mad.

Fuck him. I don't give a fuck. I don't even know the nigga, and from what I've seen so far, I rather keep it that way, because he's a fraud trying to prove to me that he's eating heavy. He don't even got a flat screen. Who still watches box TV's?

My thoughts were cut short by the phone ringing again. When I picked it up, it was Nice again. I accepted the call because I felt like it.

I'm bored and he wants to talk, so why not let time fly by kicking it with him on the phone? Anything is better than listening to this clown's lies.

We talked for fifteen minutes before homie came back in the living room and gave me the "what the fuck you doing" look when he spotted me chopping it up with Nice. In return, I rolled my eyes, ignored his presence, and kept talking to Nice like the clown wasn't standing there. I guess after the clown heard a little of the conversation, and nothing about him not wanting to speak to Nice came out my mouth, he went in his room to get dressed.

Nice told me that he would be home in two weeks. So, I gave him my info so he could hang with somebody that wanted him around.

His clown-ass man is a fraud, and a jealous nigga like that never makes it to the one spot. I don't see Nice losing out on anything by not fucking with him when he gets out.

Finally, Morgan was done getting fucked. She came out all smiles, while I was sitting there pissed off. She's lucky I had some sour with me.

"Damn, bitch you got me fucked up. You lucky I don't know my way around Brooklyn, or I would have been gone."

"I'm sorry, Toki. I told this nigga you was gonna be pissed when his man knocked the first time. So did you and homeboy kick it?"

"Kick it?" I asked while walking towards the door.

I opened it and walked out. Morgan ran right behind me.

"Wait, Toki. Damn, bitch, what's up with you?"

"Nothing. Just next time you go on one of your sex missions, leave my ass out of it. Shopping? Yeah. Jumping a bitch? I'm down. Money runs? Always. But shit like this? Leave me be. You know me, Morgan, and you know what I like. That clown back there is not my type. The only good thing about this mission is you got a stack and I met a kid named Nice."

"Who's that?" she asked with a confused look.

"I don't really know yet. All I know is he called on the phone, and I picked it up. The clown you left me in the living room with didn't really want to talk to him. He sounded as if he was about fourteen or fifteen. I don't know what it is that has me wanting to kick it with him when he gets home. Maybe because I feel sorry for him since the nigga that he thinks is his man is not really real."

"So what, you like this kid Nice?" Morgan asked with a smirk, like what I was saying didn't make sense. "Come on, Toki. Let's get you out of Brooklyn. This air got you tripping."

*****

Back at my place, Morgan took another sip of her soda.

Her cell phone vibrated, and she looked down.

"Hate to eat and run, but I gotta go, Tee," she said, hopping up. "I gotta meet up with somebody."

One thing about my girl is she never let a dime slip threw her fingers.

After she left, I finished my dinner, cleaned up the kitchen, and ran upstairs to take a shower. Then I put on my new all-red Victoria's Secret lingerie before Qwan came home. After I got extra sexy, I lit some Glade vanilla-scented candles and put the Moet on ice.

Checking the time, I noticed it was after midnight. I grabbed my phone to call Qwan. My call went to voicemail. I sat on the couch, lit my blunt, and watched the Sucker-Free Countdown on TV. Lil Wayne's "Man in the Mirror" put me in a zone.

After finishing my blunt, I got up to put the food away. My eyes were heavy, and I was sleepy and a tad bit disappointed that I didn't get the chance to impress Qwan. My face was lightweight screwed.

Hearing his key in the lock, I went to the door and smiled.

I wanted to be the first thing he saw when he opened the door. His eyes fell on me as he slowly closed the door and sniffed the air.

"I smell something good, pretty lil' lady," he said, walking towards me. "Damn, you look very pretty. Red is your color." He kissed me. "Where you order soul food this time of night?"

"Follow me," I instructed as I led him to the kitchen where the food was on the table. "Baby, you can't order take-out as good as this. This is all home cooked, and the chef's name is Toki."

He laughed. "You cooked? That's funny. You don't look like the cooking type, especially the type to cook all of this."

"Well, Mr. Qwan," I said, while pulling out his chair for him to have a seat, "that's why they say you should never judge a book by its cover. This right here is all me. Are you ready to feast?"

He smiled hard and moved his chair in close like he was a little kid excited about eating their favorite food. I fixed his plate, and he went ham on it. Next, he went ham on this pussy. From the dining room table to the bed, he gave me the business, and then we fell asleep.

When I woke up to use the bathroom, I saw Qwan sitting up in the bed, his eyes focused on me.

"Look who's awake," he said with a smile. "You look so pretty when you're sleeping, so innocent and peaceful. I just had to watch you." He kissed me on my forehead.

I smiled in response before getting up to use the bathroom. Now, I loved the way I mesmerized him, but I wasn't too comfortable waking up to him watching me. It freaked me out. But, I did like the way he showed me that he wanted me. He knew I was a keeper.

When I got back in the bed, he was smoking a nice sour blunt. He passed it to me, and I took some pulls.

"So, lil' lady, can we get an update on what you into? I

hear the streets talk. I did my homework. I mean, in the game, you always have to be careful when something this good comes your way."

"Oh, so you did your homework on me, huh? So tell me what did you learn when you completed your homework?"

Toki volunteers no information.

"From what I hear, you're the sister of the kid Nice from Bushwick. Not by blood, but by loyalty. I heard he's locked up right now with a heavy charge. I heard he was the man in the Wick. I also heard you had the last of his bricks. Oh yeah, and that you're loyal as shit. I think he called you his…lemme think…oh yeah, infamous rider."

"Hmmm." I laughed under my breath. "So you heard all of that about me?"

"Yep. I told you, lil' lady, this is my city. I find out what I want to know. So now, help out my suspicion. How much of that is true?"

"Well, most of it. I don't have the last of his bricks, though. That's been gone. Living off the earnings. Most went to legal fees and taking care of him."

"Look at you sounding like a boss bitch," Qwan said with a huge smile, like he was proud. "Do you mind me asking how he got jammed up like that? I heard he was a stand-up nigga and moved alone. We ran in the same circle. I mean, I know we ran in the same circle in our younger days, but due to my on-again, off-again relationship with breaking the law and his mishap when he was younger, we never really crossed paths. But, I know of him, just like I know he knows of me."

"Well, from what I think, he was set up. That's usually how it goes when the pigs hear your name. It's always a weak-ass nigga telling them about you; the pigs ain't psychic. Could only be somebody you fuck with that's making them aware of your existence, you feel me? We will find out who's the alley rat that set him up. Besides that, he got the best legal team money can buy. I got a street family. We eating good, and we living easy. We just been sitting back waiting until he comes home. You see, Nice would never put me in a position where I would be exposed to shit that can put me away for a while or that would put me in a casket. So, he rather not have me deal with his connect. I wouldn't know him if it was you, you got me?" I stared at him.

"I got you, and I don't blame him. I wouldn't want you involved in anything that could jam you up either. Shit, I don't even want to let you go outside without me. It's like you're a very expensive, rare, delicate diamond. I don't know why I feel like I have to be your protector, but I got you, lil' lady. I mean, I hear you got some shooters on your team, but me, I'm on the front line. You are definitely a prize in my eyes, so no worries. Save your money; let me take care of you."

We stared into each other's eyes. The chemistry was so strong that I felt my eyes gathering water. He made love to me with his eyes, and I had an orgasm.

I think he's the one.

He kissed me, and I melted in the bed. He had my legs shaking by simply kissing me. He slid downtown, and I had quadruple orgasms.

Qwan lay beside me when he finished. He held me close and kissed me on my neck.

"Lil' lady, you know you in too deep," he whispered.

Without responding, I fell asleep.

Chapter 15

After Qwan read his text, he finished getting dressed.

"A'ight, lil' lady, I gotta go. I should have enough time to pick up Numbers and make it to the airport."

He kissed me on my forehead before heading out the door.

Just before he was completely out of sight, he doubled back, looked at me with that little sneaky grin, and said, "I got a surprise for you on the kitchen counter when you get up. I love you, Toki."

Did he just say what I think he said?

"You hear me, Toki? I said I love you."

"Love you, too," I said without thinking about it.

Do I?

We had been kicking it for a while, but it was still too soon for those three words. When he said it to me and I replied, it felt right. So, I decided to embrace it until he showed me otherwise.

Once I heard the front door slam shut, I jumped out of bed and ran to the window to watch Qwan pull out the driveway. I ran downstairs anxious to see what Qwan had left me. What girl could go back to sleep after knowing there was a nice treat waiting for her? Qwan gave very nice gifts.

I entered the kitchen and saw a red box, some cash, and a note. The note read, *Here's some bread just in case you get bored and want to go shopping. See you later, lil' lady. Luv, Qwan. P.S. I hope you like the watch.*

I opened the box to find a rose gold, big-face Rolex. I smiled.

This man treats me so good.

Chapter 16

"Yo, Toki!" Qwan yelled. "Where you at?"

"I'm in the room."

When Qwan entered, he had this dumb look on his face like he had just gotten his dick sucked or some shit. He looked guilty.

"What you doing?" he asked.

"Nothing really, just cleaning my shoe closet."

"Cleaning your closet? Nah, my lady don't clean shit. Get up. I'll pay somebody for that."

My doorbell rang, and I looked at Qwan.

"I don't know who that could be. My house is not the pop-up house. Even my family knows that."

He smiled. "I don't know. Go see."

I hesitated for a minute, then smiled and went downstairs. When I opened the door, there was a man standing in the doorway with a Saks Fifth Avenue garment bag and a shopping bag with a beautiful red crystal vase that contained a long-stem, bleeding red rose.

I smiled and shook my head. I loved his spontaneous ways.

Damn, this nigga got me spoiled like milk.

I couldn't even budge.

Noticing how stuck I was, the deliveryman said, "I have a delivery for Ms. Toki Smith."

"I'm Ms. Smith," I replied.

I felt Qwan smile from behind me. Tears fell from my eyes.

After the deliveryman handed me the items, Qwan nodded his head at him, and he left.

"What's wrong, Toki? You a'ight?" he asked.

"I'm good. Just a little surprised. Thank you for the gifts. You're definitely what I would call my hood Prince Charming."

He smiled. "Anything for you, lil' lady. It's just a little weird seeing you shed a few tears. You're a toughie. Never thought you had a soft heart."

"I mean, yeah, I'm tough, but I'm also human. I always and forever will be a lady. A lady recognizes when she has a good one. I know I'm hard to impress, but I have feelings, Mr. Qwan. And I think I like this feeling."

I kissed him softly and said, "I think I like the feeling of letting my guard down and letting a man pamper me. I think moving forward it's something I can get with. Don't you think?" I kissed him again softly. "To be for real, it's a little overwhelming, but I'm a big girl. I think I can handle it."

Once more, I kissed him. This time, I slipped him some tongue and licked his lips. I sucked the bottom one softly while looking him directly in his eyes. I wanted to pull his dick out and jump on it.

"I told you, lil' lady, if you trust me, I got you. Let me take care of you," he said.

He grabbed my ass, cuffed it, squeezed it, and held it in his hand firmly. He looked me in my eyes and gave me that sneaky, but sexy grin.

"I love you, Toki, and I mean that. I love you more than anything. You're the chick I want in my life. You're the type I would love to wife. I'll ride for you as long as you'll ride for me. All I ask is that you stay true and loyal to me. Will you, Toki?" he asked in a low, sexy voice, and then kissed me softly on my lips.

"Will you, Toki?" he repeated. "Will you ride for me?"

Mesmerized, I gazed into his eyes.

"Promise you will ride it out with me, Toki." He kissed me again. The kiss was perfect.

My pussy dripped. Before he could do or say anything else, I was on my knees sucking the shit out of his dick. I lubricated it with my spit as I jerked him and played with his balls. I worked it in like lotion. I felt the head of his dick swell like it was about to explode, but I pulled away, not wanting it to end yet.

He was breathing heavily; he couldn't do shit. I had the nigga standing in the living room with his pants down, dick out and mad hard with my spit dripping off it. Once he got it together, he stepped out of his Jordan's and took off his jeans. He pushed me over the arm of the couch. With me face down and ass up, he stuck his dick in and bust his nut almost immediately, but I wasn't finished.

I backed him up, pushed him down on the couch, sat on his lap, and faced him. As we kissed, my pussy got super wet. After putting his dick inside me, I started to slow roll until it got super hard. His legs shook, and his toes curled. He couldn't take it. He tried to grab my hips to slow me down, but that was a no go. I wanted to feel him cum in me as I bounced. It drove him crazy.

I planted my feet on the floor and grinded on his dick like I was auditioning for a Sean Paul video. My pussy swallowed his dick. He kept busting, and I took in all his babies. His dick felt like heaven. Feeling my quake on its way, I put my hands in my hair and bounced like never before. I slid down, grinded up to the tip, and then bounced down.

"Oh, Qwan, I love this shit!" I screamed out.

I wanted to look into his soul when I came. So, I stared him in his eyes and gave him all the sexy I had in me. I pulled out my breasts and placed his hands on them. He hugged me as I grinded down on his dick. He stuck his finger in my ass. Woo! Liking it, I busted another nut, but he stayed hard. He slapped my ass as I made love to his big dick. That sent me over the edge, and we came together. We sat in that position for a while, trying to recover.

"Come on, lil' lady," he finally said, slapping me on my thigh. "Let's get ready. We're going out tonight."

I was exhausted, but I wanted to rock my new shit. So, I got up off his lap.

"Can Morgan come with us?" I asked him.

"Yeah. Call her. She can kick it with Numbers. He just came back in town."

"Okay, I'm gonna call her," I said before running upstairs to get ready.

I texted Morgan to meet us and then jumped in the shower.

I opened the garment bag. Inside was a red, black, and white Gucci asymmetrical, tight-fitting jersey dress. I smiled. I lotioned up with my Chanel, slipped on my dress, and finished my look with my red YSL platform pumps and a matching clutch. The dress fit me like it was made especially for me.

I sat in front of my vanity adding the finishing touches to my makeup, when Qwan came behind me.

"You look beautiful, Toki."

I smiled as I turned my head and looked him in his eyes.

"Thank you."

"You're welcome, but, lil' lady, you're missing something," he said.

"What?" I asked, looking in the mirror.

Qwan placed an iced-out diamond necklace around my neck. "This is what you're missing." He clasped the lock on the necklace. "Nine carats. Now you're perfect."

My mouth fell wide open. I was in complete shock.

I know I love him now.

"You like it?" Qwan asked.

"Like it? No, I don't like it. I *love* it, Qwan."

I stood up and tongue kissed his ass down. If I didn't want to show off all my gifts to Morgan, I would have sucked him until the sun came up.

"Glad you like it. You ready?" he asked.

"Yeah, I'm ready…now," I responded.

"I bet you are," he said, then kissed me one last time on my cheek.

We made our way out the door and jumped in Qwan's new red Porsche Cayenne truck. He said he had to get a red whip so he could match my fly.

My phone rang.

"Hello."

"Hey, y'all on y'all way?

"Yeah, Morgan. Where you at?"

"I'm in the limo. I didn't want to drive."

"Cool. We should all get there at the same time," I told her.

After hanging up, I sat back and stared at Qwan. *God, is he really real?*

*****

When we pulled up to the club, I saw Morgan standing in front talking to Black, the bouncer.

"Damn, bitch," she said after I walked up on her. She held the necklace in her hand.

"You like it?" I asked.

"Yes, bitch. That's some basketball wife bullshit right there. Damn, Toki, how much he drop on that?"

"Girl, I didn't even ask. He gave it to me right before we left."

"See, Toki, I told you that he was worth a second try."

"Yeah, you said he was my Prince Charming, too. Maybe there might be a few of them in the hood," I replied.

Of course, we were seated in the VIP area. We were

having a good time, when I noticed a light-skinned girl bombarding her way into our section without the bouncers or any of Qwan's men stopping her. Her face looked familiar, and from the way she walked up in VIP, I could tell Qwan's peeps knew her. As she got closer to us, I realized it was Qwan's baby mother, Juno.

Instantly, I got on my defense. Morgan peeped it, too.

"So, what's up, nigga?" Juno stated as she stood in front of Qwan and me with her hand on her hip.

I looked at Qwan and then back at her. "What the fuck is going on?" I asked.

"Bitch, who the fuck are you?" she asked, waving me off.

"Bitch, watch your mouth before I slap the taste buds out of it," Qwan stated through clinched teeth.

By the way the veins were popping out of his forehead, I knew he was pissed.

"Watch my mouth? Please, nigga! You wasn't saying that shit when you was up in my house beating my pussy up a few hours ago."

"A few hours ago!" I blurted out as I thought about the guilty look he had on his face earlier.

That's probably why he bought me this necklace, because he felt guilty for fucking his trash bag-ass baby mother behind my back. But, if this is how he says sorry, then he can go in the bathroom and fuck her right now, bum bitch.

Before anyone knew anything, I slapped blood out of her mouth, literally. Toki don't take kindly to disrespect.

"Next time, hoe, whenever you see Qwan and I'm with him, you should do the smart thing and park your hooptie, because you not ready for the ride this pretty bitch can give you."

I slapped flames out the bitch again while she stood there in shock from my assault. I guess she thought I was pussy because I didn't respond to her coming out her face to me. I will admit she was a little feisty, but honey didn't know me.

So, I introduced my fist to her face over and over again

"Nice to meet you, bitch," I said, before giving her one shot to the side of her head.

She fell, and when she tried to get back up, it was too late because I was on her. I wrapped my hands around her neck, trying to crush her windpipe.

"Bitch, let me warn you! I'm not to be fucked with!"

When she started to turn a little blue, I let her go, but the ass whipping was not over.

Morgan already had her hammer in her hand, ready for anybody in her crew to jump. Them hoes played their role, though, and stayed against the wall while Juno and me went at it. She grabbed my hair, but that shit didn't faze me. When she did that, Qwan grabbed her by the throat and made her let go.

I knew the bitch was bugging at that time. She barely knew me. However, when Qwan grabbed that hoe, I snatched Morgan's .45 from her hand and shoved it directly in Juno's face. I wanted to pull the trigger so bad, my pussy was wet.

Morgan slid in and said, "Toki, she ain't worth it."

She saw the viciousness in my eyes. She knew if we weren't in a club and the fight wasn't being published, I would have put a piece of hot metal in between Juno's eyes.

"Next time you see me, bitch, you better remember this ass whipping." I spit on her and walked out the club, still holding my swag.

I was mad at Qwan because, as a man, he was supposed to have that bitch in check. That type of shit didn't happen to me and bitches lived to talk about it

Morgan was right behind me.

"Call the limo," I said.

"Damn, Toki, slow up some, chick!" Morgan yelled.

"Come on with them eight-inch heels!" I yelled back at her.

As soon as the limo pulled up, I jumped in and Morgan

followed.

"Peel off, Trav," I told the chauffeur.

"Toki, why didn't you wait for Qwan?" Morgan asked.

"Why would I do that? I mean, just because he had my back, it didn't make me forget what she said. Yo, that motherfucker is crazy. He got me twisted. I didn't go through shit like this even when I was the side bitch. I was always treated like wifey. Why didn't I wait for Qwan?" I repeated sarcastically. "Trav, drop Morgan's ass off first!" I yelled.

"Bitch, you crazy!" she shouted. "You really gonna leave Qwan?"

"Yes, bitch, I'm leaving him, and no, I'm not crazy. What's crazy is that nigga thinking he can play me."

"Calm down, Toki," Morgan said. "Listen to me."

"What's up? What you trying to tell me?" I tilted my head to the side.

"I tried to stop you because Qwan was coming out behind you, but he got stopped by the bouncer. I don't know if he's okay, because I was following you..."

My phone rang, interrupting her.

"Yeah," I answered.

"Yo, Toki," Qwan yelled. "Where the fuck you go? Why you leave me, yo?"

"Leave you? You left yourself when you decided to fuck SpongeBob just before you fucked me, you nasty motherfucker! You really laid down and made a kid with that bitch, with her soggy ass!"

I hung up. "Shit, that nigga got me fucked up, Morgan."

"So where is he, Toki?"

"I don't know, but you getting on my motherfucking nerves acting like y'all best friends or some shit. You more worried about Qwan's whereabouts than how I'm feeling. I mean, if that's the case, then you should have stayed behind to make sure the bouncers didn't bounce him on his ass."

"What, bitch!" Morgan yelled. "I'm just asking because

he was right there holding you down and I saw him trying to leave with us! But, fuck it! It's not that serious. I won't ask about him anymore because you bugging, Toki, and on that note, I'm done with this bullshit."

As we rode in silence, steam poured from my ears. *The nerve of that nasty-dick motherfucker. Fucking her and then fucking me right after. He paid for it in advance, but that's bullshit.*

Morgan knew I was pissed, and when I'm pissed, I don't bow. She got out the limo and slammed the door.

Fuck it. I'll call her tomorrow.

Katy Perry's ET played through the speakers and brought me back to me and Qwan's fuck session from earlier. I was mad all over again.

"Fucking bastard."

"Ms. Toki, we are almost empty. I need to get some gas," Trav said.

"Good. I need a Dutch and a Pepsi anyway."

"Yes, ma'am," he said, then pulled over to a gas station on Route 4.

While he filled up the tank, I sat in the limo and rolled my sour. By the time we took off, I was in full blaze, relaxed, and calmed a bit. After Katy played six times in a row, and my blunt was almost done, I arrived at home. When we pulled up, Qwan was sitting on my porch. My pissed-bitch face was on as I walked toward the front door.

"Fuck you doing here?" I asked. "Why you not with SpongeBob?"

"Come on, Toki. You're feisty as fuck. Yes, I do have a baby mother that still thinks she's my girl, but I showed you in the club that I don't give a fuck about her."

"Yeah, okay, that's nice to know, but, Qwan, I'm not the one for all this bird-head, pimp-gangster bullshit, because I don't need nobody but my family. I mean, come on, honey. Open up your eyes. Look around. I'm doing real fine on my own, so running up on bitches and taking a chance with my beauty, naw. I'm not pussy in no way, and my anger is vicious. I'd rather shoot a bitch. Fist fighting, pulling hair, fucking up my swag is not what I'm into. That broke shit is not what I do. Ain't no money in whipping the ass of a broke bitch. I get money. I get fly, and I ball; and that's what I plan to do until the day I fall. I need a nigga that knows my worth 'cause I do for me. You got me? So, check your baby mother when it comes to me, because if not, her picture will be on the back of a milk carton. And that's real talk. Oh yeah, go get you a thirty-eight pack of Magnums if you gonna run around fucking scum."

Qwan stood looking at me in a daze for a moment. Then he frowned and moved closer to me. I smelled champagne and Jean Paul.

If this nigga hits me, help him, God, because my bitch is right in the drawer by my front door. I will light his ass up.

He licked his lips like was he ready to eat some pussy. He pulled me into him and gripped my ass. He knew that shit turned my hot ass on.

Damn, why he gotta look so good?

I opened the door and pulled away from Qwan. He was on my ass, his dick hard as fuck.

Damn, I'm wet and drunk. I'm gonna fuck all this anger out of me when I ride his dick.

I pulled away from him. He grabbed me again.

This time, he pushed me up against the wall in the hall and whispered, "Stop fronting, Toki. I know you feel this hard dick on your fat ass."

He slapped my fatty and turned me around with extra aggressive force. I liked it. As we kissed, he ripped my thong. I grabbed his dick, and he pushed me against the wall. He stuck that dick in me, moving it slow at first, trying to work his way in. Once I felt it all inside of me, I came automatically. He must have felt those juices on his dick, because he fucked the shit out of my pussy.

"Oooo, fuck me, nigga," I said. And he did.

He lifted me up, and I wrapped my legs around his waist. We fucked against the wall, our foreheads touching and our eyes locked. He pulled me all the way to him, and I knew he was about to cum. Not ready for him to cum yet, I pushed him out of me and pulled my dress and thong all the way off. I threw my sexy switch on and walked into my living room in my YSL's. He followed me like my ass had him under a spell.

"I want you to hit all these walls."

He pushed me down on the couch and lifted my legs all the way up as he banged this juicy pussy out.

"You like it? Huh? You like that?"

I nodded yes while biting my bottom lip and giving him my sexy face.

He replied, "Yeah, I know. Now watch your mouth next time," then slapped me lightly on my ass.

I wanted him to live in my pussy; the dick was so good,

"You know you my bitch, right?"

Speechless because he's dick had me in a trance, I nodded my head yes.

He got up, bent me over the couch, and started hitting this ass from the back while I played with my pussy with one hand, trying to squirt all over his dick. I can't front; he was giving me the business.

We switched positions, his dick still in the pussy. I rode his dick faster and faster, and I came again and again. We kept going until we both fell asleep on the couch. Qwan woke up before I did and carried me up the stairs to the bedroom. I opened my eyes.

"Hey, sleepyhead," he said. "You look so pretty and peaceful when you're sleeping. I didn't want to wake you." He kissed me on my forehead.

I smiled and closed my eyes.

He kissed me again on my forehead and pulled the cover over my naked body. Then he climbed in bed and lay next to me. He wrapped his arms around me, and we fell back to sleep.

Chapter 17

"Girl, your man had your back last night."

"Yeah, he better had if he still wanted to tap this ass again. And last night, he did a lot more than tapping it. Bitch, he smashed the pussy," I laughed.

Morgan replied, "Toki, you crazy. So what you getting into today?"

"I think I want to try out that new spa boutique that chick Trina opened up in Harlem. I heard it's off the chain. Every chick in NYC that fucks with a nigga getting paper has been there. They say it's dope, so we need to grace Trina with our presence."

"I guess we're going then?" Morgan asked.

"Yep, so get ready. I'll be there in fifteen."

Think I'll roll in the GT today, I thought after hanging up.

After I finished getting dressed, I went into my basement to grab twenty stacks for Bishop's watch. Before Nice got locked up, he had a Mexican build a vault in my basement behind the wall underneath the staircase. It's where I kept our assets.

I opened the vault and basked in its glory. I had over four million dollars under my stairs, and nobody knew anything about it. I grabbed the money and my pink .22, locked up, and went to pick up Morgan.

After pulling up to the spa, we noticed how Trina had

fixed up the place. She had valet parking, and according to Morgan, valet parking in Harlem was extra. She had a "bad bitch central" pampering theme going on.

The attendant opened my door and handed me a ticket.

He said, "It's free, just have them punch your ticket when you pay."

"I'm very impressed with Trina's work," I said to Morgan as we entered her spa and looked around, admiring the shop.

The décor was three shades of pink trimmed in chocolate, like the Juicy Couture colors.

"Hey, Toki. Welcome to my spa," Trina said, greeting me with a hug and a kiss on the cheek.

"What's popping, Trina? I love your place. This was a yummy idea."

"Thank you, Toki. You look fabulous, like always. What can I get you?"

"Thanks, girl, and you can get me the works. I want it all."

"Well, in that case, you came to the right place," Trina replied with a huge smile on her face. She turned to Morgan. "Hi, Morgan," Trina said, giving her a kiss on the cheek, as well.

"Hey," Morgan said.

Trina and Morgan didn't like each other because at one time, they were fucking the same dude. But, dude got on some lame-ass freak shit, and Morgan canceled his ass.

This chick's spa was off the chain. I loved it. She had all the goodies: chocolate-covered strawberries, all types of daiquiris, hot cocoa, cappuccinos, and frappes. Everything that makes a girl feel spoiled and special was on display to be indulged.

"Toki, you know my cousin, Stacy, right?"

"Yes. Hi, Stacy."

"Hey, Toki. You're looking cute, like always. OMG, Toki. Are those the Swarovski crystal daffodil Louboutins you got on? Them shits are mean. What they cost, like six thousand dollars?"

"Yup, and when I leave here, I'm going to cop the turquoise pair."

Stacy avoided Morgan. Stacy liked to get shit started, and Morgan liked to finish it. Stacy knew that due to a few unfriendly encounters she ended up regretting.

"Ladies, you can follow Stacy to the dressing room," Trina said.

Trina peeped the icy silence, and knew anything popping off would not be good for business.

We followed Stacy to the back behind the pink suede curtains, passing the private one-on-one nail tech stations. She had four white leather cubical booths so the customer and nail tech could have complete privacy. Before we sat in the big leather massage chairs to get our pedicure, Stacy showed us to the dressing room. Brand-new pink robes hung with pink slippers that adorned Trina's logo. I undressed down to my undies, then slid on a robe and slippers. Trina's shop really did impress me.

As Morgan and I got pampered, Stacy played her role as hostess.

"Can I get you ladies something?" Stacy asked.

"Yes," I replied. "I would like a glass of wine and a few of them chocolate-covered strawberries."

Morgan didn't respond, and Stacy didn't brother to make sure she was good.

"I wonder how long this is going to be here," Morgan stated. "You know black-owned business don't last in Harlem if it ain't selling food, and especially if it's a chick's business. You know bitches in Harlem be hating."

"Here you go, Toki," Stacy said, returning with the things I had requested.

As she handed over my treats, Morgan put on her headphones and rolled her eyes.

"So, Toki, how's that fine-ass brother of yours?" Stacy asked.

"He's good."

"That's good. I heard he was locked up. What happened?" Stacy asked, moving closer to give me all her attention.

"He's locked up, that's what happened. No offense, honey, but one, I'm going to need you to back up a few feet 'cause I can't breathe. And two, I don't discuss my brother to no chicks. I'm gonna tell you like this. Me being polite and knowing that his situation is not a secret, I answered your question as far as how he's doing. But, to sit here with you and have a convo about his case is not gonna happen. Thanks for the sweets, though" I told her before taking a bite of the strawberry.

Before she said anything else, I plugged in my headphones, took a sip of wine, and laid my head back to relax as my feet were being done.

The day of pampering was not complete without a massage. We only got forty-five minutes because I had too much on my plate. Plus, I wanted a full body wax. That way, Qwan wouldn't have any bush in his way. After our pampering session, we paid our tab and requested my car.

"Morgan, you drive. I'm not feeling too good."

She looked at me sideways. "Okay. Where you gotta go?"

"I need to stop in Brooklyn real quick. I have to go to the jeweler to pick up Bishop's AP."

"So, Toki," Morgan began, "what's up with all this car sick shit. As long as I've known you, you have never been the one to get car sickness. Bitch, you better not be pregnant."

"Come on, Morgan. You know me having a baby don't fit in my way of living. I'm always moving, so me and kids don't mesh."

"Oh, trust me, I know you don't want no kids. But, if you are, I think you would make a great mom." Morgan smiled.

"Mom? Bitch, I'm not mother material. I wouldn't know

what to do with no baby. And Qwan already has a son that comes to visit from time to time, so I'm good with being a part-time mom."

"You are one stubborn chick, Toki. I mean, you two live together, so it's not like it's impossible for it to happen. The only way to prevent it is if you're on birth control."

"Nah, I don't take birth control. I know my body, Morgan. I would know if there was something wrong with me. Maybe it's something I ate."

"Bitch, you're pregnant. Matter fact, I'm gonna stop at the drug store to get you a pregnancy test," Morgan demanded.

"I don't know why you in such bliss, because if I am, it's straight to the chop shop we go, Morgan."

"Chop shop? Girl, you know Qwan is not having that. He left his crib and moved in with you, and that's something you always said you wanted. Remember, you said you'd rather be the one that he cheated on and not cheated with. Toki, you're no longer the side bitch that always gets treated like the main bitch. You're the one that he shows he wants to be with, so why not have it? I mean, how's things with him anyways? Is he anything like Sweets said he was going to be?"

"One, I'm not having any kids. So, let's just end this discussion about me and babies. And as far as what Sweets warned me about, I haven't seen that side yet."

"So how does he feel about you running your family's drug ring?"

"He ain't got to know all that. What Qwan don't know won't hurt him."

We pulled up in front of the jewelry store.

"You can stay here. I'll be in and out."

"A'ight," Morgan said. "Ask Ofia about my diamond hoops."

I closed the car door and went inside Ball Till You Fall to pick up Bishop's watch. I came right back out, got in the car, gave Morgan her earrings, and showed her Bishop's watch.

After my long day of errands, I dropped Morgan off and made my way home to cook dinner for Qwan. Ever since the first time I cooked for him, he never ate take-out again. So, when he came in, he expected dinner to be ready.

After eating dinner alone, I was kind of aggravated because I'd been trying to call Qwan. He's probably with his baby mother. That's why I don't do relationships because of nights like this. You don't want to be mad because with the life we live, I know anything could happen, but when you already found out he cheated once, your mind won't allow you to think any other way.

I pretended to be sleep when he got home. I watched him go through his usual routine of putting up the glock and maybe some work. As he did this, beating his baby mother's ass was still in my brain, on top of the fact he had just walked in at five-thirty in the morning. The words 'you fucked me earlier' sounded off. He said he was sorry, and that was all fine and dandy, but that broke my heart a little bit.

I might have gotten over it quick, but how can I when he's doing shit like this, causing me to be suspicious?

I felt him ease in the bed.

He kissed me on the cheek and whispered, "You sleep?"

I heard him, but I acted like I was in a deep sleep. I just was not in the mood for him. Thinking I was in a deep sleep and wasn't waking up, he rolled over and went to sleep hard.

His phone woke me up at seven in the morning. He finally answered it.

Damn, he just went to sleep. That better not be no bitch. That's probably the reason why he just came home and was ignoring my calls.

I focused on his conversation. I could tell it wasn't a bitch, though, because I heard a man's voice.

Qwan sat up in the bed. "Why? What's up, son?"

I could hear the caller yell, "Yo, nigga, just come right now."

Whoever called Qwan was pissed. He sat for a minute and gathered his thoughts. A call like that at seven in the morning meant one of two things: the stash got jacked or the pigs kicked in doors. Either way, I knew he had to go handle it.

"I gotta run. Money emergency." Qwan jumped out of bed, threw on his shit, and rushed out the door.

I didn't ask, and he didn't say. I rolled back over and went back to sleep.

*****

After a long day of making my rounds and making sure I tied up the last loose ends concerning Bishop's party, I went home to cook dinner. While I was cooking, Qwan came in, and he was not in a good mood.

"Hey, boo. Is everything okay? I called you a few times to check on you, being that I haven't spoken to you since you left this morning. I know the call you got this morning was not a good one. Wanna talk about it?"

"Word. How you know? Was you on the other end of the phone?" Qwan snapped.

I looked at him in shock. "Damn, nigga, I was just asking. Whatever it is, I didn't do it to you. No need to lash out at me for being concerned. But, don't worry about it, honey. I won't ask you shit else."

I went upstairs. I was tired anyway. He made me lose my appetite when he snapped off at me.

Fuck him. Let him ask his bum-ass baby mother for some help.

*****

I woke up around seven o'clock in the morning. When I rolled over, Qwan wasn't in bed. I opened my eyes completely and sat up to survey the room.

"Qwan?"

He didn't respond, so I picked up my phone and looked at the time. Instantly, I caught an attitude. I went downstairs to see if he had fallen asleep on the couch, but no Qwan. I went to the garage; his car was missing.

Cool. I don't really give a fuck, and I'm not calling him. Wherever he went, he can stay there.

Every morning since that day, I woke up to an empty bed. That shit hurt me because more and more, I started to see a new Qwan, and this new Qwan I wasn't feeling at all. I didn't let him know it even fazed me, though. If he wanted to leave, that was all he had to say. If he was getting bored with me, we could have gone our separate ways. I loved him, and he knew it. He knew what he had at home; he knew I was loyal as fuck. Plus, I had too much other shit to worry about.

Word on the street was that Sin was back in town. I saw Bishop all of five minutes when he came home. Then, to add insult to injury, Qwan changed into a man I didn't even know.

I decided to call him one last time. This time, he picked up.

"What the fuck nigga are you on? Some type of drug?"

"What bitch?" Qwan spat back. "Watch your mouth."

"Bitch? That's what you call me? Word? Yeah, well, you can stay where you at and kiss this bitch's ass goodbye." I hung up on ten and pissed all the way off, pacing my bedroom floor, bugging over that nigga calling me a bitch.

You know what? Qwan has me fucked all the way up! He don't know me, so it's time I show him.

"Hello? Lock Smith and Smith."

"Yes. Can I have someone come out ASAP to change my locks on my front door?"

"We are booked up for the day, but I can definitely get someone out there tomorrow morning. Is this an emergency, ma'am?"

"Nah, not life or death. I just wanted to get rid of a pest, but I can hold off until tomorrow."

"Okay, ma'am. We'll set the appointment for tomorrow," he told me, then hung up.

I have some rounds to make, so I'm just gonna handle my business and put Qwan in the back of my brain.

My phone was ringing off the hook.

"Hello?"

"Need you, sis."

"What you need?"

"I need two and a half."

"A'ight, I'm on my way," I said and disconnected the call. "My phone's popping!" I yelled out, excited.

I ran to the bathroom to get ready, and at that moment, I forgot Qwan even existed.

"A money call at seven in the morning. Now that's what I live for."

Chapter 18

After running all day and arguing back and forth with Qwan, I had a big headache.

I listened to some R&B, smoked some weed, and recalculated my mistakes with Qwan, trying to think back to see if I did something to make him act like that towards me. Qwan still wasn't coming home at night, and I made up my mind that if he didn't change, he would be canceled. Another one added to my list of mistakes I could have avoided. I questioned Qwan's motive. If he loved me, he would fiend for me, not leave me sleeping in our bed alone most nights. I didn't like this new side of him and started to hate who he had become.

I knew he was fucking somebody. That wasn't what really bothered me, though, because I'm a realist. I know what comes with the fame, as long as home was where he came to lay his head at night. But, I guess Qwan and I didn't really see eye to eye. He wanted to roam free like a dog, and shit on me all day. I mean, he wasn't respecting me at all. *Staying out all night and not calling me?* Niggas get it twisted. When you got a wife at home, the hoes get treated like hoes. You eat, you beat, and then drop the hoe back off. A side hoe needed to know her place, especially fucking with me. But, from the looks of it, I was the one being treated like the side bitch.

I guess coming home to me is too hard for Qwan to do.

I tried to call him a few times, but he didn't answer. Another slap in my face. Tears dropped from my eyes. My heart was hurting because the more I called and he didn't answer, the more I felt stupid. I hated looking like the joke, but that's how I was feeling right now, and the shit hurt me to the core. I had to pack his shit and kick his ass out. I was too good to go through that type of bullshit. I grabbed some garbage bags, went upstairs, and packed his shit.

"This motherfucker thinks I'm stupid," I said, while stuffing all his shit in the bags.

I dragged his bags downstairs and sat them in front of my door. *When he decides to return, he can turn right back around and make his way back to BK.*

I pulled out my iPhone, snapped a picture, and sent it to his phone. Since he didn't want to answer, I would show him that I'm not the one to creep on. I called afterwards, but of course, he didn't respond to my text or answer. I got even angrier. I poured a shot of Patron, which didn't help. I stared at my phone, waiting for it to ring.

This motherfucker thinks I'm stupid!

I couldn't keep my mind still. I couldn't believe how gone that nigga Qwan had me. I was totally out of character. I couldn't sleep, and I cried hysterically. That's not even me.

Why am I the one that's putting my all into this relationship and this nigga is only giving me half of his? I don't deserve this type of fucked-up life, because I know I'll make the perfect wife. I know there are sacrifices when it comes to love, but I'm hurting and Qwan doesn't even give a fuck. He is bruising my heart to the point where he is beginning to leave a scar on my chest.

I sat Indian style on my couch and cried. I couldn't understand why I was getting the feeling that Qwan didn't love me like I loved him.

I stayed in the house all day the next day. While in the kitchen making myself something to eat, I heard the front door open and close.

When Qwan entered the kitchen, I smiled and said, "Oh shit, look who decided to come home."

He wasn't in a good mood. I know how shit can get when you got your bread invested in a few different areas that might not be working in your benefit. And even though I was feeling some type of way towards Qwan because of his actions, I really didn't want him to leave. Still, he needed to be taught a lesson.

"You got my shit packed?" he asked.

"Yep, you passed it at the door."

"Word," he said. "You want me to leave, Toki?"

"Yep. If you can't respect me, then I'm okay with a distant relationship. So, that way, when you don't come home, I won't know because I'll be here and you'll be out there somewhere."

"Word," he simply said, then smiled and walked out the kitchen. Suddenly, he stopped and turned back to face me. "Hey, Toki, if you think you're kicking me out or any sort of leaving me, you should rethink. It wouldn't be too good for your health. I know you know what I'm saying. You a hood bitch; you know how to read in between the lines. You got me, smart-mouth Toki? I'm gonna say this once. Don't play with me, bitch, because I'm not at all the one to play with. Go play with them little niggas you call your brothers."

"What nigga? You must have bumped your head. You're the one who stays out all night, night after night, and you got the nerve to come up in my house talking to me sideways. What did you expect, Qwan, when you don't come home? I'm not a pushover, so please don't take me for one. I packed your shit. If you can't respect me, get the fuck out."

He laughed. "You a funny bitch. If anybody is leaving, it will be you in a body bag. Now call my bluff, bitch, and I'll show you who bumped their motherfucking head. And this right here? This is my house. I pay the bills up in this bitch.

Yeah, you can take care of yourself, but you not. I am, and this is my house. You don't own shit when it comes to you and me. You got me, bitch?"

You know what? I'm gonna let him win this one. He's feeling himself. I'm not gonna say shit. I'm just gonna show him how I do when I'm on my Toki shit.

"Listen, Qwan, I'm not gonna do this with you. I really don't have time for this. I have things to do. So, before we both say even more shit we can't take back, I'm ending this conversation with you. I'm going upstairs."

"Yeah, you do that, bitch!" he yelled. "That's the smartest thing you did since I've been with you."

This nigga's straight tripping. He's extra disrespectful. Got to have a new pussy or something. He needs to be gone from my life. Toki don't need no man.

My cell rang.

"Hello!"

"Hello, is this wifey?"

"Wifey," I repeated, giggling. "And who's this?"

"Are you wifey is all I want to know," the mutt said.

Calling from a blocked number, eh?

"I'm not married," I replied, "but I'm definitely number one. So now that you know my position, how can I help you, bum?"

She laughed. "Well, number one, I guess I'm number two then. Number one, can you tell your man that he left his boxers in number two's bed buried in between my sheets," the bird said, then laughed and hung up.

I ran downstairs. There was no way I was *not* going to address that little phone call. I stood right in front of him as he watched some videos. He looked at me with an evil look. Face fighting wasn't moving me. I was too pissed to care about the damn TV.

"Yo, if you want to fuck hoodrats behind my back, then do you. Give me my keys, take your shit, and leave. I have low tolerance for shit like this. If I wanted to share my dick, I would have stayed single. So, if you don't want to end up single, get your hoes in order. If not, there's the fucking door, nigga."

He said nothing. Just gave me a blank facial expression while staring at me.

"That's my fault, though," I continued. "That's what I get for being a faithful bitch."

"What you say?" he asked, standing and facing me.

"I said, that's what I get for being a faithful-ass bitch."

Without warning, Qwan grabbed me by my throat and squeezed with all his might. Gagging for air, I tried to tear his hands off my neck.

"You wanna cheat? You wanna be a hoe bitch? Is that what you said to me?" he said through clinched teeth.

I saw maniac in his eyes. He let me go when my eyes rolled in the back of my head. I gasped for air and rubbed my neck.

When I finally caught my breath, I said, "Wow, so today is the day I meet the real Qwan."

He walked to the door, and before exiting, he said, "Exactly."

I was floored. My eyes burned from crying. I didn't know what to do or think. He disrespected me, put his hands on me, and a bitch called my phone. This was certainly not like me.

The house phone rang, jarring me from my thoughts.

"Hello."

"Listen real clear, bitch. Whatever ideas you may have of locking me out or leaving me, you might want to rethink it because I know where Morgan lives. You know what I'm saying, right, Toki? You know how this goes. I mean, I know you would hate to turn on the TV and her picture is on the news. So, be smart about whatever you're thinking. Now lay down and get some rest, so when you wake up, you'll be thinking with a clear head," he said, then hung up.

He can send one of his goons at Morgan if he wants to. She will flat-line that nigga quick, and it will be his goon's picture plastered across the TV screen. Qwan needs to fear what he doesn't know, and what he doesn't know is that I can easily pick up the phone and cancel his existence. I love him, and that's the only reason why he's still breathing after choking me. Now that's what he needs to know.

*****

"Damn, bitch, you came over here mad late last night. I was too tired to ask what happened when I saw that you weren't bruised or bloody. So what's up, Toki? Why you sleeping with me instead of Que?" Morgan asked, as I sat up in bed so she could set my breakfast down in front of me.

"Nah, girl, he's out of town. I heard some noise in my backyard, and that shit creeped me out. Not like a nigga would be dumb enough to try and rob me. I was more concerned that it might have been boys outside my window with them three letters on their Teflon vest."

"Toki, you bugging. Since when have you been paranoid? You need to stop smoking on that sea weed."

We heard a knock on Morgan's door. We looked at each other.

"I wonder who's at my door at nine o'clock in the morning?"

The person knocked again, but this time with much force.

"I'm coming! Stop banging my door down!" Morgan said.

I walked out the room and stood in the doorway to see who was knocking like the police. Morgan went in the drawer of the end table that she kept by her front door. She pulled out her .22, cocked it back, and looked through the peephole. I saw her sigh with relief as she opened the door. When she stepped to the side, Qwan and I were looking in each other's faces.

"Boy, you scared the shit out of me knocking on my door

like the police," Morgan said.

Qwan didn't react, move, or respond to her comment. He didn't even say hello. Morgan walked away.

"Toki, the door!" she yelled.

As I made my way towards him, he said, "You might as well go get your stuff and get dressed because you ain't coming back."

I played it off in front of Morgan. I walked into her room with a fake smile like I was happy he showed up to get me. It took everything in me not to tell Morgan that he hit me and didn't come home the night before. I wanted to tell her the real reason I came to her house so late. I didn't, though, because I felt like it was my problem, not hers. There was no need to upset her. I could handle it myself.

"Girl, he looks mad," she said.

"Nah, he's not mad. He just missed me. I'll call you later," I said before closing her door behind me.

Chapter 19

I woke up early the next day. Qwan was sleeping like a drunk. He reeked of Hennessy and sour. Not wanting to disturb him, I went and kicked it on some business shit with Matrix and Row over on D Street. Plus, I wanted to hang with the fellas.

When I returned, Qwan was not home. As soon as I walked through the door, he called my phone.

"Where the fuck you go?" he asked.

"What you mean, where the fuck did I go? I had to handle something, and last time I checked, my father's name was Henry. You've been bugging on me lately for no reason. If you're going through something, it might be better to talk to me, but instead, what do you do? You shit on me. That just makes it worse because you got a temper, and I'm not pussy. I never been used to a man putting their hands on me, but I know I won't fold. I'm not that bitch. Weak has never been me. So what's up, Qwan? If you want to leave, you can. I'm not holding you here. I love you, but I'm not desperate."

"No, you don't. Bitch, you don't love me, because you won't listen. And I see I'm gonna have to make you. Ain't no way I can leave. What the fuck, Toki? Don't you get it? You stuck in this for life. The only way out is in a bag with a toe tag."

When he hung up, I sat on the couch with my mouth open wide, thinking, *What the fuck did I get myself into?*

*****

It was five o'clock in the morning, and I couldn't sleep. As usual, Qwan wasn't home, and I refused to call him. I was going through it.

I think I need a drink because I feel like I'm about to hurt something. It's five in the morning and Qwan is missing in action, I thought to myself while shaking my head and pouring myself a shout of Patrón. *Fuck that wine. I need some strong shit in my system, because a bitch's anger is on ten right now.*

I needed to calm down and get some advice, so I called Morgan.

"Toki, what's wrong? It's five o'clock in the morning. Are you okay?" Morgan asked.

"No," I cried. "Morgan, he didn't come home, he ain't been coming home, and I'm tired of his shit. I don't know what to think. This motherfucker is playing me."

"What you mean playing you, Toki? What's going on? He did this before? Have you tried to call him?"

"No, for what? He's not gonna pick up. I was just trying to sleep the empty night away, but I can't get this motherfucker off my brain. What the fuck, Morgan? I don't think I like being a housewife if this is what I will have to deal with, because on some real shit, I can't handle this."

"When was the last time you spoke to him, Toki?"

"When I got home from kicking it with the boys," I said, weeping. "I know after I fed him that food for thought about how he's been treating me, he went to some club to find him a skeehoe. I know what goes on after the club, after a night of drinking and partying. If a nigga don't come back home, he's definitely creeping off."

"Don't cry, Toki," Morgan said. "You want me to come over?"

"Nah, it's late. I just needed to hear your voice because I'm in here going crazy, and you're the only one I can call who won't judge me or try to lecture me. I just needed an ear, and yours is the only one I wanted to hear my nightmare."

"Don't cry, Toki. You know how to handle this lil' nigga. Don't let him turn you into what you're not. I know you love him. I can see that all in you, but he's a nigga in the game. You should know firsthand what this life brings, and you know how to handle shit like this. Crying is not you, Toki. Brush it off. Wake up in the morning and go shopping on him."

"A few months back, you would have been right, Morgan. But, I love Qwan. I don't want his money. I just thought he was made for me. That's what's hurting me the most. I let my guard down with him, Morgan, and now I can't seem to put it back up. Morgan you know I hate looking like a fool, and me thinking Qwan was the one is what got my emotions all tangled up. I think I'm in shock because not in a million years could somebody tell me I would be going through this."

"Come on, Toki, you got me crying now. I've never heard you like this other than the night Nice got locked up."

"Yeah, I know. I never knew I had this in me."

"Yeah, well, we gonna break it before it becomes a bad habit," Morgan said. "So, suck them tears up and wipe your face, Tee. You're a bad bitch. You got too much to lose over dude. You know how niggas do when they on stage; they get happy when they start making a few extra ones. What you're forgetting, Tee, is your worth. You told me to never forget mine, and now it's time to take your own advice. If Qwan knew better, he would treat you better."

"I know Morgan and I know I'm stronger than this. But, when your heart finally decides to allow you to love, walking away is the hardest part."

"For some, yes. For you, no. Full-time love is something new to you, Toki. You always played it safe, not wanting to get attached. So, most of your niggas were always somewhat attached. Now, you got your own man and living together, so the love works full-time, and to me, that was something you weren't expecting. So, it caught you off guard. It's taking an emotional toll on you. It's time for your guard to go up. Fuck that nigga Qwan."

"Yeah, I hear you, and I took some notes. Thanks, Morgan. I feel a little better. I knew it would be you to bring me back to reality without lecturing me. I'll call you tomorrow."

I heard her, but I still felt helpless.

I grabbed a sleeping pill to help me sleep. I also sparked a blunt and drank some water. Once the pill kicked in, I was out. I woke up to my phone ringing. I fumbled around for it.

"Hello?"

"Yo, Toki, this is Numbers. Qwan got locked up."

Maybe that's why I was more emotional then pissed.

Chapter 20

"Hello, I'm here to bail out Qwan Brown," Maria told the fat female clerk sitting behind the counter.

"I need you to fill out these forms, miss," the clerk, handing Maria a clipboard.

I asked Maria to come sign for the money being that she's a business owner. I wasn't up for the, "Miss, where did you get this money" questions.

"Damn, I don't know his original address by heart," I said.

"Just put your info, Toki, and hurry up. You know Hector would flip out if he found out about this," Maria said.

"I know, Maria. I'm just gonna fill in all my info and use his name, so that way, when the check comes, it will come to me."

"Hey, Toki."

I looked up. It was Tammy.

"Hey, Toki," she said again, while waving as she made her way towards us.

"Who's that black chick, Toki?" Maria asked

"Oh her? That's Qwan's sister."

"Damn. Mommy needs to stay out the sun. She's almost well done with her Victoria's Secret sweat suit…fucking bum."

When it comes to me, Maria isn't the friendly person if she doesn't know you.

We both laughed.

"What's up?" I said when she approached us. "Tammy, this is my sister Maria. Maria, this is Tammy."

Maria gave Tammy the head nod and barely parted her lips when she said hi.

"Numbers called and told me to meet you down here just in case you needed some extra money," Tammy informed me. "He forgot that Qwan leaves a safe with me."

Maria's eyes cut sharply as she looked up at Tammy with an expression that said, *I caught that. You're trying to be funny, bitch. Don't get slapped.*

"What you mean he leaves a safe with you?" I asked with much attitude.

"They all do," she said. "Qwan, Numbers, and my brother, Mix. They all made a safety net and gave it to me to put in my safe for a stormy day."

"Hmmm, yeah? Well, I got it covered," I said nonchalantly, then passed Maria the clipboard.

Maria went to the counter with the proper information to start the bail process.

"So you good then, Toki? You don't need my little ones?"

"Yeah, I'm good. You can put Qwan's money back in your little stormy day safety net."

This motherfucker is crazy. He doesn't even leave a safe with me. She gets the safe, and I get the top drawer full with money. Nah, that shit don't sit well with me, because that means he don't trust me. Hmmm, I thought.

Maria passed the clerk twenty thousand dollars in cash.

As we sat waiting for Qwan, Tammy tried a little small talk, but I was tired and Maria ignored her. I hadn't slept well because of Qwan, but I ran to bail his ass out. Go figure.

The door opened, and Qwan walked through it. As he neared us, his face said he was not happy.

"He's cute, Toki, but he looks mean," Maria whispered.

Qwan gave me a hug and a kiss, but it was phony. I didn't

complain about it, though. I fed into it. I introduced him to Maria. Tammy stood up with her hand on her hip like she had an attitude. Qwan smiled at her.

Let me find out she wants to fuck my man.

"Numbers told me to meet Toki here just in case she didn't have enough money for your bail. He also told me to handle that with you because he won't be back until tomorrow, and it has to be done today."

"A'ight. Toki, you need some change?"

"Naw, we good, money."

"A'ight then, I have to go handle something with Tammy. I'll hit you in thirty minutes when I'm on my way home. Take me out some underwear and make me some food so I can jump right in the shower and eat when I get there."

Qwan walked off with Tammy, while me and Maria walked in the opposite direction to the parking lot where we parked.

"Toki, you trust that girl? I don't like her, and you better be careful with Qwan around her because it looks like she wants to fuck."

"Yeah, well, she can fuck him if that moves her."

I dropped Maria off at her house and headed home because I was super tired. As soon as I got in the house, I lay down on my bed and went straight to sleep.

*****

Yet again, I woke up to an empty bed. That nigga didn't come home even after I bailed him out. That was the last straw. I checked my phone and saw he didn't call me to even see if I made it home. I made up my mind that I was done with that nigga as of that moment.

I turned on the TV, and the news caught my attention. I couldn't believe what I saw. I turned up the volume.

"This is China White reporting to you live from downtown Brooklyn. I'm standing in front of Ball Till You Fall, a neighborhood jewelry store. The store was robbed yesterday afternoon, and two men were pronounced dead on the scene. As of five-thirty this morning, a suspect has been identified and captured. The police believe there are more involved with this robbery and murder. More details to come as we get them. Charles, back to you."

"Oh my God!"

The pain I felt towards Qwan was no longer on my list of worries.

That's mediocre shit compared to the storm that just shook my family. This is not the news I was in the mood to hear. Now my money? What the fuck is going on?

I picked up my phone and started scrolling through my contacts. I called Bishop and got no answer. Next, I dialed Morgan.

"Morgan, did you see the news?"

"No, why? What happened?"

"I'll tell you when I see you. I'm coming over."

"Okay. Hurry up, Toki, because you're scaring me."

"Just watch the news, Channel 12. By the time I get there, you will see why. Call Row and tell him to call Bishop. I've been trying to call him, but he ain't picking up. Tell them to meet us at Lucy's house ASAP."

If Ofia was a victim, I knew we had to take a trip. I wanted to know who had balls to order that hit, because Papito was about to declare war. I jumped in my 750i BMW and took off to scoop Morgan.

"I'm out front, Morgan. Come on," I told her over the phone.

Morgan ran outside, bag in one hand and her hammer in the other.

"Hey, Tee, you okay?" Morgan asked as she hugged me.

"Did you speak to Row?" I asked her.

"Yeah, he's on his way. Did you speak to Bishop?"

"No! He didn't call me back yet. I texted him with 9-1-1, but he didn't reply back."

"He probably getting some top," Morgan said jokingly.

"He needs to get the fuck up and call me ASAP before I have to knock on one of his hoe's doors. We need to find out who died, Morgan," I said, panicking. "I hope it wasn't Ofia."

"Naw, Toki. Don't think that way. Ofia is okay."

"Now what did they take is my next concern. The news didn't say it had to do with any drug involvement. But, for a nigga to rob Ofia, somebody tipped them off that the jewelry store was our safe house," I told her.

"Damn, niggas still robbing people. I guess the more prices go up, the more motherfuckers get hungry and start doing desperate shit like this. Even if Ofia is good, the motherfuckers will soon find out that robbing us was the wrong move," Morgan said.

Chapter 21

"Damn, Ofia did get hit."

The crew sat around Lucy's dining room table as the news constantly covered the robbery. The robbers took more than diamonds and cash. Our whole damn livelihood was gone. And the saddest part was that it had to be someone we knew who set us up. The question was, who?

"I mean, how the fuck they know where the shit was or even know it was there? That's an inside job. Something sounds fishy, and the shit is just not making no fucking sense. But, I'm gonna find out, and whoever is involved, I'm laying them down," Killer said. "I got a little word from the streets, but no name behind the info. All my man said was the robbery and gunplay was supposed to be a decoy for what they really came for."

"Came for?" I repeated. "So, basically, they came for our shit?"

"Yep," Row replied. "But, what they didn't know or expect was that Ofia would let off his peter, so they dropped him and took everything."

"So now we have a problem. I got enough in my own stash without touching Nice's share to cover what we owe. But, that means that's my last dime. With that being said, the next two months I need y'all to do it for me."

"Tee, is Papito mad at us?" Bishop asked.

"I don't know, and I won't know until I get to Dominican

Republic tomorrow. If he don't believe me, then we have some major problems. No connect and they coming for each one of us individually, starting with Nice in the can. If Papito don't buy my story, more than likely, I won't return back home."

"So, you going to Dominican Republic tomorrow?" Bishop asked.

"Yeah. I have no choice. I have to look Papito in his eyes when I tell him Ofia is dead and we got got, even though I know he already knows. But, the respectful thing for me to do is pay my respects in person. I know he's waiting for me to arrive. I arranged everything through Pat."

"You want me to come with you, Toki?" Bishop asked.

"Naw, I need you and Row to stay here and find out who the mind was behind this dumb move. I need y'all all up in niggas' hoods with it. Let Brooklyn know we're not having it. Any useful info, we'll pay for it. If Papito do second chance us, then he will hold us accountable for knocking off not only the goons, but the brain behind the jukes. So, I'm making it clear to y'all now that we have no other choice. Either way, we got some bodies to drop. So, let's pull out the study guides. Time to do some homework and plan a few motherfuckers' demise."

"Lucy and Sweets, I need you to hit the streets up. Talk to the niggas that like running their mouth trying to impress the bad bitches. Hands, go kick it with a few bitches. We have to start putting the pieces of this crazy-ass puzzle together, because if not, then you know who we have to answer to.

"I got a few bricks in the stash for a rainy day. Once they finish, give it to Hands and Fingers for the trap on D Street," I continued. "Everybody else, finish what you got and shut down for now. The shit I got in the stash is all we got left, so after that, we fucked. I'm out first thing in the morning to take that trip, and, Morgan, you're coming with me."

I continued with my orders. "Killer, put the word out all

over BK. We got a half milli on whoever had a say in this suicide mission.

"Bishop, call your gold-digging bitches Lil' Kea and Bad Trina. See what they know or what they can find out. You know them bitches fuck all the hustlers, so tell them to pick their brains, pillow talk them right out some info.

"Even though Matrix just went out of town, hit him up, Row, and tell him to shut shop down. It's time to come home. We have to make sure this setback won't make us hit rock bottom. One last important thing that we must remember, Nice can't know anything about what took place. It's a small thing to a giant, but when you're fighting for your life, that's a worry that needs the most attention. This shit I can fix with my eyes closed. I got our business. Let Nice worry about what he's going to ride home in from the courthouse when they throw his case out. With that being said, family, it's time to make the hood rock. Let's go to work."

"Toki, did you speak to Qwan?" Morgan whispered to me.

"Earlier when I bailed his ass out of jail. I got bigger bills to count than to be paying attention to how many nights Qwan's ass stays out."

"I met him the other night in the club, but I heard your boy owes some niggas a nice amount of cash." Bishop just came out with it. He got straight to the point, without cracking a smile.

"What's a nice amount, Bishop?" I asked.

"From what I'm hearing, them EMF niggas want the bread for all that work they hit him with just before the ring leader got locked up."

"What's the scoop on that?" I asked.

"Word is Qwan indebted to them. Dumb nigga assuming he didn't have to pay up because the nigga Terry was in a jam. What homie didn't know is that not all got caught. Terry's brother never got caught up on that case because they couldn't put him in none of the deals that took place, but he laid low just in case something was to come up. Once he knew he was never on their case, he went back to the A and opened up shop, but he didn't have enough bricks in the stash to handle their five-state clientele. So, he did some research to see what was owed and found out Caki's cousin was the last nigga hit with the motherload, and he didn't pay up. So, now, they're in New York looking for that money. Terry's brother was one of their main hitmen, but he was smart about his and did everything alone. From what I hear, Qwan owes enough for him to come up missing. See, Tee, I know everything."

I looked at him and crossed my arms.

"I'm a little disappointed with you, but I'll get over that," Bishop added. "What I want you to do is be careful. I know me telling you to leave homie is out of the question, but what I'm telling you is homie gained a hell of a lot of enemies since he's been home. The streets said he turned into another person. I hear he's yelling, jacking niggas, and deading niggas that throw him shit. Word, homie be moving reckless. Toki, make sure he don't be bringing nobody to the crib, because you should have never brought him there. But, you did. So, be smart about how you move around with dude. 'Cause as soon as I hear your name, no matter what it is, I'ma put one in a nigga right then and there."

My heart dropped. I knew Qwan was bugging, but I never suspected that. He got a little happy with his hands, but even after the baby momma beef, the late-night creep, even the phone games, I didn't want anything to happen to him.

I wonder how much it is. Can I get it without blowing my spot? But then that means digging in Nice's stash. Naw, I'll pass. Nice's money is his money. Hmm...let me find out my heart is turning cold. Maybe the EMF crew will be doing me a favor. Damn, my mind is running.

Bishop noticed me in deep thought. "Don't worry, Toki. I'll look for him and ask around a little bit."

I heard Nice's voice. *Family and money first, Tee.*

"Naw, fuck that nigga, B. We have to handle family. It's not that serious. He probably just laid up with a side bitch," I stated.

Bishop smiled and walked out the door.

"Damn, Tee, at least he waited to tell you until after Sweets was gone. I could see her face now, lips twisted with that 'See, bitch, I told you' look on her face. Oh yeah, I've been meaning to ask you. Bitch, what's up with the Louis Vuitton silk scarf you got tied around your neck, looking like you about to do a pinup doll photo shoot?" Morgan asked.

"I got hickeys from Qwan's ass. I hate to see a chick sporting a hickey. It just looks too trashy, so I'd rather hide it. I was mad when I saw he went to work on my neck. Hickeys are for kids. I didn't even know niggas still do that. I guess when you got the bomb pussy, it will make a nigga do a lot of shit he probably won't normally do."

We laughed.

I was glad Sweets was gone before Qwan's name came up. Hell, Sweets being the suspicious type, she probably would have asked to see my hickeys, which weren't really hickeys at all, but bruises.

"Whatever it is he owes them EMF niggas, I'm pretty sure he got it to pay back. I mean, I know they hit him with a few of them things, but I never questioned how many just so he wouldn't question how much cake I got."

"I can't believe he didn't come home after you bailed him out. And how much was his bail?"

"Twenty thousand."

"What! Toki, you put the whole shit up?"

"Yeah, I took Maria and had her do it."

"What was he locked up for?"

"A gun charge. Numbers called me this morning, so I bailed his ass out, and he left with that black bitch Tammy."

"The sister?"

"Yeah, the sister! He said he had to take care of some shit with her being that Numbers was out of town."

"What the fuck did he have to do with her black ass? I don't know, Toki, but when it comes to that bitch, I'm with Sweets when she said something ain't right about her."

"Yeah, I know. I feel that way, too. I mean, I think her and Qwan might be fucking. The only thing that might make me think otherwise is the fact that she's Number's girl."

"Naw, she's ugly and old looking. He don't want her. I think she's just a grimy bitch. She looks like a chick that can't be trusted, and if Qwan is fucking her, that's just disgusting."

"Yeah, well, pussy ain't got no face. If they not fucking, they doing something."

"Are you going to tell him you're going to Dominican Republic?" Morgan asked.

"Nope, and if he don't come in tonight, he won't see me until we get back from visiting Papito."

"Now that's the Toki I know. Fuck a nigga. I got my own dough. I guess one day they will get it that their attention is only needed for a quick beat and some good top."

We laughed.

"Morgan, you're a nasty bitch, I swear. So you ready to take this trip?"

"There's no choice in this. So, yeah, I'm always ready," she replied.

Chapter 22

"Hurry up, Toki. We gonna miss our flight."

"Flight? You mean jet, bitch, but I'm coming!" I yelled.

I ran out the front door with two Chanel pulleys in my hand.

"Damn, bitch, I thought you said this was a U-turn and not to bring any clothes, but here you are with two big ass pulleys," Morgan said as she grabbed one from me. "I know one of these shits better be filled with clothes I can fit," she added, while switching with her big ass.

I love my cousin. She's crazy.

"OMG, Morgan, with your extra ass. These are not filled with clothes. This is all cash," I told her as I set the home security alarm and closed my front door.

Trav grabbed the pulleys from me and Morgan and me, and then he hurried to go open the door to our limo. Once we got in, he closed the door and threw the pulleys in the trunk. Then he got in the car and took off.

"Damn, bitch," Morgan said. "All that bread is for Papito?"

"That's why he sent a jet. Papito has low tolerance for disrespect. So, for us not to show our face after his family died because a motherfucker took our shit, that's saying fuck you, and having no respect means no connect. So, I'm going to personally deliver him his ones and pay my respects for our loss."

Papito was an old-fashioned gangster. He came up in the era where all a nigga had was his word. He didn't fuck with phones or computers. If you wanted to speak with him, you better get that passport stamped and take a trip to Dominican Republic or track the lawyer down.

"Morgan, did you leave your phone at home?'

"Yeah, girl. I know the rules."

"Good," I replied as I sat back to enjoy the flight.

*****

We descended into Dominican Republic.

As we landed, Morgan asked, "Who's picking us up?"

"Pedro should be out there waiting for us."

"Pedro, with his fine ass," Morgan commented. "I don't know, Toki, but if I get some of that Dominican rum in me before we leave, I might get a quickie. Hit Pedro off with some of this New York pussy," Morgan stated.

"You might just want to give him head, Bloody Mary."

She laughed. "Oh yeah, I forgot."

When we stepped off the jet, Pedro and two guards greeted us. The guards grabbed our luggage and put it in the trunk.

"Hello, Toki. How was your ladies' flight?" Pedro asked.

"It was great, very upscale. I'd rather travel by jet than deal with the airlines. But, then again, who wouldn't?" I replied, then embraced Pedro and gave him a kiss on his cheek.

"Well, hello, Pedro," Morgan said with her fake, seductive Spanish accent.

"Hello, Morgan," Pedro responded with a sexy smile.

Morgan winked and got in the car.

I enjoyed the weather and the view as we drove through the town of Puerto Plata. We drove past beautiful acres of freshly cut, perfectly manicured green grass. Papito's home was located at the top of the mountain.

Papito's estate was bigger than Grand Central Station. Papito was like a father to Nice; he raised him and taught him everything he knew about the dope game. He lived in Bushwick for fifteen years, and he supplied the whole east coast until picked up by the government on an 848-conspiracy case. Being that Papito was like the president in his country, no one would rat on him. He never used a phone or did any drug talk indoors. That made the government's case weak. All they could do was deport him back to Dominican Republic, but Papito never stopped making money.

When we pulled up, Papito's servants met us in front, all lined up like I was the President.

"Hola, Señorita Toki," the head maid greeted with a smile.

"Hola."

"Hola, Señorita Morgan."

"Hola."

"Welcome to Puerto Plata, Dominican Republic. Señor Papito has been anticipating your arrival. Follow me, please," the head maid said.

The maid led us into the house where a beautiful Dominican chick stood in front of the door. She wore all black, so I figured she was security. She took our bags and completely frisked us. Once done, she stepped to the side, and the maid led us through the home.

"Ahhh, Señorita Toki!"

"Hi, Papito," I said, embracing him with a big hug and kiss.

Every time I saw Papito, he made me feel like a little kid. I smiled so hard that my face ached.

Papito instructed the maids to show us to our rooms to change for dinner. That trip was my fifth one, but it was the first time I came without Nice.

Every time we went, a feast was prepared just for us.

After dinner, Papito and I went to the lawn, while Morgan chased Pedro around. I admired the court-sized living room as we walked through it. The home was decorated with antiques. I fell in love with it all over again.

"So, Toki," Papito said, "how's my boy doing?"

"He's good, Papito. He's hanging in there."

"Is he worrying? You know that boy thinks more than he forgets. I always tell him to live and let go, but he'd rather get headaches than let shit fly. He always lets the street talk get to him."

"You know Nice, Papito. He has the world on his shoulders. If he was the President, he would let everybody eat."

"I know that boy's heart is bigger than his chest can hold. Did anyone tell him about the store getting robbed or Ofia losing his life as a solider while protecting his family's investment?"

I watched Papito's body movements as he talked about Ofia's death. I knew death didn't faze Papito, but I thought the death of his nephew might hit a soft spot. However, his body language said, *Charge it to the game.*

"I made it clear to everyone that Nice is not to know about this at all. I told them if he calls and tries to pick their brain, not to let him fool them, 'cause you know Nice is the best at mind games."

Papito laughed a little and fell into a daze.

"Damn, I miss that boy," he said, while shaking his head. "Why him? Why did he have to be the one to get caught up?"

"I know, because every time I hear his name or his voice, I shake my head and think the same thing."

"So, Toki, I know you're not to blame for the robbery and Ofia's death. But, what I plan on blaming you for is murdering them that took my bloodline's life and the food from off my plate. Whoever did this to our family must be taken out, Señorita Toki."

"I'm already on that one, Papito. Trust me when I say I got you."

We sat in his white wicker lawn chairs as the sun beamed down on us. I knew by the time I returned home I would look like I tanned on an island for a month.

"So, Señorita Toki, the reason I wanted to sit with you is…"

His butler, who handed me an 8x10 envelope and a glass of mojito, interrupted Papito.

"Don't open it until you get home," Papito told me. "Keep this close to you until you and Bishop are alone. This is the key that will end Nice's worries as long as you follow the plan I have mapped out for you. If you play it right, when Nice goes to trial, the judge will throw his case out for lack of evidence.

"Now, for business, Toki. I already packed the jet, and it's about to take off. You will be following the jet in my G5. You got me, Toki?" Papito asked.

I nodded my head yes. Then we hugged and kissed before I left.

*****

Morgan and I boarded the G5 and headed back to New York City. The trip back seemed faster than the one going. It probably seemed that way because of all the Moscato we drank.

I sat back to rest. I had too much on the brain. So much had happened in a week.

Qwan and I started strong, but then he flipped. My stash house got hit and Ofia died. He owed niggas money and didn't tell me. I mean, he could have told me. I could have helped him. I guess he didn't want to bring shit my way.

His mood change makes sense. I guess I can be more sympathetic without him knowing that I know. I guess I'll just leave his street shit alone and stop trying to wear the pants, flaunting my money. A real man doesn't want their bitch to help them out financially without fucking with his pride. So, I'll leave Qwan's worries about his finances up to him and worry about my own.

"Toki!" Morgan yelled.

"Huh?"

"Why you always blank out? What's up with you? What's on your mind? Is everything really okay at home, because just now, your brain was in a different zone? The only time I see you do that is when something's wrong."

"Oh shit," I said, laughing. "Naw, I was just counting some numbers in my head. My bad, Morgan." I laughed again.

She cracked a smile and said, "You is crazy. I was calling your name for a minute."

"Well, you know when it comes down to making sure that money's right, I don't hear or see shit until the numbers in my head add up."

"You sure, Toki?" Morgan asked with a worried look.

"Yeah, I'm sure. Everything is okay."

I'd rather keep Morgan in the blind for now about my problems at home with Qwan.

Chapter 23

When the driver pulled up in front of my house, I looked around for anything out of place. I didn't see Qwan's car in the driveway.

"See, Morgan, just like I thought. He's not here, and he probably hasn't been here. Shit, I bet he didn't know I was gone."

Wow, Qwan is something else, and he claimed he loved me. Whatever.

"Toki, are you okay?" Morgan asked just before Trav drove off.

"Yeah, I'm good. Go on home. I'll meet you later."

I walked in my house, disarmed my alarm, and looked around for signs of Qwan. Then I grabbed my phone from the drawer. There were a lot of missed calls from Qwan. I didn't care to call him back, though.

I turned on the jets to my Jacuzzi and added my Chanel bubbles. Next, I went downstairs, grabbed my Glade vanilla-scented candles, and placed them around the tub. I also made some tea to help settle my stomach and rolled a blunt.

I dropped my dirty clothes to the floor and stepped in the water with my tea in one hand and blunt in the other. I lit my blunt with the flame of one of the candles, sat back, and let the jets and bubbles consume me.

What if I am pregnant? I've been feeling funny and

nauseous lately, and on top of that, I'm emotional as hell. Shit, being a mommy ain't my thing. So, it's time for the clinic. I can't shake the feeling.

I soaked for thirty minutes, grabbed my towel, and dried off. I lotioned up and sprayed on some calming smell goods from Carol's Daughter. After sliding on my undies, I went downstairs to pour a glass of wine. I thought about the envelope Papito gave me.

I need to get next to Bishop, I thought before drifting off to sleep.

*****

When I woke up, I got dressed and headed for the door. I had to run back upstairs because I forgot my phone on the dresser. When I entered my bedroom, I heard it ringing.

"Where you at, baby girl? You Gucci?"

"In the car now, B. On my way. Call Sweets and Lucy and tell them to meet up at the spot. Morgan already knows."

Bishop was already waiting for me when I walked in.

"Hey, baby boy," I said.

He hugged me. "What's in the envelope?"

"I don't know. Papito gave me this and told me not to open it until I got next to you."

"Shit, open it."

We sat on the couch in the office. I opened the envelope and pulled out its contents.

"Yo, I knew that nigga was a snitch," Bishop said.

I read the letter Papito included, which said, *This is the last time I will be in contact or in business with your crew, which is the reason why I loaded you up. The next time we get up, Nice will be home, and he will be handing my money, but as of now, handle this and make sure it goes down smoothly for Nice. If this happens to fuck up because you did not listen, you will never hear from me again. So, make your move wisely. Once you finish reading this letter, make sure you burn it.*

Just as we finished reading the letter, the crew walked in.

After the greetings and hugs, I said, "Now that we're all here, let's get right down to business. We got about a hundred birds to let fly."

"Damn! Why Papito send so much, Toki?" Sweets asked.

"Less trips. We've got to double up and get our spots running ASAP. A day or two with no work is crucial."

"It's a great loss," Bishop said, "but our fiends are loyal."

Lucy interjected. "Yeah, they are, because we got the best shit. The little homies in the Wick need to get going tonight. It's haywire over there."

"Yeah, the fiends have created pandemonium on D Street," Sweets commented.

"Morgan, call the Golden Girls. Tell them we need the whole crew to get busy."

The Golden Girls were a crew of bad bitches that got money bagging, cutting, and transporting.

"Done," Morgan replied.

"Okay, family, time to make the hood rock."

Bishop and I didn't mention the envelope, its contents, and the loss of the connect. When lifestyles change, so do people. We didn't want to put it in the minds of the family to do anything sneaky. Betrayal happens when motherfuckers know shit's running low, and betrayal destroys families. As far as Sin's ass really being the rat, it became my problem when Nice was locked up, but I just needed to make sure.

I got this one by my lonesome, just so I know it gets done right. I'll let the family handle the niggas that robbed us.

Chapter 24

A week passed since he got stupid and put his hands on me. Qwan was up my ass, always in the house trying to be extra nice. He promised me that he would never lift his hand to me ever again, claiming to be a changed man. But, Toki ain't no fool. My guard remained on defense.

He went out of town that morning. I was shocked he left me, but he knew I was going to my friend Shaunie's funeral. I couldn't believe Shaunie was dead. When I saw her picture on the news, it floored me. Her and her cousin were reported missing, and they were found in Shaunie's trunk. They had been tortured and beaten. Shit was fucked up.

Shaunie and me were cool, but I didn't know her family. So, I asked Lucy to go with me to her funeral. That way, I wouldn't be completely alone when I went to pay my respects.

As I looked around the church, I made eye contact with that nigga Joke.

Damn, I hope he don't bust on himself. He looks like at any point he's going to cream-pie in his pants, staring and drooling like he's never seen pussy before.

"You see that?" I whispered.

"Who?" Lucy asked.

"That clown of yours drooling over you right there." I pointed at Joke.

"Oh shit, I didn't even see him."

"Did you tell him you were coming?"

"Yeah, he knew."

"Well then, that explains how he spotted you amongst all these people. But, then again, you're the only white bitch in here."

We chuckled.

I focused my attention on the lady who was reading the sympathy cards. Shaunie and her cousin had a double funeral. They had many flowers, casket sprays, and stand-alone wreaths. Huge custom-made bleeding hearts sat on top of their caskets.

I thought about the last time I saw her. I remembered she told me that Sin's ass popped up again and that she thought he came back for her. And since I was attending her funeral, it looked like she was right. She was a good bitch that fucked with the wrong nigga, and he made her die slowly.

"Okay, we're going to have the friends of the family come up first to pay their respects," the preacher said.

After debating whether or not to go, I decided I couldn't handle seeing her son cry because his mother was gone.

I spotted Joke posted by the door as Lucy and I left the church.

"So are you going to kick it with the Joker?" I asked Lucy.

"Naw, I got things to do," she responded. "Besides, I haven't been checking for dude. The only reason I contacted him in the first place was to let him know I would be at the funeral. He's a broke-ass clown. Not to mention, homie be rocking fake shit. That fucks up my rep."

I noticed the watch on Joke's wrist. The only person who had that specially-ordered watch was Nice. Ofia got those diamonds from Africa, and Nice was the only nigga that got fifty-pointer flawless diamonds all over the Bezel. It took six months to get it done, and when Nice got popped, he told me to take it to Ofia to be put in the vault.

That nigga couldn't afford a rare AP like that. So, for this nigga to have the same watch on, it told me that he was in on the robbery. I knew it wasn't a replica either, because only one was made in the fucking world.

"Toki," Lucy said. "You okay? Why you stop like that?"

"Yeah, I'm good," I replied.

I looked Joke in his face as he stood fronting on the wall, perpetrating like he was getting money.

"My bad. I just can't get over this watch your boy got on," I said.

"Damn, that is nice," Lucy said as we approached him.

Noticing us staring at his wrist, Joke smiled and replied, "Custom made, mama." He was cocky with it.

I laughed. "Yeah, nigga, we see you."

Lucy gave him the 'I'll call you' gesture. We laughed because we knew she wasn't going to call him, and he did, too.

After we walked to the car, I drove to the end of the block and watched people file out of the church.

Lucy slipped on her gloves and checked the clip of her .9mm. She screwed on the silencer and then cocked it back. I drove down the street, and we pulled in front of Joke as he stood with a few niggas. Lucy rolled down her window and smiled at him. He walked to the car real cocky, like he had won something. When he got close to the car, Lucy sat up and hit his ass with three quick ones. No one had a clue.

As soon as his body dropped, Lucy stepped out the car and backed everyone down. She took the watch off Joke's wrist and hit him in the head just in case he was a fighter. Niggas stood in shock.

She put her pointer finger up to her lips. "Shhhhh," she told them.

Then she got back in the car, and I drove off slowly while Lucy examined Nice's watch.

"A little bloody, but that can be fixed. Can't say the same

for Joke's ass," she said, smiling as she wiped blood off the watch.

I smiled with satisfaction. "One down and however many more to go. I bet Joke didn't think today was gonna be the day he met up with his maker."

I wondered how Qwan would feel when he heard his human holster was dead. *He will probably feel nothing, because he don't care about nobody but himself.*

"Toki," Lucy called out, jarring me from my thoughts.

"Yeah, what's up?"

"You got everything all set for Morgan's party tomorrow?"

"Yup, you know I went all out," I said while pulling up in front of Lucy's house to drop her off before heading home.

Chapter 25

So hard to breathe this air we call love. Ain't nothing worse than the hurt you receive from a love. When you get hurt by the one you're living for, it can make you want to hurt no more.

When I got home, there was still no sign of Qwan.

I guess he's staying out again or maybe he's just not coming back. Either way, I'm too tired to care.

I stripped off all my clothes down to my underwear, jumped in my bed, and went to sleep.

I woke up feeling the sting of a slap.

"Nigga, did you just fucking slap me?"

"Next time you pull a disappearing act like that without asking me first, I will snap your neck," Qwan said.

This nigga's fucking crazy. He's the one gone for days, but I get slapped. What the fuck?

I was shocked. My face burned.

"What do you mean ask you? Ask you? Why would I ask you? I'm a grown-ass woman, nigga. You don't fucking own me," I said.

"Bitch, who you talking to? I don't own you?" he said. "I do own you. Remember that, bitch. You better know who you're talking to. My word is my word when it comes to the streets. It's my word when it comes to you, and it will be my word that I will find you at any given place you decide to call home."

He slapped me with the back of his hand.

Oh, hell no! I jumped out the bed and charged him in rage. We got it popping. I was fed up. I gave that nigga a couple of blows to the face. I took his blows like a champ, until he punched me in my stomach. I threw up from the pressure of the punch. He finally let me go, and I dropped to the floor in excruciating pain. All I could do was cry, and all the bastard did was walk out the door and didn't look back.

I lay on the floor in that same spot until the pain eased up a little. Then I got up and grabbed my car keys, my weed, cell phone, and a bag. I drove to the Hilton Hotel.

He won't find me here unless I'm being followed, I thought, while looking in my rearview mirror to check my surroundings.

Once I checked in, I drove to CVS and bought some painkillers, Epsom salt, a Dutch, a Pepsi, and a pregnancy test.

I pray to God I'm not pregnant.

Upon returning to my room, I rolled my blunt in pain. *I don't deserve to be treated like shit.* I went in the bathroom and ran water in the tub, adding some Epson salt so I could soak.

I turned off my phone. I didn't want to speak with nobody. I knew when he made it home that he would wonder where I was. He needed to learn a lesson. That nigga was getting out of hand.

I soaked in the tub and smoked my blunt while Melanie Fiona's "4 A.M." was on repeat. I relaxed in my thoughts, trying to make sense of how a nigga could go from being *the* one to being the *psychotic* one. Tears streamed down my face. I knew I needed to let him go, but I couldn't hate him. My thoughts raced on. I couldn't stop them. And I knew that while I was crying and dry heaving, he was probably getting his dick sucked.

Once out of the tub and lying across the bed, I finally drifted off to sleep.

*****

I woke up from pain and the housekeeper wanting to service the room.

"No, thank you," I yelled, walking towards the door.

"Okay, no problem," she replied.

I took the pregnancy test, and it was positive. So, I called the clinic to schedule an abortion.

I hope I'm not too far along to have a termination, because I need this baby out of me today.

I told the front desk to charge me for a few more nights since I needed a hideout until the bleeding stopped.

Not wanting to go through it alone, I powered up my phone to call Morgan. Qwan had sent me several 'I'm sorry' and 'Toki, please forgive me' bullshit-ass messages, but I didn't have time for him.

After leaving the hotel room, I went to the nearest MAC counter to get my makeup done. Then I went to the Juicy Couture store to purchase a cute little sweat suit to wear after the procedure, because I knew I wouldn't want to put back on some tight-ass jeans. Afterwards, I picked up Morgan.

"Hey, boo," Morgan said as she got in the car and kissed my cheek. "What's up? What happened last night? Did Qwan ever come home?"

"Damn, bitch, you didn't even put on your seatbelt and you're already in my business!"

"Oh please, I know you're dying to tell me," she said.

It's not like you got another close cousin you tell everything to. I mean, who else are you going to call? Sweets? She's not trying to have a conversation about Qwan not coming home at night."

I didn't reply.

"So where we going?" she asked.

I smiled. "Chop shop."

"Chop shop?"

"Yes, bitch, chop shop. Toki's pregnant, and Toki's not keeping it."

"So you really are pregnant?"

"Yep, and I'm booked to see the doctor in an hour. I cannot have a baby right now, Morgan. I got too much going on in my life, and a baby does not fit into my plans. Besides, Qwan has been getting on my nerves. I don't know if I want to be attached to him for the rest of my life. He has control issues, and I have a problem with listening, so we're not mixing good."

"So, basically, he doesn't know you pregnant?"

"No," I responded, "and he don't need to know. That's why I made this call before he could even get a clue that I'm knocked up. Now all I have to do is pray I'm not too far along to have the procedure done today."

"Today?" Morgan shouted. "You crazy, Toki. If Qwan finds out that you was pregnant and didn't even tell him, not to mention you're about to kill it…" Her voice trailed off. "Naw, Tee, you crazy."

"I'm not crazy. I'm being smart. Come on, Morgan. He don't really even know me. He don't have a clue who he barely comes home to. But, you do, and you know the life we live. We don't got no room for no kids We in the streets, giving it up and eating off of any boss man buying our shit. Morgan, we're on their income list; we're not the average bad bitches that go to work for yearly salary. Why would I want to have a baby when I'm living fast? I'm not with that housewife bullshit. I'm a street bitch, so me bringing a child into this world would not be fair to the kid. Besides, all this sleeping around on me, not calling, and not picking up the phone…Qwan has no respect. So why would I want to lock myself down with him and have to deal with his bullshit? Love fades. Babies don't. My mind's made up, and we're on our way to the chop shop."

“Toki, you’re crazy, but if this is what you really want to do, then you know I’m riding with you.”

When I got back to the hotel, I ordered some room service and then called the CVS pharmacy to have them deliver my meds.

Qwan blew up my phone. I answered and told him that I went to Delaware and would be home tomorrow. He knew Morgan’s party was the next day, so he was on my back.

Besides, 45 Milford Street is my house. If anybody is leaving it’s him. He needs to get the fuck out.

*****

The phone rang at eight o’clock in the morning.

“Who the fuck is calling me this early? I hope nobody died!”

“Hello! Wake up, bitch. It's my birthday!” Morgan said.

“Bitch, it's your birthday, not mine. I need my beauty sleep. Call me back at eleven.”

“Toki! Come on! Don't act like that, bitch. We got a lot of shopping to do today,” Morgan said.

“Now you talking my language!”

“Word, Toki? Shopping gets your attention? You’re fucked up,” Morgan said.

“You know I'm playing. It's your birthday, and we gonna party like it’s your birthday!” I sang.

“That’s more like it. Be ready by ten,” Morgan said.

When I turned over after hanging up, Qwan was up staring at me.

“Where you think you going, Toki?” he asked.

“Sorry if I woke you, baby. I'm going shopping with Morgan. Today’s her birthday.”

“A’ight, but before you do anything, get my dry cleaning from Brooklyn on Utica,” he said.

“Que, that's across town. Ain’t you gonna be on that side? Why don't you pick it up?”

“If I wanted to pick it up, I wouldn’t have asked you. Just

do as I say, and stop testing me," he said, pointing his finger in my face.

I wanted to bite it off, but knew I wanted be going to the mall with Morgan if I did.

This nigga is fucking crazy if he thinks I'm going out of my way to pick up his shit. If I make it on time, then I'll get it, and if not, tomorrow is another fucking day.

Being punctual, Morgan was outside blowing the horn at ten o'clock, just like she said.

"Hurry up, bitch! We got a full day ahead of us," Morgan said as I walked out my door.

"I'm coming," I yelled out to her.

When I got in the car, something in my head told me to look up at my bedroom window. As soon as I did, I caught Que looking at me all crazy like Norman Bates in the movie *Psycho*.

"Niemen Marcus got this Theory shirt that screams 'It's all about me!'" Morgan said as she approached the register and gave the sales girl her name.

As she waited, I spotted two dresses that were a must-have for me.

"Look, Toki," Morgan said, holding up a blue, backless, ruffled shirt. "You like it?" she asked.

"Like it? I love it. That's perfect for you."

"Yeah, I think so, too," Morgan said as she gave the sales girl her cash. "What you find, Toki?"

"I'm copping both these dresses. You like?"

"Yeah. Them shits were made for you."

"Word. Now all we have to do is hit the Loub store, but first, I want a pretzel with cheese."

"Alright, I want one, too," Morgan said.

"Toki, is that you?" I heard a familiar voice ask as I reached for my pretzel.

I know this bitch knows it's me, but why the fuck is she talking to me?

I turned around and said, “Yeah, it's me. What the fuck you want?”

“Damn, Toki. I just wanted to hash out our problem and explain my side of the story,” Summer said.

“Bitch, I don’t care to hash out shit or hear your cheap explanation.”

“Toki, please,” Summer said.

“Toki, please what, bitch? Ain’t shit for us to talk about. What you need to get through that empty head of yours is that I don’t like you and I never will. I mean, why is it so hard for you to see that me and you ain’t never been in the friend zone.”

“Damn, Toki. It’s like that?

The sound of her voice, the smell of her cheap perfume, and the look of her knock-off bag and clothes ticked me off. So, my reaction was my best reaction. I smacked the bitch with my pretzel. The cheese dripped all down her face.

“Now you can call it hashed. Get the fuck out my face!” I said, pushing past the hoe.

“I don’t know what’s wrong with that girl! She must like getting smacked and barked on because she keeps sweating us,” Morgan said, confused and shaking her head.

“She has to be! For the life of me, I can’t understand why any chick that keeps getting dissed and hit on keeps setting herself up like that. She has to know she will never win when it comes to us.”

I was pissed off. Not so much with the fact that Summer had approached me, but because she was shopping where I shopped.

Nah, that’s not sitting well with me.

I walked towards the exit. “Yo, Morgan, let’s get the fuck out of here. This mall is dead to me now. I need to be exclusive in whatever I decide to wear. Fuck Short Hill Mall!”

“Why? You just bought two dope-ass dresses, Toki.”

"I'm not wearing them shits! If that bum bitch made her way out here to shop, I can imagine how many more bum bitches with a couple dollars are shopping in here. Nah, fuck that. We're going to my favorite place to shop. Next stop, the Americana Mall. I know I won't bump into no broke-ass bitches. They can't afford them price tags!"

Once I got home, I remembered I forgot Qwan's dry cleaning. *Oh well, I probably won't see his ass until tomorrow or the next day*. I shook it off and got ready to party hard with my bitch.

After ripping the mall apart, it was time to hit the nightlife and show the NYC who was in charge. *I'm gonna light up the club for my bitch Morgan tonight. Ace of Spades only!*

As we pulled up to the club in our limo, everyone was looking like, *Who the fuck is that?* Trav got out and opened the door for us. Me being who I am, I came out last. The looks on bitches' faces were like *I hate her!*

I just smiled and stated, "I did it again, bitches!"

"Yo, Morgan, what you drinking tonight?"

"Only gold bottles," Morgan said, while we made our way in the club.

The Green House staff set the place up just how I wanted, with everything gold down to Morgan's name across the wall.

"Toki, I love you, girl! Couldn't ask for a better friend than you!" Morgan said.

"I couldn't ask for a better friend than you. I'm blessed with you and Sweets. But, enough of this soft shit. Let's show out!"

My girls and me partied, putting our footprints in the couch. The music was blasting, and everybody was dancing. That feeling came over me. You know, the feeling when your life feels perfect, and the ones you love are with you for real. Life was great, but I still wished Nice were there.

"I'm so fucked up, Toki. This was the best birthday ever!" Morgan said.

"Your birthday ain't over," Sweets said. "We going to the after spot!"

"Where at, Sweets?"

"This new shit in Harlem. We going back to our stomping ground," Sweets told her.

"Oh yeah, home sweet home," I said as we exited the club.

The limo was right in front, but something else caught my attention.

"Oh shit! What the fuck is he doing here?" I said.

"Who?" Sweets and Morgan asked.

"Qwan's ass! He knew tonight was ladies' night!"

"He looks pissed off, Toki," Morgan commented.

"Toki, fuck him. Let's go, 'cause I'm ready to shoot his ass. I can't stand him," Sweets said.

"Chill, Sweets, Morgan. He's not mad. I'm just going to go home and fuck his brains out. I love y'all bitches! Have fun!"

"Okay, Toki. love you, too," Morgan responded.

"Toki, if that nigga acts up, hit my phone and I'll come take his top off. I love you, too," Sweets said.

I just laughed. *My friends are crazy*.

"Hey, baby, what you doing here?"

"Get in the fucking car, Toki," Qwan said.

"What's wrong, Que?"

"I'ma show you what's wrong. Get in the fucking car, and don't make me repeat myself again."

I got in the car, and as I buckled my seatbelt, the car door locked. I just looked at him. His face did not seem familiar. He definitely wasn't the man I met. He sped off, eating every light for at least twelve blocks. I just couldn't understand why he be so mad when it comes to me. He was just kissing my ass, and now he back on his mean mugging shit.

"Why didn't you get my dry cleaning?" he finally asked.

I didn't respond or bother to turn my head to acknowledge

him speaking. Instead, I looked out the window as if he wasn't even there, but when he slammed on the brakes, causing my head to hit the dashboard, I realized his existence. Then he pushed my head into the window. I was too drunk to fight back, so he took that as the green light to go off on me.

Instantly, pressure and pain engulfed my face from him punching me. My head jerked back so hard it felt like my neck broke.

"Bitch, didn't I tell you to pick up my dry cleaning?" Qwan said.

I felt a knot forming on my face, and I just knew I had gotten whiplash when my head hit the dashboard. Blood dripped down into my eyes from the gash on my forehead.

Oh my God, he's trying to kill me!

I had no strength to look up or move. My body was slumped over like dead weight. I could hear Qwan's voice. I felt dead, but the pain that ran through my body let me that I wasn't. I felt the car moving fast, smelled the scent of his cigarette, and heard the sound of the wind.

I guess he's done hitting me. Thank you, God.

When the car came to a stop, I figured we were home. My door opened. He lifted my head and repeatedly punched me. I felt my jaw shift to the side as Qwan repeatedly hit me in my face.

He kept saying, "You're gonna learn to listen, even if I have to beat it in you."

He's gonna kill me. At this point, I don't even care. I can't go on living with this man in my life. I don't trust him. Every word is a lie. 'I won't hit you no more. I promise. I'm a changed man, Toki,' he said. Fucking liar.

"Fucking bitch!" Qwan said and kicked me in my back. "You will die with pride, bitch, knowing you in a battle you can't win. You won't even shed a tear."

He slapped me across my face. I hit the pavement and my head hit the curb. I was dazed. My head was spinning like eighty miles an hour. I felt my body being lifted. I believed God had come for me.

I felt the pavement, a huge pressure, and the worst pain ever in my body. He stomped me out with his size eight boot. I felt my ribs break. I could taste the blood spitting out my mouth.

It's going to take a lot for this motherfucker to kill me!

My mind was getting stronger and stronger; my thoughts got more evil and ruthless.

He's just turning me into a monster like him.

He put me back in the car and started to drive.

He's in control of my body, but not my mind. When I get the chance, I'm going to kill him.

"You think you tough? You ain't let a tear out them eyes? We'll see when we get home!" Qwan said.

Shit, ain't nothing more he can do to me.

"We home, bitch. Get out!" he said. "Oh, so you don't hear me?"

The car door flew open and my body hit the ground.

I felt the rocks in my driveway as he dragged me into the house. I couldn't scream; I was too drunk.

He picked the perfect time to do this to me.

The burns and cuts from him dragging me wasn't shit to me. Once he got me in the house, he dragged me up the stairs to my bedroom. He ripped my clothes off and left me there for a few minutes, but it felt like a lifetime. When he returned, the bastard poured some kind of liquid on me. The liquid burned and had a strong scent.

This nigga is pouring alcohol on me. Is he really crazy?

As the alcohol burned me, I felt a belt across my chest.

Is he beating me with a belt? God, give me the strength to live through this, because I'm going to kill him!

Once his arm got tired from swinging, he picked me up, carried me in the bathroom, and dropped me in my Jacuzzi filled with scorching hot water. I screamed to the top of my lungs as I jumped up. He pushed me back down in the tub, and I jumped up again. This time, I got out the tub, but I slipped and hit my head on the side of the tub. I wasn't out, but that put my movement on pause. The pain was unbearable. My body was giving up on me.

Dear Father, forgive me for I have sinned...

I closed my eyes slowly and the pain faded. Qwan noticed, so he snatched me by my hair and dragged me down the stairs, as I hit my head on every step. Once downstairs, Qwan tied me to a chair in the room, and began to torment me.

"Toki, you scared?" the nut asked, bending down and trying to look me in my face.

My head hung. *I'm not giving up. I'm holding on. I will die a horrible death before I fold.*

"See, bitch, this is our problem right here. You don't listen. You think you tough? I'm a man, bitch. If I want to snap your neck, I can without a sweat, so you need to fall in place and play your role before your stubborn ass gets peter-rolled. You can act like you not scared, but, bitch, everybody is scared to die."

With one eye closed, my head bleeding, and dazed, I lifted my head with everything I had in me.

I'm not throwing my towel in yet. I got some shit to say to Que.

I looked him in his eyes with my one okay eye and screwed up my swollen, bleeding lips. "I'm a G. I ain't crying or begging you not to kill me, but you, on the other hand, will be."

I spit blood out my mouth, than sat back all cocky with my chest poked out.

"Come on with it. Is that the best you got, Que, you pussy? You look silly beating on me. Won't you see for yourself?"

I nodded my head at the wall behind him. He turned

around to look in my ceiling-to-floor mirror.

"So what's up? Do you like what you see?"

He turned back and smiled at me. "Yeah, I think the view motivates me."

This nigga is fucking crazy.

Chapter 26

I was missing in action for two weeks. Qwan's crazy ass was babysitting me. If I blinked, he caught it. He wasn't trying to let me out of his sight. He even had a private doctor come out to tend to me. Shit, I missed meetings and money. I made Morgan handle everything, fronting like Qwan took me away for some one-on-one time, while I was actually at home tending to my battle scars.

Qwan watched my every move; he made sure when I was used the phone, he was right there to hear who I was talking to and what I was talking about. I knew he was scared I would fold and call the police, but Toki don't vibe with the police. Shit, he didn't sleep one bit. He sat up all night, ever since he almost killed me. Smoking weed and watching me. I did the same; he just didn't know it. I slept with one eye closed because I thought with my brain. I decided to pretend to be sleeping just so he wouldn't catch me off guard with one of his sneak attacks, at least until I executed my plan.

The first day I went out it was cold as shit. It was winter and the day of Bishop's party, which would be the biggest event of the year. I'd been waiting for this day. So, there was no way I was going to miss it. Shit, I planned it. Qwan would have had to lock me up to keep me from going. I figured he must have felt bad after all the shit he did to me and decided to let me go. He kissed my ass and even hinted that he was going to come to Bishop's party.

"Where you at, lil' lady?" Qwan asked when I finally answered my phone.

"On my way from the mall. Why? What's up?"

"I'm hungry, and you know how much I love your cooking. Can you hurry up?"

I laughed. "A'ight, I'm coming."

"Who was that, Toki?" Morgan asked.

"Qwan crying 'cause he's hungry."

"You got him spoiled, huh, Toki?"

"If you say so," I said, while peeking at Sweets through the rearview mirror.

Her face was exactly the way I knew it would be, evil-looking. I don't talk about Qwan around Sweets because I knew she didn't like him.

When I turned my music all the way up, Sweets leaned from the backseat to lower my tunes.

"Damn, Toki! You like a nigga! Music on fifty. I can't even hear myself think. You love bumping your gangster bitch music."

Morgan replied, "Bitch, you know Toki's a nigga with a pretty face and sexy body."

Once I dropped them off at home, I told them I would see them later that night, then headed home to handle my business.

*****

Our limo pulled in front of Club Amnesia on West 29th Street in Manhattan. Glad that my brother was home, I went all out for Bishop.

"So, ladies, you know Nice is going to call us for a conference call. In the middle of the party, we have to go in the office. He wants to be on speaker so he can do our toast."

"Damn, I haven't heard his voice in a minute, so that would be a treat for me," Morgan expressed. "I miss that nigga."

"He just needs to hurry home," Sweets said.

The hood showed up for my brother. After Trav opened the door, we stepped out the limo. We walked down the red carpet, smiled for the cameras, and waved at a few chicks we knew and niggas who wanted to get to know us. Some called our names, trying to get in. I mean, if they weren't already inside, more than likely, their paper wasn't long enough, and after one o'clock, it was bottles only. If somebody was stuck outside, then that's where they belonged.

We walked through the club acknowledging the bitches and niggas. As we approached our VIP section, I saw Bishop looking fresh to death with his D squared jeans, Hermes belt, and Hermes t-shirt and hat to match. He was iced completely out. Matrix came out Gucci down to the socks, which was shocking because even though this was an event we all had to show face at, Matrix still would have just probably stopped by since he didn't really party. My whole team was in the building, from the youngins to my white bitch. It was definitely a family affair. I hugged my boys, and we partied.

The gold bottles came ten at a time. I paid a hundred stacks to have them flowing all night. After a few glasses of Ace and a few sour blunts, I noticed Qwan never showed up. That was a good thing for me, because it made my night of partying with my family go much smoother. Qwan would have fucked my mood all the way up. Besides, at that point, Toki was on some new shit.

I shrugged. *Wherever he's at, that's where he needs to stay.*

"Yo, it's time, y'all. Nice will be calling in ten minutes," I said, while looking at the new iced out Rolex that Nice had sent me.

The DJ threw on some reggae music as the family made our way up the stairs to the rooftop office, where eight bottles of Ace of Spade sat on the table. My phone rang as we settled in the room.

We all gathered around the table as Bishop and Row popped the corks and passed the bottles out. We each had our own bottle because that's how we moved. Share? We shared money, not bubbly.

Nice's voice came through the speaker. "What's popping, fam? Good to hear all your voices. First and foremost, I want to say welcome home to Bishop. Congrats on kicking that case in the ass. Toki, you already know I'm proud of you like a motherfucker. You really holding down the fort like I knew you could. That's why I chose you."

I smiled at his satisfaction.

Nice addressed each of us individually. Sweets was a little standoffish. I knew she wasn't still mad.

Something is fucking with her emotions.

"Toki has a little something for you, Bishop. We felt like it was the best way to show you that we love and appreciate you."

I handed Bishop his iced-out, big-face Audimar Puget. Bishop flashed a big smile showing them all white teeth.

"He's smiling from ear-to-ear, Nice," I told Nice since he couldn't see him.

"That's what I live for," he replied. "Shit like this. A smile on the faces of my family is a priceless work of art. I want y'all to know I appreciate the loyalty. My family keeps me breathing, and as long as I make sure my family stays from behind these walls, I'm all the way good. Loyalty doesn't come in packs, but we do. Loyalty is rare in the game; we got a special gift. I would never trade my team for nothing in the world. A good boss acknowledges his peers and rewards them for their good works. A real boss is happy when his team eats heavy. Loyalty will never be just a word in our family. It's our lifestyle; it's our way of living. With that being said, raise your bottles in the air. I want to toast to us. For those who love us, the bastards who hate us, and the lucky motherfuckers who got to meet us! Toast to love, loyalty, family, wealth, and more money. I love you, family, until the day they bury me."

We toasted with our bottles and took a little sip. Then Nice hung up.

A tear fell from my eye. I missed that nigga something bad. It was killing me inside, but being a trooper, I wiped that tear away before my family peeped it.

Bishop gave me his Rolex to hold while he showed off his big-faced AP to the whole club. As we turned to leave, Sweets stopped me.

"Aye, Toki. Lemme holla at you for a second," she said.

We sat at the table.

"What's up?" I asked.

"Toki, you know I love you, right?"

I nodded.

"You know I would die for you, right?"

"Yes. Why?"

"You know I would never lie to you, right?"

"Sweets, spit it out. The questions are killing me."

"Okay. You know my friend Trina?"

"Yeah. Morgan and me went to her spa when it opened. Cute shop."

"Well, her man was from Brooklyn, so she knows a few chicks that know Qwan."

"Why would there be a conversation about whether or not she knows Qwan?" I asked.

"Because I asked her, that's why," Sweets said. "Toki, she told me that she knew his baby mother and that his baby mother used to be in and out the hospital from all the broken bones he caused her."

"Yeah, well, did your friend Trina tell you that his baby mother is a hoe?"

"No."

"Did she tell you about how many niggas ran through her friend?" I said, standing and waving my hand.

"Listen, Toki," Sweets said, grabbing my arm.

I snatched away from her and stood still.

"Toki, I told you when I met him that he's not for you. You and him live in two different worlds. He's a jacker; he robs celebrities and drug dealers. And from what I'm hearing, now he's robbing people in the hood. If he's turning on his own friends, what the fuck do you think he's going to do to you when he finds out you're the queen bitch behind the dope game? Come on, Toki. Think. You're not dumb at all. You're smart as hell, but your problem is you never want to listen. It's like you think listening to a motherfucker will make you lose your respect in the streets."

"Listen, Sweets," I said. "I got this. I'm good. Whatever Qwan did to his baby mother, he is not and will not do to me. We're two different breeds. He don't know nothing about my position in the game, and that's the way it's going to stay."

"Yeah, okay, Toki. You can try to act like word don't spread like wildfire in Brooklyn if you want, but that motherfucker is nuts. If you fuck with him after my hundredth warning, then you and me are through. I can't live my life stressing over you when you're not stressing over yourself. Qwan is a grimy-ass nigga. Watch, you'll see. Satan will reveal his horns," she warned.

"Sweets, slow your roll and watch your mouth, 'cause you bugging if you base our friendship on who I sleep with. If so, then you were never my bitch. That's how I see it. Maybe if you get yourself some dick some time, you would be a little less stressed. Smile a little. Stop always screwfacing, because the misery is showing. Qwan and me are good, bitch. If you and Trina wanted to borrow him, all you had to do was ask."

"You know what? Fuck you, Toki," Sweets said as she flipped her middle finger at me and walked out the door. She stopped before totally exiting. "Oh yeah, Toki, one more thing before I forget. She also told me when Qwan is not home at night that he's sleeping with the ugly girl that he calls his sister. Ummm, what's her name? Oh yeah, that's right. Her name is Tammy, Number's bitch. That may be why he ain't here with you now."

"Whatever, bitch. I think you need to go home. Seems like you had too much to drink."

"Naw, bitch, I ain't drunk. But, what I am doing is leaving."

Sweets walked down the stairs and probably out the front door. I brushed it off. If she fucked up our bond because she didn't like my dude, then that told me a lot about our bond. Maybe it wasn't as tight as I thought.

After I made it back downstairs, Morgan asked. "Where's Sweets?"

"She left. I'll tell you why later," I told her, then continued to party.

After cutting Bishop's cake, I received a text from Qwan telling me that he was outside to pick me up. He never said he was coming to get me, but since the party was ending, I called it a night. I kissed my family and hugged Bishop. When I walked out the club, I saw Qwan waiting in an all-white Camaro, his face all screwed up like somebody had just crushed his world.

If I didn't know any better, the way he's looking, I would think he's mad at me again.

I opened the door and got in.

"Hey, boo. Whose car is this?" I asked as I leaned over to kiss his cheek.

He backed away from me and looked me up and down like the sight of me disgusted him. He was really angry. We rode home in silence.

Tonight is not the night for Que to play hitting games. I swear, I'm gonna flat-line his ass. I'm not drunk tonight, so if he wants to act up, then what's up? First, it was 'Toki, I'm sorry,' and now we back to this shit.

Once we walked in the house, I took my shoes off.

"You hungry?" I asked.

"Naw," he said, following me to the kitchen, where he stood in the doorway watching me.

I could see the jealousy appear on his face when he spotted the new watch Nice sent me.

"Where you get that watch from, Toki?" he asked.

"Oh this?" I said like it was nothing. "Nice sent it to me."

"Why would he send any bitch he's not fucking a watch like this? That watch cost about thirty thousand."

"Well, actually, it was fifty."

"You was fucking that nigga when he was home, Toki?" Qwan asked.

"Nah, there's just some niggas out there that appreciate a bitch like me on their team. I mean, if you would treat me right, you would see what Nice sees in me. But nah, you want to be mean. All day you want to fight with me. Que, I'm tough, but that's not what my life is about. I'm loyal to you no matter what you did to me. I've been loyal to you, but you rather take your street shit out on me."

"Nah, you got a big-ass mouth. You don't know when to shut up. Like now." Qwan moved in closer to me.

"So what now? You want to fight me because I asked you was you hungry?"

"And still you didn't listen, because I said I wasn't fucking hungry," he responded through clenched teeth, sizing me up.

I looked him up and down, stepped back, and yelled, "What did I do to you? What the fuck is wrong with you?"

"What's wrong with me?" he asked.

"Yes," I replied.

"What's wrong with me is I have a problem with what you have on. That's how you show me respect? The one night I let you go out alone, you made sure you looked like a hoe!"

"Hoe?"

"Yeah, hoe," he said, then slapped me to the floor.

Damn, I'm not up for all of this tonight. Maybe if I surrender, he won't hit me again. Nah, fuck that.

I turned around swinging like a mad woman. He couldn't hold me, so he went for my hair and dragged me around the house like a ragdoll.

"Get the fuck off me, Qwan!" I scratched him just to leave behind some DNA just in case he killed me.

With one hand around my neck, he picked me up off the floor. My feet dangled, and my face turned red. I hit him in his face with all the energy I had left. I couldn't breathe, and I felt my body getting weak. I had no more energy to fight back. My body went limp. Once Qwan felt like he was satisfied, he let me go, and I fell straight on my face. Blood gushed from my mouth. I gasped for air through blood.

He bent over me and whispered, "Next time, bitch, have some motherfucking respect." Then he walked out the door.

When I got enough strength, I crawled in the bathroom and grabbed a washcloth. I wet it and pressed it against my mouth to control the bleeding. I tried to call Morgan, but it went straight to voicemail.

I didn't know what to do. But, I knew I got myself in some shit that I needed to get out of. And I knew I couldn't do it by myself. It was time to wake up. That nigga was never going to change. After another attempt, I still couldn't get Morgan on the phone.

If he follows me over there, he can say hello to Morgan's .9mm, I thought, but as soon as I opened the door, there he was.

"Going somewhere?" Qwan said. "No need to leave. I found what I was looking for."

In his hand, he held a welding torch.

Oh my God! This motherfucker is crazy. I'm definitely going to die. This is some other shit. I know I wasn't the best bitch, but damn, what did I do to deserve this?

"Are you crazy, nigga?" I asked him.

"Yeah, well, you seem to mistaken me for a fool, a soft-ass nigga. You like fighting back, so I decided to show you who's the boss. You want to run and tell your fucking cousin and your fake-ass brothers, Toki? I'm not a pussy," he said and handed me the phone. "Call them. Just remember, I got good aim, too. Bitch, you gonna learn who wears the pants in this relationship."

Again, he grabbed me by my neck, and I grabbed his. He squeezed; I squeezed. He squeezed harder. I bit my bottom lip and stared him in his eyes while squeezing with all my might. I wanted him to see what he was making me.

He needs to know this bitch is crazy.

But, my strength was nothing compared to Qwan's, even with all the anger in me. He overpowered me probably because he liked the pain, but I wasn't enthused. As I began to get weak, I heard my momma's voice saying, *Think with your mind, baby girl, and not your heart.* I realized that to stay alive, I had to quit fighting back.

"Qwan, please, let me go. I know who's boss. Just please, stop choking me."

Finally, he let me go. I fell to my knees, balled up like a baby, and moaned helplessly.

"I knew you would see it my way," he said. "But, just in case you forget, I'm gonna leave you with a reminder. Lay down, Toki."

I was about to refuse, but then he put the Glock to my head.

"Take off your shirt and pants."

I did as I was told.

"Now, lay on your back."

I guess before he kills me, he wants to rape me. Whatever. At this point, I don't even care no more. Whatever he's gonna do, he needs to get on with it.

He pulled the duct tape out, ripped off a piece, and said, "I don't want to hear you scream, so I'm gonna tape your mouth shut."

I didn't reply. There was no sign of fear in my stare. He fired up the torch. I didn't move. I lay there as he branded me. I didn't make a sound, not even a grunt. I didn't flinch.

I'm never gonna see Nice again.

Que moved the torch around on my body. The damn nut burned Q's all over my body, and I didn't make one noise. All he saw in me was hate, because by then, I was numb. I had no more fight left. If my life was supposed to end that way, cool. Qwan stared into my eyes. He realized he didn't break me. He backed up and looked at me as if to say, *Who are you? Are you even human?*

"All that, and you still have no fear of me?"

I looked him in his eyes and shook my head.

"That's dangerous," he said.

Then his eyes shifted from me to my watch. He smiled and snatched it off.

"Tell Nice we said thanks, but no thanks."

As soon as the door closed, I cried like a baby. I waited a few minutes before I got up. Then I took the tape off my mouth and ran in my kitchen to grab a knife. However, he had taken them and anything I could use to hit him. I looked out the window; his car was gone. I locked all my doors and windows before calling Morgan. Thank God! This time, she picked up.

"Morgan!"

"Toki? What's wrong? Are you crying?"

"Yes. This motherfucker hit me. He busted my whole mouth and more. Where are you?"

"I'm at dinner with Row."

"Can he hear me? Did he hear you say my name?"

"No. I'm in the restroom."

"I need you, Morgan. Please come to my house, and bring your gun."

"Okay, I'm on my way," Morgan told me.

"Make sure you come alone."

I tried to clean myself up a bit so Morgan wouldn't see me too messed up.

Morgan arrived ten minutes later. She took one look at me and tears fell from her eyes.

"Toki, what the fuck did this nigga do to you? Did he find out about the abortion?"

"No. He beat me up like this because of what I had on. I can't do this shit. I can't hide it no more. I've been trying to sweep this under the rug for too long. Protecting him and acting like I'm so in love, when I'm really crying out for help. I need to see Nice. I need to talk to him face-to-face. I have a lot I need to tell him, and I won't do it through a letter. Morgan, I need to tell him I fucked up. I need to tell him that I'm not perfect," I cried.

Morgan hugged me. "I'm here, Tee. I'm here."

I stopped hugging her. "I need to tell Nice that I love him. I do, Morgan. I love him. It's fucked up that I had to go through hell to see it, but I love him, Morgan."

"You always knew you loved him. It was just a lot at stake in your head, and you felt your friendship wasn't worth the risk. That's not a bad thing. That's just being you, Tee, a real bitch."

Morgan called Pat, but he didn't answer. So, she left him a message.

I rolled blunt after blunt, smoking back-to-back, trying to numb the pain in my heart.

I can't believe this is happening to me. I never pictured it, but I guess it happens to the best of us. I guess this is my life's test to see if I'm built for this shit.

When Morgan sat back down next to me, she was extra quiet, and she tried her best to avoid looking me in my face.

"Morgan, why you so quiet?" I asked.

"All this is my fault. I pushed you to it."

"Don't blame yourself. You didn't make me call him. Oh

yeah, maybe you did," I said, then laughed. "I'm jus playing."

"Toki, this shit isn't funny. Look at your face. This is crazy."

"I know, Morgan," I said, dropping my head in shame. "But you didn't force me to sleep with him. You didn't make me give him a key. You didn't make me fall in love with him. I was in love and in denial. Me? Get beat? That shit don't happen. It just sounds crazy."

Morgan looked at me as she took my face and held it gently in her hands. She turned it from side to side, examining me.

"Listen, Toki. You know I've been through this before, and being all too familiar with abuse, I saw the signs but ignored them. I saw the black eye you were trying to hide when we went to see Papito, even though you tried to cover up all the battle marks.

"A victim of abuse knows all the signs like she knows the Ten Commandments," Morgan continued. "I looked abuse right in its face, and I ignored it. I was too busy being a friend and not a sister, in fear of pointing it out to you. I know the feeling. No matter what my ex did to me, I didn't want to hear it. As a result of that, I never wanted to be the girl that said 'Leave that nigga.' I always valued that I would never come in between love, but this shit right here is unavoidable. Toki, this ain't love. Love don't hurt you like this. You may love him with your heart, but his so-called love ain't it. The only way out of his love is six feet deep. You know you can't leave, Toki. It's either you or him. If you don't do it first, he will. It will be you who they carry away in a bag, real talk," Morgan said.

"You know what, Morgan? I learned something in this game. The streets are easy to be told. You can take a lie and run with it in the streets. If you're somebody, everyone will carry it back and forth, just wanting to be in the know. Qwan let that fake shit go to his head. He's spending before he gets it and letting dick-riding niggas and bitches get into his head. He ain't got no stash; he ain't got nothing but cars, clothes, and jewelry. He believed the picture the streets painted for him, and now, his run is over. It's time that nigga knows who really is boss."

Just then, the door swung open.

"Get down! Get down on the floor! Police!"

We took a dive like we were on the swimming team, as boots trampled through my door.

"Toki, you got anything?" she whispered.

"Qwan took my hammers, and the other shit they won't find. You got your hammer?"

She nodded.

"Okay, follow my lead," I told her.

I got shortness of breath at that moment.

"I don't know what's happening, but my chest is tightening up," I said.

"Toki, what's wrong?" Morgan asked, then yelled, "Officer, please! She can't breathe! I have to get her pump!"

They ignored her.

I wheezed louder. My lips became dry, and I started coughing and crying. My lips even turned a little blue.

Morgan yelled louder. "Please, officer, you gonna just stand there and let my sister die? Her pump is in the garage. Look around. With all y'all around everywhere, where can I go? I just want to go get her pump."

I tried to sit up and dropped back down, acting like I was too weak.

"Come on," the officer finally said.

He escorted her like she knew he would. She ran ahead like she was in a hurry. As she opened the passenger door, she dropped her hammer from her waist and put it under the seat. She then ran back in the house to my aid. She pumped three times, and we went through the routine.

After a glass of water and twenty minutes of sitting on the

couch, the captain walked through the door.

"Don't I know you ladies from somewhere?"

Morgan responded, "Maybe, maybe not. But, what I want to know is why you kicked in this door?"

The captain, who was carrying a folder, handed us our lawyer's card. Morgan took the card.

"So, by you giving me this, it tells me you already contacted him," Morgan said.

One of the rookie cops who had been searching the guest room said, "I got something, Captain."

The captain returned and said, "So, Ms. Smith…"

I looked at him, wondering how he knew my name.

"…where is your boyfriend?"

"I'm not saying shit," I responded.

"I knew you was the more loyal one between you two. I mean, he just came back from a trip with a chick, and sorry to say, Ms. Smith, but that chick wasn't you. From that bruise around your eye and the marks on your neck, I would say you must have just found out that your boyfriend is who you thought he was—a motherfucker that only loves himself. So, if you can just tell me that this kilo of dope is his and not yours, then we will be on our way. I mean, either way," the captain said as he pulled out a photocopy sheet with Qwan's mug shot, "your boyfriend is wanted by the government."

Pat walked through the door. "No more questions. Are my clients under arrest?"

"If she doesn't answer my question the way I want her to, then, yes, they are," the captain said with a grin.

Morgan and I looked at each other. We stood up off the couch, turned around, and put our hands behind our backs. The cops slapped the cuffs on and we rode to the precinct in two separate cars, with Pat tailing behind.

Chapter 27

The detective put a folder down in front of us. He opened it up and lined all the photos of Shaunie and her cousin's dead bodies on the table in front of us. The pictures were graphic, but I looked at them with no reaction. My heart bled and cried for Shaunie. I couldn't believe Sin had done her like that. The detective also showed pictures of Cookie's dead body.

"You remember her?" the detective asked.

"Yeah, we remember her," Pat replied. "I remember my clients not having anything to do with her murder, as well."

"Yes," the detective said, "but what you don't know is something came up. Didn't Morgan say if something was to come up, y'all weren't hiding, right? So, I decided to share with you the 'something' that just so happened to come up."

Two detectives walked in with a TV and DVD player, hooked it up, and left.

So now what? Somebody's gonna bring us some popcorn with extra butter? I said to myself. *"Like them putting these pictures in front of my face and acting like they got me on tape will make me roll over on Qwan. I mean, I don't even know where he is right now, and I don't care. But, even if I did, I'm mute when it comes to the pigs. As much as I hate him right now, I can't see me signing no statements or talking shit about Qwan. Naw, that don't fit my description. If they want Qwan as bad as they're acting, then they need to do their job, because I ain't helping.*

The fat captain came in with a DVD, popped the disc in, and pressed play. Pat and me sat back and watched the movie they wanted me to see. I knew Morgan was flipping out on the inside. But, they couldn't ask any questions because Pat was representing both of us.

The video showed Qwan talking to me, and Morgan walking out of the club. We walked to the corner out of sight. Then Lucy and Joker appeared. Joker pulled some money out of his pocket and put Lucy in a cab. Joker stood around, and Qwan walked back into the picture. He and Joker got into a black minivan. People filed out of the club, not paying attention to the minivan. Shaunie and her cousin walked out with Tammy, which shocked me because I didn't remember seeing Tammy that night. They walked to the corner, and Tammy nodded. Two men wearing black hoodies jumped out on the ladies, grabbing Shaunie and her cousin. Tammy hopped in the driver's seat, and the van sped off.

Rage brewed inside me. I should have listened to Sweets. She said she had a bad vibe about Tammy and Qwan, but being Toki, I just had to do what I wanted to do. Qwan was nothing he portrayed himself to be. I was in love with the enemy.

I wonder if he knows that Sin turned state's evidence.

"Listen, Mrs. Smith," the captain said. "We've been on your boyfriend since he came home. I put together a special task just for him and his crew. I know you know what happened to these two young ladies. One was a mother of a little boy, and the other one was getting ready to go to college. Your boyfriend had a hand in that. Be smart about this. You can put an end to your unhappy life. He's a dangerous dude. He doesn't care about you, so why protect him?"

I stared at him, but didn't speak. He got agitated as he tried to stare me down, but I didn't budge.

"I'm pretty sure Nice would be happy if we let you trade

in Qwan for Nice's freedom."

He paused and watched me, almost like he was studying for an exam. He looked for a change. Nothing.

Death before dishonor, and besides, I want Qwan dead.

The detective got even madder. His face turned red, and he spit when he talked.

"His time is up. His crew is dropping like flies, and if you're not careful, Ms. Smith, you can get caught up in his shit."

I rolled my eyes at the pig and looked away from him.

"I mean, either way, Ms. Smith, you and your cousin are in a fucked-up situation. The dope we found will land you both ten years," he said.

"They will both get bail. Anything else?" Pat asked.

"Well, that's up to the judge, and most times, when a body is involved, a judge usually denies bail."

"True, if they are being charged with murder. Before you can throw bodies on my clients, you must have proof, and in their case, you have none," Pat said. "So, charge them if you are going to charge them, but it won't be for murder."

"We won't charge them yet. It's her boyfriend we want, not them. But, be real careful, Ms. Smith."

I smiled. "Careful?"

"Because if you're not, your boyfriend will add another body to his growing tab, and it will be yours," he said before walking out the room.

Chapter 28

"I think Qwan is the one who robbed us."

"You think so, Toki?"

"Are you blind, Morgan? Or was my mind playing tricks on me? You know our trademark, and that brick had our stamp on it. Besides, did you not see the fucking tape? Not only did he rob us, but he killed Shaunie, which means he knows Sin's rat ass."

"Maybe he bought it off a nigga."

"Naw, Morgan. Qwan is definitely the mastermind behind the robbery and Ofia's death."

"So what you gonna do?" Morgan asked.

"I don't know. I mean, even though all the signs were pointing in Qwan's direction, I just never spoke on it because a big part of me didn't want to believe it. But, now, how could I avoid it when it's in my face? As soon as I laid my eyes on that brick the cops found that I didn't even know was in my place, my mind started to play all kinds of flashbacks."

"Like what?"

"The night we got robbed, remember Qwan didn't come home? Then we find out that clown Joke was in on it, so Lucy knocked his ass off. Neck's involvement, the Rolex that he supposedly brought for me that I think he took back, because for the life of me I couldn't seem to find my watch and my necklaces, and it went missing not too long after he got that bad money call. I know for sure that Rolex was Cookie's. It's all clear now."

"So how you wanna play it?" Morgan asked.

"I don't know yet," I told her. "Let me make it official, because with a nigga like Que we have to move careful. Qwan don't know the jewelry store was our spot, so let me pick his mouth and see what he tells me."

"But you don't even know where he's at."

"Yeah, I know, but he'll be back."

"Okay, Toki. Just don't get caught up in feeling sorry for the nigga, if he's really the person that did this," Morgan said.

"Naw, my days of feeling sorry for Qwan are over. All he's done is fucked up my life. I know Nice is mad at me. He don't want to see me, so I guess I'll just write him a letter."

"Okay, cool. I'm going home for a little while to change my clothes. Do you want to come with me?"

"Naw, I'm just gonna sit here and write this letter."

"Are you sure, Toki? If not, then I won't even go."

"No, go do what you need to do. I'm good. I have to wait for the locksmith anyway. I'm good. I'm gonna take a Percocet to go to sleep. I'm fine, Morgan. Call when you're on your way back. Just in case they come and change the locks, I can open the door for you."

"Okay, I'll be back in like two hours. If Qwan comes before I get back, call me, and I will be here in a flash."

"Okay. See you in a little while."

After Morgan left, I decided to roll a blunt, smoke a little, and write my brother a letter.

Hey brother,

It's your sister, Toki. I hope this letter greets you in good health. To keep it all for real, let's just get to the point. This bullshit I got myself in is breaking me. I can say I'm done with it, but if he's still alive, he will always be in my backyard lurking, itching for that right moment. Sometimes, I take a long drive in your Bentley, trying to get a feel of what you would do if you were me. I'm sorry for all that has happened, but brother, I've fallen way under. Please send someone to pull me out alive. I don't want to die. The way things have been going for me lately, it looks like I might see my maker sooner than I think. Not sure what's going on, but I know I'm in trouble.

I thought I should write this letter because I know you are mad at me. I miss you, and I wish you were home. Life would be so much better. I hate my life right now. I just want to make this nightmare disappear. When I look back and envision all that I have lost, I can't believe I let my head hit the floor.

I don't understand how I allowed myself to get in a situation like this. I thought I did a background check. Nice, I did! But, there was nothing in there that told me he would treat me like shit. I hate myself for falling in love with this dick. And now that I don't love him no more, he can't handle it.

The funny shit, brother, is this nigga showed me many times that the love he claims to have for me is a bunch of franks and beans. He doesn't love me or anyone else for that matter. He loves and only cares about one thing, and that's money. I thought I was doing the right thing by putting him down with us, thinking more business for us. But, I was wrong. I'm tired. I need you, brother. I'm lost without you. Everything on the outside looks good, but behind closed doors, my life is a big ole mess.

I just felt the need to let you know how sorry I am, brother. I'm sorry I let you down. I'm sorry I let my heart think for me. I'm sorry I didn't live up to what you see in me. I'm sorry I didn't listen and decided to do my own thing, thinking I know everything. Now look at me. I'm damn near dead 'cause I'm sleeping with the enemy.

If this letter doesn't reach you in time, or if you happen to turn on the news and the headline picture is mine, I just wanted to tell you that I love you with all of my heart. I never meant for this bastard to take over my soul, giving him total control over my life. Nice, I know you're the only one that can pull me out of this hell I'm living in alive.

Till death,
Your baby sis, Toki

*****

I woke up in a strange place. I tried to move my arms, but couldn't. I realized I was tied up.

What the fuck?

I felt the duct tape over my mouth. I tried to scream as loud as I could through the tape. I tried to make some noise so I could see the face of my takers. Knowing who got me would help me know my level of danger. I squirmed around, trying to get a feel for my surroundings.

Okay, I'm in the back of a van.

I saw Qwan's devilish grin, and it gave me chills. He got me when I was helpless.

I knew I should have put a bullet in his head the very first time his bitch ass hit me. A damn second chance landed me in this damn van. How the hell did I fucking slip like that?

"Rise and die," Qwan said, looking to be two steps shy of the loony bin. "You finally woke up. Just in time for the grand finale. We're going on a little trip. Oh yeah, bitch, whether you are dead or alive, you're going. It's whichever you choose."

He smiled, and I swore I looked into the face of a psychopath.

"So, stay here and don't act up. Be a good girl, and I'll let you live. I'll be right back, okay?" he said, acting like I was in kindergarten or something. "I have to go get something for us," Qwan's crazy ass stated just before closing the door to the van.

Then he stuck his head back in and said, "Oh yeah, I just saw your family. They pulled off right before you woke up. I think they was looking for you. But, fuck it. They gone now, so stay here and I'll be back."

He slammed the door.

What in the hell did I get myself into? How the hell did I get in this shit? Hardhead-ass Toki, the gangsta bitch.

Qwan wasn't gone a whole two minutes before he opened the back door. This time, he wasn't the happy-go-lucky nut who had just gone in the house. He was on some extra insane, deranged type shit. Something was wrong with his brain.

He grabbed me by my hair and looked me in my eyes. His mouth foamed, and his eyes were bloodshot red. Hate spewed from his eyes.

"Where the fuck is my shit, Toki?" he asked me calmly.

I knew what he was looking for, but I looked at him with no emotion. I wanted him to rip the duct tape off my lips so I could scream.

His shit? HIS SHIT? How about my shit? That brick the cops found was mine.

I wanted to give him a piece of my mind. I mumbled a little through the tape like I was trying to tell him where I put it.

When he rips the tape off, I'm going to tell Qwan where he can go put his dick.

Qwan punched me in my eye, and it immediately started to swell. I felt the puffiness grow tender as he picked me up and carried me into the house.

He opened the door and stepped inside. He slammed me on the hardwood floor with as much force as he could muster. I landed on my side. The pain shot straight to my head. That's how bad I hit the floor. I felt as if I couldn't move. My whole body went numb, and my head pounded profusely. I screamed loud enough that he heard me through the tape.

This nigga is rag tagging me off some lightweight work

that didn't even belong to him. This nigga is fucking sick. No way is he in his right state of mind.

I never saw anyone that mad in my life, especially if I wasn't the cause for his insanity.

I wanted to scream, cry, and kill Qwan, but he knew me. That lame-ass nigga handicapped me so he could beat me…seriously beat me. He beat on me while I was tied up and helpless. That proved he was nothing but a sucker.

A manmade bitch is what Qwan is. I swear if God gives me one free minute, I'm taking it. One to the head will put Qwan in a nice deep sleep, because love don't hurt like this.

"Where's my shit, Toki? I'm not gonna keep asking you."

Again, I tried to speak, but I couldn't.

"Are you trying to tell me something?" Qwan asked.

I knew he wanted to hear what I had to say. I knew he hoped I was going to tell him where his shit was.

"I can't hear you, Toki. You trying to say something?"

I nodded, and he snatched the duct tape off my mouth. If I wouldn't have been used to getting my mustache waxed, I would have screamed, but instead, I gave him a cold, blank stare.

He grabbed me by my hair and forced me to look him in his face.

"Listen, bitch," he said. "I'm not gonna keep asking you. Where's my shit?"

"Untie me so I can get it," I told him.

I knew the pigs took that last brick he left after he robbed us, but I did have one to spare if it would make him happy and keep his hands to himself. I needed an exit strategy.

He nodded his head okay, and then he walked into the living room. He grabbed the remote control, powered on the entertainment center, and turned the music all the way up.

Putting the Glock to my head, he said, "Now, listen to me clearly, Toki. I know you think you're a little tough cookie and you like fighting me back, but if you even think about trying to sneak me in any way, I will make it quick. You got me, bitch?"

I nodded. Not a dumb chick by far, I knew trying some stunt girl shit would not be smart, especially when Qwan had the only gun. From the looks of his dilated pupils, I knew he was on the edge and waiting for me to give him a reason. So, I played it smart and did what he said.

I knew Qwan had robbed me. I just wanted to hear him say he did it.

When he untied my hands, I spit in his eye.

"No, motherfucker, you mean my shit," I said and spit again.

That fast, I had forgotten to do what he told me. I had to be Toki.

He slapped blood out my mouth. "Bitch, you spit in my face!"

Then he backhanded me right to the floor. He kicked me repeatedly in my ribs and stomach until I threw up. He even kicked me a few times after I vomited.

"If you ever spit in my face again…" he said as he dragged me up the hall and back again, making sure I hit every wall.

He eventually untied my hands, but my feet were still tied together. Thus, I was still hopeless and tortured.

"You only doing this because I'm helpless!" I yelled. "You got my feet tied up. You know otherwise, we can get it rocking, you bitch-ass nigga."

"Oh really?" he said. "Matter of fact, I'm gonna go upstairs and give you a second to get some strength. When you ready, give me a holla. I know my shit is here somewhere, and you're gonna tell me where you put it, bitch. Did you give it to your fake-ass brothers?" he asked, before walking up the steps.

This nigga is crazy as fuck. He's really acting like that work is his. I know he heard me when I told him it was my shit. My words didn't faze him, though. Let me find out Qwan was lining me all along.

I have to find something to protect myself, because the nut got his gun, and there is no way I'm catching bullets with my teeth. That shit only happens in movies.

I was in so much pain that I needed a break. Sitting on the couch, I was bent over untying my feet, when I heard my front door open.

Dumb nigga left the door open.

Quietly, I stood to see if it was Morgan, but she would have called my name out as soon as she walked in the house. The footsteps sounded like men's boots. I knew better than to yell, so I lay on the couch and closed my eyes. I didn't know who came through my door. It wasn't the police, because no one yelled for me to get down on the floor. I prayed it was family coming back for me. I was beaten halfway to death, so lying still was not hard to do.

As I heard the footsteps getting closer to me, I tried my best not to move or breathe. My intruders didn't buy my faking dead act, though. Instead, he greeted me with a cold .9mm barrel and pressed it against my face. I opened my eyes and closed them again.

This shit cannot be real, I thought as I opened my eyes again.

The nine was still in my face, and the nigga holding it there was ski masked up with a black hoodie on.

"Damn," I said. "You niggas must be from another country, because robbing me is not a wise thing to do. When my family finds out you put a gun in my face—"

The gunman slapped me across my face.

"I would pistol whip you, but you're too pretty for that, ma. Besides, it looks like you just went to war. Play your role and get the fuck up. Oh yeah, one more thing," he said, before backing up to give me some room to stand. "Please, bitch, don't try me. I heard about you, so be smart in your thoughts.

You hear me, shorty? No sudden moves, because I would hate to have to do it to you."

I got up as the goon instructed.

"Now get on your knees," he told me.

I looked homie straight in his eyes, trying to look in his soul. I wanted him to know that yeah, this bitch was bold. I grilled the nigga without blinking. I never have shown fear. If it's my time, then it is what it is.

"Please don't get happy and think I'm scared of you and your gun just because I obeyed your command for me to stand up. I will die slow before I suck your little-ass dick, homie."

The goon chuckled. "Nah, ma, this ain't about no pussy or a nut. This is all about my cash."

The goon completely untied my feet and gently stood me up. The second goon brought Qwan downstairs bleeding.

Nigga can't beat a nigga, huh?

I assumed there would be a struggle, because I knew Qwan. He wasn't just going to let a nigga tie him up. I hoped he would had forced the goon's trigger finger, but lucky for Qwan, he just got an ass whipping. The goon gun butted him when he brought Qwan in the living room and tied him up. Blood gushed from his head.

From the way the nigga who slapped me moved and talked, I knew who the boss was. He instructed me to stand up and then led me towards the basement. The other one pulled Qwan up with force and pushed him towards the basement door. He never spoke; he never made a noise. All his actions were done physically. Whatever the leader did, the silent killer followed suit.

"You know what to do, shorty," the head goon said, nodding his head at the fuse box. "Open it," he said.

I did as I was told. I flicked a switch in my fuse box that opened a little slot in the wall that hid a scanner. I put my hand against the scanner, and my basement door opened. I was definitely thrown off and confused as to why they wanted us in the basement. It never crossed my mind that they knew I had a stash. But, to my surprise, that's exactly what they came for.

"Put that nigga in a chair," the leader said to his goon.

The goon placed what appeared to be a white pillowcase over Qwan's head.

He said to me, "You know what I want. Let's just make this nice and quick. No one needs to die over what I came for. You balling shorty, right? Yeah, you balling. So, this ain't shit. You can definitely afford the loss. Nothing personal, ma. You should thank your man for this. He's lucky he had you. Being that you're the big homie's sister is what spared his brains. You should watch the company you keep, ma. You're worth too much," the goon stated as he untied me.

Whoever these niggas are, they know too much of my personal business to be goons from the EMF crew. How would they know which door led to my basement? How did they know I had a safe behind my wall? How the fuck they know only my handprint could open the door?

The leader walked over to Qwan and said, "You got to be the dumbest motherfucker in history to not know who you was beating on. Just a dumb nigga."

There was no denying that these motherfuckers did their homework. I gave the head goon a double take. I was confused as to how they knew me. The head goon winked at me to let me know I knew him from somewhere. I tried to study his voice, but I couldn't connect it with a face. He sounded familiar, but I figured that was because I wanted him to be familiar.

Although they robbed me, they helped me at the same time, because I would choose the goons over NYPD any day. I made up my mind that they could keep the money. What they took was light, and I wouldn't die from it. The little hit would not starve me; it just gave me energy to go even harder. I know I owe everything to Nice. He taught me well.

The leader found it hilarious that Qwan never knew my real profession. He thought I was just a lucky girl from the Bronx who met a nigga named Nice from Bushwick that took a liking to me and put me on because I'm a rare one. He failed to realize I was true to the game. I'm a G. I ride for mine. He didn't know I was a chameleon. Adaptation is a learned skill. He never knew I was a gunner known to bust with my niggas. He didn't know I was a Black Widow and would put a nigga straight to sleep when they thought they robbed Nice.

"You deserve to die. One to the head for stupidity," the leader said to Qwan as he mushed his head like a bobble doll. "Don't sweat it, though, homie. Some things you know and some you just don't. But, let me take this opportunity to reveal to you who your bitch really is."

The silent goon removed the pillowcase from Qwan's head. His eyes opened wide. I thought they were going to pop out of his head when he saw a whole wall filled with money on top of money on top of bricks.

"She's who we call the black Griselda Blanco," the head goon said, smiling like a Cheshire cat.

Tight beads of sweat the size of raindrops gathered on Qwan's nose. If looks could kill, the head goon would be dead. He was tied up and being punked, but none of that mattered. I got upset because I thought the goons would help me. Instead, they robbed me blind.

"What's wrong, lil' homie?" one of the goons asked when he noticed Qwan killing me with his stare. "What, you didn't know Toki is the Queen Bee?"

They both laughed.

"Well, now you do. Too bad for you that you found out about it when you won't be able to spend it."

I guess it was hot in my basement, because the silent goon unzipped his hoodie to reveal a big white YSL logo on the front of a plain black t-shirt that basically said, "Hello. My name is Stupid."

I smirked in my head, not wanting to tip him off to his deadly mistake. When they were done taking my shit, I was bone dry, but they left me untied. Qwan, however, wasn't so lucky. I was the only one who could untie him. I smiled when I realized our roles were reversed. Now, I'm the one in control of Qwan's soul.

To Be Continued…

In the Field We Play for Keeps

Chapter 1

A lot had been going on in Qwan and Number's relationship. Qwan was getting greedier and meaner by the minute. The last two jobs they did, Qwan had been on some sneaky, grimy shit, pocketing extra profit. He had Tammy lining other dealers up for him to rob behind Number's back.

After Qwan lied about getting robbed for everything him and Numbers had, Numbers started to see the change in Qwan, so he started investigating. The more he searched, the more he found out Qwan wasn't really for him. Qwan had taken every dime of his and Number's stash and fucked it up. He wasn't trying to re-up. Nah, he partied it up, drank it up, smoked up it, and E-pilled it up.

Numbers was the brain when it came to moving keys. He wasn't toting his hammer looking for trouble like Qwan. Numbers would rather sell drugs than rob and kill. But, when you let your so-called man call the shots in your life for so many years, it's hard to rock him to sleep. So, now, Numbers was moving sneaky.

All the moves Qwan had been making lately were all the wrong ones. Numbers had a loyalty that no one could have broken, but when his three-year-old daughter told him that she saw her mommy sleeping with her uncle Que while he's gone or sometimes when he's sleep, that was on another level. Numbers knew that when you're dealing with a nigga like Qwan, you have to move carefully. Qwan was on a road to destruction, and Numbers was not in for the ride. They were joined at the hip, but Qwan's greed is what was making them split.

When Numbers arrived at the prison, he got processed and searched. Numbers sat on the no-contact visiting floor waiting to talk through a glass window. When the doors opened and the inmates started to pour in the room, Numbers watched as he waited for his visit. When the last inmate came in, Numbers was a bit confused as to why the person he had come to visit didn't come out with the rest. He sat for about twenty minutes before he heard the buzzer go off again, letting the inmates know their visit had to end quick. Once the visiting room was clear and only Numbers remained, in walked a familiar face that Numbers was not expecting to see.

The familiar face sat down, smiled, and said, "Surprise! My man Junior felt we should talk first."

"Talk about what?" Numbers asked, confused.

"That's on you, son, but whatever business you're trying to do with Junior, you have to go through me first."

"Oh yeah?" Numbers said, as he leaned back in his seat in disbelief. He couldn't believe he was really holding this conversation with Nice instead of the nigga he had paid to come see.

"Yeah," Nice shot back. "You see, up in here, I'm something like an authority figure. You know, niggas gotta ask my advice regarding all kinds of shit. So, Junior stepped to me the other day and said this nigga Numbers, who he don't even know, has been sending him cash money to get on his visiting list. So, then, he asked me did I know a nigga named Numbers. I said, 'Yeah, I know a Numbers very well.' You know in Brooklyn, everybody know everybody, right?

"Hold up. Let me help you find your tongue," Nice said to the speechless, confused Numbers. "You're trying to get next to Junior because it seems you're the only nigga out of your crew that didn't know your right-hand man wasn't really all for you. On top of that, Junior is also the connect for the EMF crew, who has put a bounty on your head for that bread you and your man kept. So, you do the smart thing and seek out Junior, trying to kill two birds with one stone. One is to get word to them that you didn't have anything to do with deading them on their bread. I get it. You want to have a line of your own, and you want your man gone. But, you're too scared to take him out yourself, so you do the businessman move. You negotiate your safety like a businessman would do. Right?" Nice asked as he shook his head.

"I see the pup is trying to stray away from home," Nice continued. "You sure you want to do that? Can you handle a connect like Junior? Better yet, can you handle your man if your plan doesn't work in your favor? I mean, I like the idea of you wanting to have a mind of your own, but after all this time, it became a little too late. Even though you're smartening up, you rode with him for so long that, as of now, your rebellion is meaningless. What would it matter that you're against him now? The damage has already been done."

Before Numbers could respond, Nice interjected, "Let me make it plain and get to the point. As far as a connect, that's not going to happen. What will happen is you're gonna give Bishop four hundred thousand long, and maybe I won't let my city kill you."

"Word? Four hundred thousand?" Numbers repeated.

"Yeah. I think that's a good price to pay for your life. What you think? You see, Toki is a priceless picture. She's my delicate other half. When she's not being handled as such, then that's a problem for me and my whole team. So, I'm giving you two days to get that bread to Bishop, and if you don't, say bye to your family."

Nice got up and walked off the visiting floor, leaving Numbers sitting there looking dumb, trying to figure out where he could get four hundred thousand dollars from in two days.

*****

When Numbers' plane landed at JFK, he went to the parking garage where he had parked his car. Once inside the car, he went straight for his phone in the glove compartment. While waiting for it to power on, he started the engine. Text messages and voicemail alerts came through before he pulled out his spot. But, he only returned the call from Mix.

"Hello."

"Yo, what's up, Mix? I see you hit my phone. I was handling some shit."

"Yeah, nigga, I need to meet up with you and that nigga Qwan tonight. Remember the little situation I was telling I had lined up for us?" Mix replied.

"Yeah, I remember," Numbers said.

"Well, the plane just landed."

"Word, son," Numbers said, smiling from ear to ear.

"Yeah, son. It's going down tonight, so we need to kick it ASAP."

"A'ight, yo. I'm on my way home now. Meet me at my crib," Numbers told him.

After hanging up, he put the pedal to the metal, excited because he just found a way to get that four hundred thou. He smiled the whole way back to the BK.

Chapter 2

The night of Bishop's welcome home party it was cold as shit. Winter had just arrived.

"Damn, Mix, why we park on this dark-ass block? This shit seems like some setup shit," Qwan stated, checking his surroundings.

Living life the way he did, he always had to look over his shoulder.

"Nah, Que, we good. Matter of fact, there them niggas go over there."

"Where? In that all-white Camaro with the B-more plates?" Qwan asked, while stuffing his Glock in the waistline of his pants.

"Yeah, that's them, but, Que, we said no guns," he replied. "Just stick to the plan. Trust me, that's just going to fuck the whole deal up."

"So what, nigga. I'm more than certain they got their hammers," Qwan replied, not giving a fuck what Mix said.

Qwan didn't play fair in the streets. He stayed attached to the only thing he was loyal to other than his pockets, and that was his Glock, which he called his bitch.

Mix knew Qwan behind a gun, with his hot hands, made for the worst nightmare. So, he tried his best to convince him to leave it in the car.

"Nah, son, let's just get in and out," Mix said to Qwan. "Come on. We're not trying to catch no bodies. Just leave it here with our hammers," Mix suggested, trying to convince Qwan that they were good.

"Naw, what the fuck we going to do if these niggas think like us? Fuck that, son. You know I trust no one. No mother, no girl, no sisters or brother, friend or foe," Qwan expressed, while waving his hand to brush Mix off.

"So what's that supposed to mean, son?" Mix asked.

"That means I'm bringing my bitch."

Numbers interrupted Mix and Qwan's debate about him being strapped, but he made sure he was careful with his input because he didn't want to give Qwan any reason to believe he wasn't riding with him no more. Numbers played his role, siding with Qwan like his supposed to.

"Word, Mix," Numbers said. "We need at least one hammer just in case niggas get stupid."

"Listen, son," Qwan interjected. "At the end of the day, I don't know them niggas and they don't know me. Before I walk up in some building in Queens to make a deal with some niggas from B-more without my bitch, that's the day they should bury me alive."

"Que's right, Mix. What if shit goes left? What we gonna do with no ammo? Tell them, 'Hold up a minute. Before you jack us, let us go get our hammers out the car that's parked around the corner?' Nah, we need at least one so we can have a fair one."

Mix did not let up, because he knew the deal was not life threatening. If he felt he couldn't trust his family, then he wouldn't fuck with it. Mix played it safe. If the money was right and the come up was easy, he was with it. But, if he felt death might be the outcome, Mix was smart enough to pass it up. Unlike Qwan, money didn't make Mix.

"Bringing guns was not what we planned. I told them niggas to leave their ammo, so we good, five. If we bring our shits, they might think they getting jacked. We're trying to do long-term business with them. We need to make them trust us enough so they can feel comfortable with hitting us with the motherload, and then we ride out. That's the plan, so let's stick to it."

Qwan walked a little closer to Mix and said, "I've really never been too good at taking orders from another man. I let you slide back at the crib when you got on your Toki shit, but I'm not letting it slide again. I'm bringing my hammer for my protection. I don't know these niggas, and last I checked, B-more don't fuck with New York."

"Alright," Numbers said, interrupting Qwan checking Mix. "Chill. We don't need these niggas in our business. Let's do the transaction and get the fuck out of here."

All Numbers was trying to do was get his hands on that bread before somebody got a hold of his ass.

"Fuck it. Just let me do all the talking," Mix said, giving in to Qwan's resistance about bringing his bitch to the meet and great.

Satisfied with Mix's suggestion, Qwan bowed at the end. "Nigga, you know I'm no talker. That's why my bitch needs to be right by my side."

They walked up on the B-more niggas with their Maryland accent and New York amateur style of dressing. Mix slapped five with his cousin Trap, whose swagger made one presume him to be the boss. Since there were only two of them, the other nigga had to be his goon. He never cracked a smile. He slapped five out of respect, but he never talked. His stare blank and cold, he never showed one bit of emotion, and the .9mm that was sticking out the side of his shirt let Qwan and them know he was not in the friend zone.

Qwan noticed the gun on his hip and automatically thought, *I told this fat nigga at least one of these motherfuckers was gonna be strapped up. I mean, why wouldn't they if they holding a boat load of shit? And this nigga Mix's cousin was iced out, so he had to be strapped coming around me looking like a few laundry bags of money.*

I should bitch slap his fat ass. That's why I follow my own lead. I do as I feel, and what I felt was that I needed to be strapped. I never sleep on a motherfucker. I just hope for the sake of them, if they happen to have a few sneaky tricks up their sleeves, they better make it do what it do. B-more niggas like pumping lead in niggas with no question, but Mix said no weapons. Qwan smirked a little at his thoughts.

After they entered the apartment located on the third floor of the building, they all sat down in the living room to chop it up. The spot they were at was a trap. There was a big 62-inch flat screen television hanging on the wall, a long table, a black leather sectional sofa, a few chairs, a PlayStation, and an entertainment system. They had black shades on the windows instead of curtains. There was not really much to the crib; the apartment was definitely only used for work and getting a quick nut with a side bitch.

Mix attempted to start the transaction by saying, "Let's get straight to business. Okay, so we got four hundred and eighty thousand as previously discussed for ten joints."

"Yeah, as previously discussed," Trap stated nice and calm, almost like he was high on a Percocet.

Trap did all the negotiating; he was all the way business. He made it clear by his actions that he was about his profit. Even though they knew Mix and him had some type of family connections, Trap was strictly business. Their personal relationship was left outside.

"The product is in the trunk of our ride," Trap continued, then explained the instructions on how the deal will go down. "Once we see the money is right, my man will go transfer the product from my car to yours."

As Mix attempted to respond, Qwan interrupted him. "Nah, that's not a good idea for me. I don't follow rules when it's my bread we spending."

"You mean *our* bread," Numbers said, talking up once again.

Qwan ignored him and kept his eye on the money. *Whatever Numbers is talking, he won't be talking long,* Qwan thought.

"This is how we're gonna do it. We all count the money together, and then *I'm* going to make the switch from my car to yours."

Mix attempted to intervene. "Chill, Que," he said. "This family." He tried to keep Qwan at a cool level because Mix saw he was antsy.

Qwan looked at Mix with a look that said, *Nigga, shut the fuck up,* and proceeded to tell them his new plan. "I'll do the switch and leave my mans here so you know we're not about no funny shit. Once I give Mix the call that everything is what you niggas say it is, then we good and everybody's happy. You dig?"

"A'ight, my man," Trap said. "Ain't nobody on no funny shit. I'm always on my money shit. That's just how we always did our shit. But, fuck it. Let's get to counting this bread together."

Everything added up right. So, Qwan grabbed the money off the table, and the goon gave him the key to their ride to do the switch. With no hesitation, Qwan snatched the keys and the money, and in less than five seconds, he was out the door.

"Damn! Only if they know who they just gave their shit to," he said under his breath with a smirk.

As Qwan walked towards the car, he thought, *Who the fuck do these niggas think they're trying to get over on? I guess Mix didn't tell them who the fuck I be. They gotta be some nothing-ass niggas, 'cause niggas know worldwide that I'm not the one to try. How can you sneak me when the definition of sneaky is me?*

Qwan chuckled as he hit the alarm to the B-more nigga's Camaro. Then he checked the trunk for what Trap said was theirs. Once he saw the trunk was full, he switched the work and threw the knapsack of money in the trunk of Number's car. Next, he jumped in Trap's Camaro and left Number's car running with the keys in the ignition. Before he drove off, he made a call.

"Yo, where you at? That shit is in your baby father's whip. All you have to do is jump in it and pull off. And hurry the fuck up before they suspect something and catch your dumb ass. If so, then that's your ass. Make sure you're checking your surroundings and then meet me at our spot. I have something to handle, so I'll meet you there later."

"What the fuck do you have to handle? You going to get that bitch, Toki. Right, nigga?"

"First of all, watch your fucking mouth when you address me about my bitch. All you need to do is make sure you get this work and bread to the spot. I'll see you when I get there. And remember this one thing. This thing with us is more business than personal. Yeah, you get wet as fuck, but Toki is my bitch. So, let's stick to the plan and get this money. A'ight, yo? Now hurry the fuck up," Qwan said before hanging up.

Meanwhile, Numbers and Mix were sitting preparing for death, and they didn't even know it.

"Yo. Mix, where your man at? It's been over ten minutes. What? He got lost going right out front to the car?"

"I don't know, but don't worry. He's coming back to finish the deal. I mean, he did leave us here," Mix said with no doubt. "Yo, Numbers, call that nigga Que and see what the fuck is taking him so long," Mix ordered.

Numbers called Qwan's phone, but it just rang and then went to voicemail. "Damn, son, he didn't answer."

Growing leery, Numbers thought to himself, *"I know this nigga didn't do no dumb shit while we still up here.* Numbers felt his stomach drop and his body temperature rise. He tried his best not to raise any doubt with Trap and his goon regarding Qwan coming back.

Still in the blind and never thinking Qwan would leave

them behind, Mix kept trying to call Qwan, but eventually, the phone stopped ringing and started going straight to voicemail.

Tension grew and niggas eyebrows rose. They got antsy; there was no more laughing and joking. Numbers sat up on the black leather couch that him and Mix were just sitting so comfortably on. His stomach began to do all kinds of flips. As time passed, it was getting harder for Numbers not to show the B-more niggas that he was worried.

Numbers mumbled to Mix, "Yo, what the fuck is that nigga Que doing? Word, he's making me nervous on some G shit."

After ten minutes came and went with still no sign of Qwan, Mix knew Qwan's ass was up to no good. *This nigga is doing some real dangerous shit. Did he forget we was the ones that didn't bring our hammers?*

In a pissed tone, Trap asked Mix, "Yo, what's up with your man? You think something happened to him? 'Cause I know he didn't just take my shit and leave y'all here."

While laughing, the goon said, "Nah, he didn't do that. Nobody's that fucked up in the head that they would leave their mans here to die. This is the part of the game I live for. Time to feast."

With a big-ass smile on his face, the goon showed Mix and Numbers that murder was his life's pleasure.

Responding to their accusations, Mix said, "Naw, something ain't right. Qwan's not that cold-hearted that he would use us as bait."

Mix was in denial. At the same time he tried to convince Trap and his goon that Qwan hadn't swapped them for the cash and the stash, he tried to convince himself that Qwan was not that fucked up in the head. However, in Mix's mind, he started to second-guess the response he had just given.

But what if he is that fucked up in the head that he would abandon us? Mix thought. *Nah,* he said, giving Qwan the benefit of the doubt.

"From the way homie was moving, I knew he was on some funny shit. I mean, maybe it wasn't your intention to dead us, but your man had his own plans. The sad part about this shit is y'all going to pay the price with your life," the goon stated with a devilish look.

Numbers and Mix looked at each other with the 'we're fucked' look because their so-called man left them there for dead. Numbers put his head down and shook it in disappointment, while Mix prayed on his family.

Pulling out his .380 and pointing it at Mix, Trap told his goon to go downstairs and see what happened. Right at that moment, Mix knew that family shit didn't hold any weight in the game.

Numbers whispered to Mix, "You know that nigga Qwan is gone, right?"

Mix agreed, but he didn't really want to believe Qwan would do something so ice motherfucking cold hearted.

Numbers was more hurt than mad. Trying to make sense of it, he put his head down and said, "Damn, did he really leave us here?" As a tear rolled down his cheek, he didn't care who saw it. Numbers' feelings were numb, and at that point, his whole life flashed before his eyes. He repeated to himself, "My brother, my homie, my motherfucking other half. The nigga I thought was the only one who had my back, the only nigga I trusted with my life just traded it in for a quick up."

Numbers was more shocked that Qwan managed to plan his demise before Numbers could plan his. *A nigga that would trade his man in for some cash is the same nigga that would bend over and let a nigga fuck him in the ass for a few stacks.*

The goon came back upstairs with his .45 already out. He cocked it back and said to Trap, "Not only is he gone, but he took our shit, car and all."

Trap turned toward Mix with a look that said, *I'm gonna kill you.*

"Damn, family," Trap finally said. "What kind of niggas you bringing around me? Why would you handle me like that, family? You knew your man was an unpredictable, foul-ass nigga. You should have never brought him around me. Now look at you, sitting here preparing to take all these bullets in this clip that your fake-ass man should be taking. I guess you was the only one that didn't know he was a crab. I read homie when my eyes landed on him. That motherfucker just robbed me with no conscience, and you call him your man." Trap chuckled. "And you was going hard, justifying his loyalty. Now how I don't know this ain't no set up? Truthfully, I found it quite fishy when you said don't bring no hammers, but of course, my goon don't follow stupid orders. He would never let me come to another state to do a transaction without being strapped up. Listen, homeboy, you're fucked up in the head. Man is gone," Trap said, when he peeped that Numbers kept trying to call Qwan's phone, only to get his voicemail.

"Damn, son, I should have known Que was up to no good," Mix said as he prepared himself for what would happen next.

"Yeah, well, that's the way this game was made to play out. In a room full of heathens, good niggas die alone."

"You got to admit it, though. Que played his role to the T." Numbers smirked a little and said, "Well played, Que. Good move. You got me. I guess my common sense ain't no good, because I would have never thought I would be a target in your no-good moves."

"So this is the day you find out your man wasn't really your man all the way," the goon said to Numbers and Mix.

Trap raised his gun, pointed it in Mix's face, and squeezed the trigger four times. It seemed like Trap and his goon let off every bullet they had into Mix, the shots sounding like war. Numbers watched as his family got hit up with them hot ones, one after the other. It was obvious the goon was enjoying himself because Numbers noticed the look of satisfaction on his face. As he let each shot off, he smiled more and more. Once they blew Mix's face off, Numbers braced himself because he knew he was next. The goon spun around and squeezed without thought, and Trap joined in.

But, Numbers was quick. He jumped up, ran, and ducked around the living room, trying to dodge the storm of bullets. He went down when the goon lay on the floor, aimed, and hit him in his ankle. God was on Numbers' side, though, because they both ran out of bullets at the same time. Still, that didn't stop them. They commenced to kicking Numbers' ass. But, Numbers was fighting; he wasn't going to just let them kill him. After watching them take Mix's life and Qwan leaving him there to die without a fucking care, he was distraught. He was hurt, and if he was going out, he was going out fighting.

He went ballistic, uncontrollable on them niggas. But, they overpowered Numbers. After the goon gun-butted him, Numbers went down, and they continued to fuck him up. They wanted Numbers to die from blunt force trauma. He went down fighting, but there was no way he would survive.

Damn, what's up? A nigga didn't even get a chance to kiss my baby girl goodbye. You know I understand and respect the game and the code we live by. It only promises us two things: death or jail. I knew either way, my time was coming near. But, up until now, no one could have told me that my blood would be the one handing me my death sentence. I would have never figured Que to cross me. I guess I slept on him, thinking my homie had love for me. I guess when it comes to money, Que never had no picks. Too bad it took for me to become a statistic to see it. I never thought my life would end this way. My motherfucking right-hand left me for dead for some small change. It is what it is, I guess. Life is strange.

Chapter 3

"Hello."

"Hello, Sweets."

"Hey, Pat, what's going on?"

"Nice asked me to call you."

"Is he okay?" she asked.

"He's fine. He's requesting for you to come see him."

"Okay!" Sweets said, confused. "Why does he want me to come and not Toki? Is she okay?"

"Yes, she's okay. As for why Nice requested your presence, he didn't say. He just asked me to arrange it and to also let you know this is not up for discussion."

"If Nice calls, we have no choice. I think I'm more shocked because Nice doesn't change or break rules. For as long as I've known him, he always bid alone. No visits and no calls other than to talk business. So, his request worries me."

"He has you scheduled for tomorrow. I made the reservations. You will be leaving out of JFK to Quantico, Virginia, bright and early in the morning. Seven o'clock is the time the flight takes off. When you get there, a driver will be waiting to take you to the prison, and he will wait until your visit is over to bring you back to the airport."

"Okay. Do you have the flight confirmation number?"

"Yes, I already sent it to your email," Pat told her.

"Okay."

"One more thing, Sweets. He said not to tell anyone, not even Toki."

"Okay, I won't. Thank you, Pat."

"No problem. Just make sure you make that flight. I will talk to you when you get back."

Damn, I wonder what it is that Nice needs to see me and not Toki, Sweets thought after hanging up. *And I can't even tell her. What the fuck do I do? Should I just leave Toki in the blind and do as I'm told, or should I just say fuck it and bring her with me on the visit anyway since we're all family? Maybe seeing Nice would wake her ass up. But, if I don't listen, Nice will be furious because I went against his wish. I mean, even though we are all equal and we all eat the same, Nice is still the boss. So, a bitch has to go alone.*

*****

The next morning when Sweets arrived at the federal headquarters in Quantico Bay, she was nervous and anxious. She hadn't seen Nice in over a year. And now, after all that time, he broke his rule. Sweets sat patiently waiting for Nice to come out. She noticed his profile and his two long braids hanging past his shoulders. His dark skin was tatted up like a comic book. Seeing Nice in the orange jumpsuit and shackled up like an animal, and knowing his hand didn't call for none of this bullshit, it ripped through Sweets' chest like a two-edged sword.

"Damn," Sweets said when she realized the visit was going to be through a glass partition. Trying not to show her pain, she put on a fake smile.

"Sweets, thanks for coming to see me."

"Come on, Nice. You're my brother. Nothing would have stopped me from coming up here if you sent for me. If you ask me, this is a privilege. You know how you do when you bid. You isolate yourself from your loved ones. But, I get it. I would be the same way. From the deer-in-headlight looks you were getting from the inmates and COs as they cleared the visiting floor, it's like they had seen a ghost."

"I guess they were just as shocked as you, but with a little bit of mixed emotions since I cut their visit short. But, when you gotta find out some things, and you can't do it through the phone or through the mail, you have no choice but to schedule a visit. When it's your family that you live for, you do whatever it is you have to do. You feel me, Sweets?"

"Yeah, I feel you. So what's up?"

"What's up is Tee."

"Who, Toki?"

Nice gave Sweets the 'duh' look. "Who else? Yeah, Toki. What's up with her? I've been hearing some things that disturbed me. One, nobody told me the store got robbed and Ofia died–"

"But—" Sweets said.

"Hold up. When I'm done, then you can take the floor and state your claim."

Nice didn't play that over-talking bullshit. He talked in a low voice. He hated yelling, so any time he sat down to chat with someone, he made sure he spoke first.

"I know Tee is handling shit like I knew she would. Business wise, we up. I heard she handled our crisis like she was supposed to. But, this is not about our pockets; this is about our heart. Toki is in trouble, and from what the streets is talking, none of the family has stepped up. Why ain't nobody making noise? What y'all doing out there?" Nice asked Sweets. He was mad, and it showed in his face and body language.

"Now I know how Toki can be. I know when it comes to these niggas, sometimes you have to force her to see every nigga ain't for her. Don't get me wrong, I know Toki knows how to hold her own, but she's sneaky. So, you can't really tell if she's keeping some shit from you, thinking she could handle it on her own. At this point, motherfuck all that Toki tough shit. This ain't that.

This shit ain't about putting in work for the block, Sweets. This ain't that. He owes money. Go take that nigga's head off," Nice said with bass in his voice. "This is all about family. This is our blood; Toki is us. Ain't no fair ones when it comes to home. You got me, Sweets?"

Sweets shook her head yes.

"Good," Nice continued. "So you already know what it is. Homies life line has been cut. Sweets, he has to go. I know Tee is grown and all, and she likes learning from her own experience. Yeah, at times, that's a good thing. But, when it's a situation like this, we have to *make* her listen. Ain't no beefing when family is in trouble. Now this is what the fuck we gonna do. You know Toki's best friend from school?"

"Who, Ashley?"

"Yeah. Her brother is my bunkie. His name is Junior."

"Huh?" Sweets said like Nice was speaking another language.

"Ashley's brother is my cell mate. He's about twenty-one years old. He's been locked up since he was fifteen. He controlled the biggest drug trafficking ring of all teenaged kids. The worst part about Junior's cartel, they feared nothing. They was trained to run drugs across the country and kill anybody that tried to stop them."

"I never met him. He was in jail when we met Ashley, but I heard stories about him. She said he had life for killing his best friend in the airport," Sweets explained.

"Yeah, so you know of him. Good. Ashley has a parole hearing coming up that nobody but Junior and I know about. Being that Ashley doesn't respect the law, she is being treated like a dog, which included her first parole hearing automatically being denied. I changed that. Pat is going to arrange everything for her to be released after the hearing, but of course, you know everything costs. So, I need you to take three hundred thousand dollars to Pat as soon as you get back, not tomorrow. As soon as the plane lands, I need you to get right to it. Oh, and one last thing, Sweets. Homie got a week to live only because you have to do it carefully because of Tee. I can't afford her getting hit by mistake. Other than that, homie's food. You hear me, Sweets? I want him dead," Nice said with the most serious expression she had ever seen.

It seemed more like he was talking to her soul. He never blinked or cracked a smile. He looked Sweets in the eyes and let her know he wanted Qwan to die.

"I need Brooklyn in a frenzy until he's gone. Sit on niggas; make his peeps speak his whereabouts. If not, leave them, too. Nobody is exempt, and nobody eats in Brooklyn until I'm happy. That means niggas' blocks should be lit up like the Fourth of July. All Tee got is us," Nice said. She saw the mixture of pain and hate in his eyes as he spoke. "So, let's make it count, Sweets. Oh yeah, and this conversation don't leave your mouth until you are with Ashley."

Nice got up without saying a word or even letting Sweets speak. He nodded at the female CO, who escorted him off the visit, leaving Sweets sitting and thinking.

Damn, he's mad and hurt, and he don't want me to see his pain because I know how much he loves Toki. I know Toki and Nice were destined for each other, but they have to put the brother and sister routine to the side and take love for a test drive, Sweets thought.

She flashed back to a time when they were all one big happy family. A single tear fell down the right side of her face. She wiped it away quickly when she heard the CO call her name to leave, interrupting her flashback.

Walking through the steel doors and having to leave Nick behind as she went back out to face the real world hit a soft spot in Sweets' heart. She didn't cry for no one, but the feeling she felt as she walked away from the visit was one she had never felt before. Her sister was sleeping with the enemy, and they were not speaking.

I need to get next to Toki so I can apologize for being so cold instead of being there when she needed me the most.

Sweets slept during the whole flight home. She knew that when she landed, she would have a long day ahead of her.

Chapter 4

Today is the day I say goodbye to lockup, Ashley thought to herself upon waking up. *A day I told myself would never come. Doing that much time as a teen has turned my heart cold. I have no patience for talking. My temper is more like rage. I blame myself for not reacting faster when that bastard was killing my mother in front of me; I blame myself for not building the courage I had to kill him sooner. Maybe my mother would still be here. Yeah, I heard it all before. If it was her time to go, there was nothing I could do to change that. But, now that I'm older, wiser, and have had a decade to deal with life as a motherless child, my motto is 'Kill Now, Motherfuck Later'.*

After my mother died, all I had was Toki. Her and me were more like sisters. She's been there for me since we was twelve years old. Only she knows how close me and my mother were. My mother was my best friend, so I would never regret my actions, not one bit. I never bowed down in the can; I'm not sorry for shit. So, they labeled me as crazy and had me going to therapy, as if I needed rehabilitation. All I had to do was show some remorse, and they would have let me do my bid like a normal inmate. But having remorse for a muthafucka who killed my mother was something I couldn't fathom. So, the government kept me caged up like a wild animal. I hated the treatment, but I would die before I folded. He deserved to die, and the older I got, the more I truly understood that I had done the right thing. Everyone kept saying my actions weren't justified because I wasn't the one whose life was in danger. But, fuck everybody who thought the government was right by saying I was supposed to just sit back and watch my mother die. I did what I had to, and if it was me, my mother would have killed him, too. The difference is she would have killed him before he killed me.

Surprise swept over Ashley's face when she spotted Sweets standing next to the limo while the driver held the door open. Ashley was all smiles as she walked towards Sweets who had been waiting for her just outside of the prison gates.

She has really grown up, Ashley though while admiring the flashy, tall, slim, brown-skinned Sweets, who looked like money.

"I love to see my bitches doing well," Ashley said to Sweets as she gave her a long hug that let her know she had missed her.

"Welcome home," Sweets whispered in Ashley's ear.

Ashley's jet black, healthy-looking hair was cut short in a bob. Her light skin was radiant. Ashley looked like she hadn't aged at all; she still looked fifteen, and she had the glow of a girl that had a lot of beauty sleep. Ashley's beautiful ocean-blue eyes told the tale of a beautiful, heartless, "don't give a fuck" killer that the walls in the maximum prison turned cold-hearted. She was twenty-three and ready for war. She knew why she had been released early, but she didn't think it would happen. Now that they proved her wrong, in her mind, it was on.

"So what's up?" Ashley asked Sweets, as she sat back and relaxed inside the limo.

"We got some jobs to fill. You know how me, you, and Lucy use to do, but this time, it's personal."

"Yeah. I heard a few details, but not enough. So where's Toki? Why didn't she ride out with you?"

After Sweets filled Ashley in on what was going on with Toki, she was stuck for a second.

"Ten years of lockup in ADX Max is too much to even recall. The loneliness, the abandonment, locked down twenty-four hours a day, seven days a week for the past ten years. Every day spent there took a little bit more of my sanity away. It was bullshit. Day in and day out, it was the exact same. The only thing that kept me going was that Toki was out here doing her thing. Her loyalty never wavered when it came to her riding this bid out with me. Even though I denied my visitations, she still kept me stocked with stuff from commissary. Now you're telling me that she's in some shit that might cause her her life? Toki? That doesn't even sound right, Sweets. But, nowadays, nothing is unpredictable. I never thought I would be sitting here talking to you after ten years. Nah, I never even dreamed of it."

"Well, what can I tell you, Ash? The world is full of surprises."

"So where are we headed?" Ashley asked Sweets.

"We're going to meet up with the rest of our family."

Chapter 5

All the infamous gangsters in Brooklyn sat around a table inside an empty dimly-lit damp warehouse by the navy yard in downtown Brooklyn.

"Here's a picture of what he looks like. They say he gained weight, but trust me, when you see him, you will know it's him. He is always screwfacing, trying his best to intimate a motherfucker. But, don't play with him. He's trigger happy, so stick to the plan and do it the way we discussed. Don't give him a second to try and pull his hammer, because it might not go the way we want it to. Then it will be your funeral we plan. He's quick. Once you got the drop on his ass, just let your hammer loose. Use your silencer if need be, 'cause it might be in broad daylight since the order is to kill him on sight.

"Now, for the other nigga, we want him alive and kicking. But, if he gives a nigga a hard way to go, then fuck it. Kill him, too. Once you leave him, pull off slow. If you get caught, that means you fucked up and didn't listen. And you already know the outcome if you bitch up and start singing. You can wait in your crib for my little niggas to come pay you and your peeps a visit.

"And we will be brief with all you motherfuckers," Killer stated.

"Do we all agree?" Row asked.

All the gangsters present at the emergency hood meeting agreed.

"Yeah, well, I ain't going to jail for killing a nigga over a bitch. I mean, who's to say them bitches won't roll on me if shit gets stupid?" The fat nigga was referring to Sweets and Ashley. "I mean, Nice is my man and all, but I don't really put my trust in a bitch. No offense, mama," the loud mouth motherfucker said, talking out of place.

"So what? You snitching?" Sweets asked him. "I mean, you in our meeting taking in our plan."

"I didn't know this was over a bitch, though."

Before Row or Bishop could comment, Ashley was on him. She turned two lips into four when she whipped out her blade and cut homie's lips in half. They bled like crazy. He tried to scream, but his lips were hanging. Ashley grabbed his face and squeezed it as the blood poured out his mouth. She sat on his lap face-to-face and squeezed his jaws as hard as she could, causing blood to run down her hand.

While staring him in his eyes, she said in a low tone, "Watch your manners, boy. There's a pissed-off bitch in the room that controls your breathing ability. So, watch what you say in my presence, 'cause next time, instead of your lips it will be your neck that I slit. And it would please me to watch you die by choking on your own blood."

Row grabbed Ashley's hand. "Chill, Ash."

He and Bishop laughed at the nigga who thought Ashley was a "yes" bitch. Now he knew she killed shit. Before Row let her go, she grabbed his .45 off his hip, and with one hand, she turned back and hit homie in his shoulder. He screamed.

"Now I can chill," Ashley said to Row with a smile on her face.

She handed his gun back to him and left all the gangsters in the room speechless. The gangsters drooled as they watched Ashley's fat ass walk back to her seat.

Row laughed hard because Ashley moved him. The others

all sat in silence for a second, watching how she put her feet up on the desk, sat back in her chair, and pulled on the blunt Row had passed to her, acting as though she didn't have a worry in the world.

Without warning, Killer jumped up and finished the job by putting two in the middle of the fat man's eyes. He fell out his chair. Standing over the lifeless body, Killer unzipped his pants, took his dick out, and pissed on him.

"Killer, what the fuck you doing?" Bishop yelled out. "That's DNA, lil' nigga."

While zipping up his pants, Killer said, "I needed to piss bad, and I couldn't hold it. Saved me a trip to the bathroom. You know kids aren't supposed to hold their pee in. Damn, B. I'm only fourteen," Killer shrugged his shoulders, gesturing that he didn't know any better.

"Yeah, well, have that shit cleaned up, you lil' crazy motherfucker," Matrix said.

Even though Ashley had just met the boys, they embraced her like she had been around forever.

*****

"Lights, camera, action!" Ashley said, while stepping out the limo dressed to kill in her red Herve Leger dress, red YSL pumps, and black mink crop jacket. She was killing them with her hot red lipstick.

"Yeah, it's definitely a zoo out here," Lucy said, agreeing with Ashley.

Lucy and Sweets loved a good party.

"I'm loving being free," Ashley stated as she looked, admiring all the halogen lights pulling into the parking lots and the niggas stepping out the Bentley GT's and Aston Martin, sporting that real bling that real niggas be sporting.

They approached the red velvet rope separating the crowd from the club's front door.

"Which guest list are you on?" the Caucasian brunette asked.

"Whose party is it?" Lucy said all sassy, with her hand on her hip and her rich-kid pout going on.

"It's Kode's party," the doorman replied with attitude, as he rolled his eyes at Lucy.

"Then we on that list."

The doorman, dressed in all black, searched the list for Lucy's name plus two. As he searched, Sin walked up on them.

After taking a double look at Ashley's fatty, he said to the promoter, "No worries. I'ma pay for me and them." He pulled the knot out his pocket and counted off the bills, thinking he was teasing them.

Lucy's thirsty ass stood there watching. Her gold-digging ass wanted him, but Sin was on Ashley's heels. He had already chosen the one he wanted to leave with; Ashley's ass had Sin's name written all over it.

Looking Sin up and down, Ashley noticed the lustful expression on his face. He bit his bottom lip like he was hungry.

Ashley giggled and said, "Naw, we good, honey. But, thanks for the gesture. We don't pay for anything."

The doorman opened the rope to let Lucy, Ashley, and Sweets in. Just before he was about to hook the rope back on the pole, Ashley turned back, looked at Sin, and said, "You can come with us, if you like."

Sin smiled and thought, *Damn, I'm gonna fuck the shit out of that fat ass tonight.*

As usual, the ladies balled out in the VIP booth. Sin tried to impress them by flashing his money every time the hostess came to take their order, but what Sin didn't know was Sweets was the bitch to call a motherfucker out quick, especially if she felt one was being fake.

She said, "You showing your bread. You gonna spend it or not?" She then turned to the hostess and said, "Let me get five bottles of Ace of Spade," trying Sin's hand.

She knew if he was getting money, he could do more or at least match what she ordered.

Sin grinned and said, "A'ight, ma, match her order."

They were partying hard. Ashley and Sweets danced all on Sin.

Before things got too heavy too soon, Sin decided to take a walk around the club to mingle a little and converse with a few gangsters, while Sweets tried to convince Lucy to take some Patrón shots. Sweets tried to convince Lucy to stay with her and Ashley a little longer, but Lucy refused.

"Naw, I can't," Lucy told them. "I got some shit to take care of in the morning, so I'm out. I'll get a cab to Brooklyn."

When Lucy left, Sweets and Ashley took a trip to the ladies' room. As they walked down the stairs that led to the dance floor, they noticed Sin having an intense conversation with a familiar face. Once he spotted Ashley and Sweets, he grabbed Ashley by her waist and pulled her close to him.

"Where you going? You leaving?" he asked her.

Ashley replied, "Naw, we just going to the restroom. We'll be right back."

"A'ight. Hurry up and bring that fat ass back to daddy."

He slapped Ashley on her fatty, and she made a little seductive "Ooooh" sound that made Sin grab his dick. Ashley gave him a little blonde, white girl giggle as she walked away switching her hips.

When Ashley and Sweets got back to the VIP section, Sin was still off in the crowd. So, they poured some more champagne and started drinking, dancing, and enjoying the music. When Sin made his way back to the VIP booth, Sweets and Ashley were dancing on each other all seductive and sexy.

Sin was stuck in his tracks. His mouth dropped open and drool damn near poured out.

"Damn, I was gone that long? Looks like I'm gonna have two pussies in my bed tonight. Damn, theses bitches is nasty," he stated, while walking over to Sweets and Ashley, who were kissing and feeling on each other.

He grabbed Ashley by her waist and pulled her fat, round ass towards his hard dick. Then he whispered in Ashley's ear while licking it.

"Damn, ma, why didn't you wait for me?"

Ashley stopped kissing Sweets and turned around to grab Sin's dick through his pants.

She seductively leaned into him and whispered back in his ear, "It will be enough time for that later."

She let go of Sin's dick after she felt it rise in his pants from her caressing it.

Ashley turned and looked at Sweets. "Come on. We're out of here."

Sweets and Ashley walked off, leaving Sin standing alone looking horny and dumb. Ashley stopped in her tracks, looked back at Sin, and put her hand on her wide hips.

She shifted her body to the side and asked, "You coming or not?"

Sin followed behind like he was hypnotized, thinking how he was about to have two bad bitches in his sheets. Exiting the club, Sweets called for the limo to come around and pick them up.

Ashley and Sin were too busy getting to know each other better. They couldn't stop lip locking. His hands caressed her whole body and palmed her ass, or at least what he could grab of it.

Ashley stopped kissing Sin and said, "Before we get caught up in this fire we're starting, I forget to ask for your phone number. Let's make the switch now, 'cause all that's gonna be on my mind when we get in the limo is your dick." She licked her lips seductively. "Have you ever had a threesome in a limo before Mr.—" Ashley paused, remembering he never told her his name.

She knew his name, but he didn't know she knew his

name. But, he would real soon.

"It's Sin. My name is Sin," he said with lust-filled eyes. "What's your name, beauty?"

"Yeah, that's what you can call me—Beauty," Ashley replied seductively. She had him on that dope fiend lean; he was high off her beauty.

"Now that we have formally introduced ourselves to each other, Sin, I want you to get ready for this ride me and my bitch is about to take you on. When we get back to the hotel for round two, we're going to go down on each other while you jerk your dick." Ashley teased him with all the sex talk. "So, Sin, before we get freaky, let's exchange numbers so we don't forget."

Ashley had him hooked. He couldn't even focus on storing Ashley's number in his phone, so she helped him.

"Let me do it," Ashley said, reaching for his phone. "I can operate these iPhones with my eyes closed."

Sin handed Ashley his phone. He was in a trance; his mind was stuck on what he thought was about to go down. Sweets stood at the curb and looked out for the limo.

As Ashley continued to seduce Sin with her sexual comments, she attempted to store her info in his phone. She looked up from the phone and moved in close to Sin, making sure her lips touched his lightly.

Seductively, she asked, "Have you ever had a black and Columbian girl at the same time before?"

Sin looked like he wanted to bust a nut in his pants. "Naw!" he replied.

Ashley licked Sin's lips and kissed him while still holding his phone in her hand. As Ashley sucked Sin's bottom lip, she noticed the all-black Audi with the tinted windows creeping up on them from behind. She kept kissing him, being real nasty with it. Her focus stayed on the black car. She continued to watch as it got closer. Sweets stood off the crib to get a better view. She reached for her gun strapped on her leg underneath her dress.

Ashley closed her eyes and began to kiss Sin more passionately. Then she stopped kissing him and started to nibble on his ear.

“Snitches get put in caskets,” she whispered to him.

Sin backed away from Ashley with a confused look.

“Bitch, what did you just say?” he asked.

Ashley smiled at him. Then she drew her gun and pointed it in Sin’s face.

Trying his hand, he reached for his hammer, but Sweets’ hands were quicker than his. She was on him with her .9mm all in his face.

“You a little too late,” she said. “You slow, you blow.”

Sweets smiled and turned her attention to the street as the all-black Audi crept up. The driver’s window rolled down, and the barrel of an AK was slowly reveled.

By the time Sin caught on to the ambush, it was too late. As soon as he caught a glimpse of the Audi, lights flashed from the sparks of the bullets busting out the barrel and hitting him in his face. Once his body dropped, Lucy pulled her AK back in the car, rolled the window up, and drove off slowly. Sweets and Ashley stood over Sin and both took a turn to hit him once in the head.

Sweets stood over his dead body and repeated the same words Ashley had spoken to him only moments before. “Snitches get put in caskets.”

They walked away smiling and laughing, leaving Sin laying dead in front of the club from nine shots. The block was deserted because the party was still going on. Besides, nobody would have heard the shots since silencers were a must.

The limo driver met Sweets and Ashley at the corner. Once they got in, they poured themselves a glass of Spade from the mini-bar.

“Let’s toast for making Nice’s situation better,” Ashley

said, raising her glass.

"Word!" Sweets said, agreeing with Ashley. "Stupid motherfucker let pussy distract him. He got caught slipping, so we pushed him."

They clicked glasses and took a sip.

After the limo dropped Sweets off, she sat on her bed and took Sin's phone out her bag to scroll through all of his contacts. She looked through his phone until she came across some texts from Numbers complaining about Qwan. He mentioned how his daughter told him that Qwan was fucking Tammy and how he was glad he got down with Sin when it came to him and Sin deading Qwan on his split from the jewelry store robbery.

I was right! Tammy's is a foul bitch. I should make my niggas torture that bitch! But, first, I have to tell Toki about her fake-ass man and how he was Sin's man. Then maybe she'll wake up, because, as of right now, he got my girl in a coma.

Chapter 6

"Row, where you at?"

"I'm at the bar with Matrix. Why, what's up? You Gucci?"

"I just need to get next to you ASAP," Morgan told him.

"A'ight, yo. We're here. We're waiting for Bishop to come through."

"Good, because I need for all of y'all to hear me. So, I'm on my way."

Morgan raced to Brooklyn to let the family know what Qwan had done to Toki. *I have to tell Row that Qwan was the one who robbed us and that Toki is in trouble. This shit is going to take theses niggas to another level, but fuck it. It is what it is.*

*****

"Damn, Morgan. You came running in here like a rapist was after you," Matrix joked, as he, Row, and Bishop laughed.

Once they noticed Morgan wasn't laughing, their smiles disappeared.

"What's wrong, M?" Row asked. "Why you looking like you just seen a ghost?"

And just like that the tears fell.

I know I promised, but promises are made to be broken. Every time I picture Toki's bruised face, the more I want to blow Qwan's head clean off his shoulders. I can't hold this secret in anymore; it's killing me. I ain't sweeping this under the rug, so fuck it. Here we go.

"I promised Toki that I wouldn't say anything, but Toki is getting abused," Morgan blurted out.

Row looked at Morgan like she had two heads and fire was coming out her mouth.

"What you mean Toki's getting abused? Who's dumb enough to hit her? I know not that nigga Que?"

Morgan looked at Row while the tears continued to fall down her face. "Yes, he's abusing her."

"And how long this been going on?" Matrix asked her.

"For a while now. At least that's what she told me."

"And you're just telling us, Morgan?" Bishop shouted.

"What the fuck, Morgan?" Matrix added. "That's not something you should have hid from us. We family. If a nigga violates her, they violate us. Why the fuck would we want a nigga to think he can mistreat Tee and we not do anything? Nah, that nigga gotta go," Matrix expressed with deep sincerity.

"I mean, I knew for a while, but Toki didn't know I knew. No one told me. I just knew. I know the signs of abuse because I'm a victim."

Morgan didn't like to share that bit of information about her life. The only ones who knew were Toki and Row.

"When I went through that in my life," Morgan continued, "I didn't know y'all. I know when a nigga is controlling a female like I know the back of my hand, but I didn't want to believe that's what was going on with Tee. I didn't know for a fact that he was hitting her, but I knew everything wasn't all peaches and cream at home."

"So what makes you sure now?" Row asked.

"Remember the other night after Bishop's party?" she said to Row.

"Yeah."

"Well, remember I was in the restroom at the diner and

when I returned to the table, I told you that I wasn't feeling good because my period came? Well, that was a lie. Toki had called me while I was in the restroom and told me that he just beat her up and that she needed me to come over, but she begged me not to say anything."

Row jumped up out of his seat. He was pissed that Morgan didn't tell him and that she had lied to him. "Damn, I thought we had a bond. We tell each other everything, and you couldn't tell me that Toki is getting her ass kicked by that pussy-ass nigga?"

Morgan cried harder not only from the guilt, but because she blamed herself for pushing Toki into Qwan's arms. She also felt fucked up because she had never lied to Row.

"She asked me to come alone," Morgan said through her tears.

With anger in his voice, Row said, "I don't give a fuck what she said. That's not something you're supposed to keep from us!"

Row was pissed. He paced the floor while gripping his gun, wanting to blow Qwan's head off.

Morgan cried so hard that she started weeping like a little girl. Her heart was torn apart and the fear she saw Toki had for Qwan was really fucking her up.

Toki's known to be a rider, the girl with the strong will to control her life. But, now, she's a victim of abuse, and it's all my fault.

"Damn, Morgan, you should have said something or took me with you," Row told her.

"Listen, if I had taken you with me, she would have never told me anything else. And when you are in an abusive relationship, your trust level is low. You start to think the world is against you and nobody is for you. You start to isolate yourself from the world, which only makes your world revolve around your abuser. You become accustomed to the hits and verbal torture; you think it's the way life was planned out for you. You start to believe you were made to be an example of what can happen if you let a man control you. But, in Toki's case, she's not letting him just hit on her; she's fighting back. And that's what I'm more scared of, because one wrong blow, and I can see Qwan blowing her brains out. We all know Toki is not backing down, but when she has no protection and she feels like no one loves her, it's hard to defeat the man that controls her. The more he puts it in her head that we don't love her, the more submissive she becomes to him, but the reality of it is, she needs us now. The most important thing to do is show Toki that she got us. In her condition, it's her feelings that are fragile, not her jaw. So, when she asked me to come alone, I had no choice. Because if not, she would have never told me anything, and the next time we would have seen her, it might have been in the paper."

"Why didn't Toki just shoot him?" Bishop asked.

"He took her ammo. Besides, before we got locked up and found out who the real Qwan was, she was still in love with him, in my opinion."

"So that means what?" Bishop said.

"That means it would have been harder to push his shit back when she still had a soft spot in her heart. However, the detectives showed us the tape from the night we met him in the club, the night Cookie Carter was killed."

"Cookie Carter?" Bishop yelled.

"Yeah, you know her?" Morgan asked.

"Not personally, but while I was in the can, I heard some nigga from the A had hired some niggas in New York to knock her off. I heard her husband was in a great deal of debt, so they took his wife's life as payment. But, I didn't think about it again until the shit actually happened and I saw it on the news with my own eyes. I knew where it came from. I just didn't brother to find out who they paid for it. So Que was the lucky goon, huh?" Bishop said sarcastically. "That's why they hit him with all them bricks when he came home. Wow! Shit makes sense. So Toki was the next hit on his list."

"From how I take it, Bishop, yes," Morgan said. "But his plan went left when he fell in love with her. It seems the more he took a loss, the more he took it out on Toki."

"Yo, Morgan, did you say y'all were locked up? When, how, and for what?" Matrix asked.

"That same morning around seven. The pigs kicked in Toki's door looking for Qwan. They had a warrant; they came in swinging their AK's, screaming and yelling for us to get down on the floor. Toki and me were in the living room when they came in. We got down on the floor while they ransacked the crib. I asked Toki was there anything in the crib, and she said nothing they could find, but my dumb ass forgot I had my hammer on me. So, she faked having an asthma attack so I could convince the officers to let me go get her pump from the glove compartment in her car. Me acting like she was really dying, I ran up ahead to hide the hammer underneath the seat before pulling out my asthma pump. After Toki recovered from her *fake* asthma attack, the captain, which was the same captain that questioned us at the club the night Cookie was killed, talked to us again. So, after a few hours of them searching and fucking the crib up, the captain came in the living room with a whole brick of our Code Red. But, after talking to Pat and looking at the surveillance tape, they let us go."

"What Code Red? The shit they killed Ofia for?" Row asked.

"Yeah, that Code Red."

"So what? Toki had one in the crib she didn't know about?" Bishop stated.

"Come on now, Bishop. When have you known Toki to leave anything outside that vault other than her two hammers that are now gone?"

"We knew some shit was shaking with that nigga Que,

because a lot of bodies we dropped behind the jukes was part of his crew. But, we didn't speak on it until we knew for sure. The only thing that kept me guessing was the fact that he was Tee's nigga, so I had to make sure. So that means Que's team is food. Yeah, I already have the little niggas sitting on Neck's block waiting for his mother to come outside as we speak. When they catch up to Prince and Flea, they're gonna unleash like beasts."

"We found out a lot when we got locked up, including Qwan has been fucking Tammy."

"Tammy? Numbers' baby mother?" Bishop asked.

"Yeah, and that hoe lined her own friend that night she got killed."

Bishop shook his head. "Damn, son. How you know all that?"

"You know when the pigs want a bitch, man. They pull out the gut busters, thinking the more they hurt her, the more she would want to hurt him. But, you know Toki. She only spoke once, and that's when Pat walked in. I mean, they tried real hard, showing Toki pictures of Qwan with mad different bitches."

"So what are the charges?" Matrix asked.

"One kilo of dope. But, don't worry about that. I don't have a record, so I'm gonna wear that," Morgan stated.

"So what is Pat saying?" Bishop questioned.

"He actually wanted speak to Toki alone while I went in the crib, but we was so tired that when she came in, we just went straight to sleep. She is really in trouble, y'all, and she's hurt because she thinks she let Nice down."

Matrix asked, "So where is Toki right now?"

"In the house. She wanted to rest some more and write Nice a letter. I'm about to go back over there now."

"Yo, and where the fuck is Sweet's ass?" Matrix yelled out. "Get her ass on the line and tell her and Lucy we need some assassinations in Brooklyn."

"Time to put some money on Qwan's head. He wants to violate, then we might as well let the hood know a million is what we paying if he's alive. But, if he doesn't come willingly, like I know he won't, then fuck it. Do him in right then and there. Let's make this happen," Bishop instructed.

"Yo, when you get with them little niggas, let them know it's code red, sound the alarm. There's money to be made in Brooklyn for the capture of a few grimy-ass niggas," Row stated as they all left the bar.

Row went with Morgan, and Bishop went with Matrix.

Chapter 7

"Row, ain't that Flea and Prince in the courtyard?" Killer asked, as him, Row, and Morgan sat in a parked car across the street from Brevoort Projects.

"Yeah, that's those niggas."

"So what's up? You ready to do this?" Row asked Morgan, while sliding on some black leather, dirt bike gloves.

"Yup," Morgan replied as she screwed on her silencer.

As they got out the car, Row threw his keys to Killer. "Yo, lil' nigga, I'll meet up with you later."

Row and Morgan jumped on Killer's KLR dirt bike. Once their helmets were on, Morgan gripped her .45.

"Let's make this count," she said.

Row drove off into Brevoort Projects where the old timer's winter basketball game had taken place earlier that day. Row drove the bike on the court, making a movie real quick with a few 360's, a couple of wheelies, and a lot of burning rubber. Once the court was smoky enough, Morgan aimed at Prince and Flea. Their bodies dropped when she squeezed the trigger. It happened so fast those niggas never saw it coming. By the time the smoke cleared and the crowd of people realized a double homicide had just been committed right before their eyes, Row and Morgan were already out of sight.

*****

Hands, Fingers, and Killer jumped in an all-black Ford Expedition and crept down Shaffer Street heading to Crown Heights. Nice' gave an order: *Everybody's body drops until Toki is found.*

"This nigga must be on a different type of high. If he knew what kind of war he started, he wouldn't want to breathe. Fucking nigga don't want this beef," Hands said, biting on his bottom lip as he loaded his clip. "Nigga can't handle what's in store for him and his peeps."

"I hope we catch a few niggas snoozing on his block, thinking shit sweet, because I'm in the dropping bodies mood," Fingers said, while pulling on the blunt he had in his mouth as he sat in the back of the truck loading his extended clip. "Niggas disrespect; now we gonna do him in."

When they approached Qwan's block, it was definitely cold out, but the block was packed. Niggas were dropping like flies, and every hood nigga was trying to find out what happened and get descriptions. Some niggas, who were holding a dice game in the middle of the street, a few nigga's poured liquid out for the homies that had already fallen. For the boys, it made for the perfect ambush Brooklyn would ever witness. The boys circled the block a few times just to make sure they had a few different openings to get away.

"Yo, son. I know Nice sent the word to always use your silencers, but what good is making a movie if nobody can see or hear the shit? Nah, fuck it. Let's pull off a west coast drive-by," Killer said.

"A drive-by?" Hands repeated.

"Yeah, like them niggas be doing out in Cali."

"Drive-by for what?" Fingers asked. "We don't need to when we got infrared beams and silencers on our shits. We can sit here and pick them motherfuckers off one by one without breaking a sweat."

"True, but this is what we live for. If we gonna send a

warning, I want them to know the crew is not having it. We drilling shit, period," Killer said.

"Fuck it. Let's just bury this block. I'm gonna use my silencer. Y'all niggas can do whatever. I like the way my shit spit," Fingers replied.

"If you really want to make a movie, then use the AK," Hands said, handing it to Killer.

"Okay, let's make it rain," Fingers said, then got out and bent down behind the mailbox that sat on the corner. He aimed at his target, a nigga betting in the dice game. Once he had a clear shot, he squeezed and said, "Wherever there's a red dot, a body drops."

"Man down!" Hands shouted when Fingers dropped his target with a headshot.

Killer jumped out the truck, letting that AK go like Rambo. His little ass had that pipe in control as he walked all cocky, letting his shit vomit, dropping whoever he felt.

Hands followed suit. It was like a domino effect.

As they cleared Que's block, Killer said, "Fuck west coast in BK. We aim to hit a nigga, you heard?"

Then he slapped five with Hands before they hopped in the truck and drove off, leaving Que's block in complete pandemonium, not knowing what earthquake had just shook them.

*****

"Yo, Lucy, where you at?" Ashley asked.

"I'm on my way home. Why? What's up?"

"Toki's missing."

"What!" Lucy yelled through the phone.

"Toki's gone, bitch! Meet us at the crib."

They both hung up without saying goodbye. Lucy lost focus, but she moved fast when her Audi swerved over into the other lane heading straight toward an oil tanker.

"Damn, Toki got me fucked up," Lucy said, realizing she almost lost her life. "I'm killing this nigga. No more chances.

That nigga is out of here. If he did anything to Toki, I'm gonna make him pay."

When Lucy pulled up to the house, Ashley and Sweets were already in front. She parked her car, loaded her nine, and put it in her Berkin bag. Dressed in an all-black cat suit and all-black spiked motorcycle boots, Lucy hopped out her truck.

"So what's up?" Lucy asked as she approached them, ready for whatever.

"Where's everybody at?"

"Out kicking in doors looking for Toki, But, if the feeling I'm getting is right, then I know where she is. I can feel her," Ashley replied. "I bet my life if we go back to New Jersey and sit on her block, Mr. Que is going to pop up, because this is all over greed, and Que knows Toki has the key to the treasure. If he's gonna kill her, he's gonna do it in her house, thinking she will give him what he wants."

"Toki's not doing that," Sweets said.

"Yeah, you right," Lucy agreed. "So that means our sister is going through hell until he kills her. She's not giving up Nice's cash. Her loyalty to Nice is on another level, like some husband and wife type shit. It's until death between them. Toki's not giving in to Qwan. She will never be the cause of Nice's setback. Naw, Que is going to have to kill Toki, because she's not going to fold."

*****

Meanwhile in Flatbush, Brooklyn...

"Yo, nigga, where you at?"

"On the block. Why? What's up?" Neck replied.

"Prince and Flea got popped in the park at the game," his worker informed him.

"When?"

"A few hours ago."

"Who did it?" Neck asked.

"I don't know. They said it was some niggas on a bike.

They hit both of them lil' nigga's using silencers."

"They in the hospital?" Neck asked.

"Nah, son, they dead, laid out. Head shot. I was trying to hit you, son, to find out what the fuck was going on? First, Joke gets laid out in front of the funeral home after Shaunie's funeral. Then I heard Sin was found shot the fuck up all in his face and shit in front of the club. Son, shit is getting spooky out here," the worker said.

"Word."

"From what the streets are saying, it was retaliation for the jewelry store getting robbed and the owner getting killed. I heard they sent the word. Anybody that was in on the juke or knew about it is a dead man."

Neck paused for a second. "Yo, have you seen that nigga Que? I've been hitting him up, but his shit's been going straight to voicemail."

"Naw. I was hitting the nigga up myself, but like you said, only voicemail."

After ending the call, Neck's mind flooded with thoughts. *If Killer and them was in fact the ones that killed Flea and Prince, then Nice sent that message for me. Damn, I wonder where that nigga Que is? Niggas is just dropping like flies. I gotta get to my crib, pack up some shit, get my stash, and bounce until shit smoothes out. I think I know what storm just hit Brooklyn. Nice got word that I was in on the jukes.*

"Damn! What the fuck?" Neck said, as he jumped in his car to go get his stash so he could flee Brooklyn before a member of the family got next to him.

When Neck pulled up in front of his crib, before getting out the car, he looked around to make sure everything looked the same as it did any other day. The corner store had the two usual drunks holding up the wall, and all the cars were familiar to him.

"A'ight. So far so good," Neck said as he exited his car.

He hit the alarm and looked around once more before

walking in his building.

All I gotta do is pack my knapsack with my stash. Fuck clothes; I can buy whatever I need when I get to where I'm going. As of right now, all I need is my money.

He put the key in the door. Before he unlocked it, he looked up and down the stairs to make sure he was not about to be ambushed. When he saw he was good, he unlocked the door, entered his dark crib, and hit the lights.

"Welcome home."

Neck lost his breath. He knew his escape from death was not going to happen. He saw Matrix sitting on a crate with his dreads in his face, with Bishop standing beside him wearing a black hoodie. Bishop's head was down, and he stared at Neck like the Grim Reaper. His eyes told Neck that he was about to die.

Being a loud-mouth fuck and a half-ass gangster, Neck asked, "What the fuck y'all niggas doing in my crib, and what the fuck is all this plastic and white sandy shit on my floor?"

"Paint protector plastic and the white sand is acid. That way, it will eat up anything that lands on it. You know, like your flesh, dick, or tongue. You know, stuff like that," Bishop said, sounding very convincing.

"So what's up?" Neck reached in the waistline of his jeans. "You two motherfuckers got this shit all fucked up. Y'all came to my door with this shit! I got a wife and kids. I know y'all can't be that stupid!" Neck yelled, thinking his words would shake them.

He was reaching, but he had no wins. So, he bluffed and they let him.

Neck saw their calmness and played on it. "How the fuck y'all even get in my crib? Where's my wife and kids?"

Neck's baby's mother walked in the living room and said, "I called them."

"Why? What happened?"

"Nothing major. No need to worry, baby daddy. They're

here to do some home improvement. You know, out with the old and in with the new," she responded in a singsong tone and with the biggest smile Neck had ever seen.

"What, bitch? You must have lost your mind!"

Neck momentarily forgot who he was in the living room with. All he knew was that his baby's mother had betrayed him. He pulled his hammer as he attempted to grab her. Silly move. Matrix was already on him and popped one in his knee. Neck fell down in the chair that Bishop put under him.

"Now have a seat," Matrix said calmly as Neck screamed and cried like a bitch.

Matrix looked at Bishop, who handed him the zip ties. Matrix tied Neck to the chair, then put another chair in front of Neck and sat in it backwards so he would be face-to-face with him.

"You screaming? Scream louder that. Shit, it boosts my adrenaline to hear a nigga scream like a bitch and begging for his life," Matrix stated with ease.

Neck's baby's mother had the music blasting like he used to when he would whip her ass.

"So where the fuck is your man Que at with my fucking sister? And where's my fucking bread, nigga? What? You shocked? No need to be. You know how we give it up. What, just because we not outside on everybody's corner yelling about how many bodies we dropped, you forgot who the fuck I am? Why would you think you could violate us and we not come knocking on your front door? Luckily, your baby mother was tired of your hits and kicks. So, she made it easy for us. What nigga? I know you not scared. You yelled all day asking who wanted it, and now you scared." Matrix smirked at Bishop, who nodded with a smirk back at Matrix, agreeing with him.

"So what's up? Are we gonna make this death a long process, or are you gonna tell me what I want to know now so I can make it quick. One shot to the head should take you out of your misery quick, because I know that knee is killing you," Matrix said, smiling.

Neck was weak with it, but that's what they expected. He didn't even let them enjoy playing with him. He gave Qwan up quick. He told them everything. How Sin introduced them to the plot on Ball Till You Fall, how Qwan made the blueprint, and how Sin had been plotting since before Nice went to jail.

"I know he hates Nice with a passion to the point where he ratted him out. Word, that nigga killed his baby mother and her cousin in front of us so she wouldn't blow his cover. As far as my friendship with Nice, that shit was genuine," Neck said, trying to be sincere, but who can't fake it when they were already crying and in a lot of pain.

Matrix wasn't buying the plea Neck was selling, trying to buy his life back. They didn't give a fuck about Mix, Numbers, or Neck. All they wanted was to know Toki's whereabouts and have Qwan's head on a platter. And until they found her, Brooklyn was going to continue to be a battle zone. Toki's disappearance turned Brooklyn into Afghanistan

"You slapped fives with the rat; you plotted with the rat; you chopped it up more than once with the rat; and you went along with the rat's plan to rob us. So, that makes you a rat, nigga."

"Naw, son, I'm a G. I don't eat cheese. You can blame me for murder and robberies before you label me a rat. When it came down to it, this shit was all about business with me. With Sin, it was personal. He wanted to wear the crown. He was gonna try anything in his power to gain reign over Nice's empire, and he did whatever he could to take it, by anyone's expense other than him." Neck spit some blood out his mouth and said, "Fuck! A nigga going through all this, and Sin was the only man to gain off his plan."

"Yeah, well, Sin's pushing up worms right now," Bishop said, as he poured bleach on Neck's gunshot wound in his knee.

"Ahhhh!" Neck screamed. "What the fuck? Kill me already. I told y'all what the fuck I know and what my role was in this whole shit. I don't know where the nigga Que is. If I did, motherfuckers, I would have been gave him up. The lil' nigga been wilding. I stopped fucking with him because a lot of the shit he do, I don't agree with."

"But, you agree with him putting his hands on my motherfucking sister!" Matrix shouted and then slapped Neck in his mouth with his hammer, knocking all his front teeth out.

Blood poured out Neck's mouth as he screamed, "What the fuck? Damn, son!" Neck spit out more blood. He cried, bitching up. "I don't know shit. I didn't know Que was hitting Toki. I didn't even know they was together until recently when he was looking for her. Word, son! Come on, son! Don't kill me! Tammy is the bitch to blame for all this. She's fucking everybody. She played everybody against each other. She was the bitch that brought Sin to us with the fucking plan. She pointed Toki out to Que in the club. She sent Joke to holla at the white bitch. She was the brain, nigga. Her and Que was on some Evel Knievel shit. Word, they was running around like savages, violating whoever. They had no picks."

"Yo, that nigga is sick. When I get next to him, he's gonna die slow," Bishop stated.

"So where that bread at?" Matrix asked Neck.

"I don't know. I never got shit out the jukes. Sin took all that shit. Him and Numbers deaded Que, and acted like Sin robbed them both. But, in reality, Sin robbed everybody," Neck cried out, weeping like a bitch.

"Word," Bishop said with a big-ass smile.

He shot Neck in his shoulder as he moved in close to him. Neck screamed, begging for them not to kill him.

"Fuck all that shit. I don't give a fuck about y'all niggas killing each other. Who gives a fuck who y'all nasty niggas is fucking? Where's my motherfucking sister?" Bishop asked, as he grabbed Neck's dick and pulled it, causing Neck to scream out in pain.

"Que got her!" he said. "He's going to meet Tammy to split the money from him and her trading Mix and Numbers' life in for an up. Then he said he was leaving Brooklyn and Toki must go with him."

Bishop yanked his dick harder. Neck screamed louder.

"Please, that's all I know. Please, son," Neck begged, while sitting in the chair half dead from the pain. "Please don't kill me. I told you everything I know and what I was in on."

Neck pleaded, but they weren't hearing him.

"Come on, son! I got kids! I'm not ready to die! What? I got money," he told them, trying to buy his way out of the unhealthy situation he was in. "You can have all that shit, my jewels and all. And I got a few bricks. If you let me live, I will leave Brooklyn and you'll never see me again. You can keep all that shit," Neck cried out in pain.

"Yeah right, nigga. Your ass will find your way back here, kicking my ass and getting into everybody's business but your own. Truth be told, Neck, you can't change no more than I can. So, your ass gotta go, nigga, and ain't no way around it."

"That's the game. Take it like a man," Neck's baby's mother told him.

Neck was drained and dying slow. Bishop and Matrix made sure they gave him a beating on his way out.

Once Neck gave them all he knew, Bishop cut his dick off with a weed whacker. Neck screamed so loud that Matrix had to put his lights out. One shot between his eyes stopped the screaming.

"Shut the fuck up, you bitch-ass nigga," Matrix said when Neck's head drop. He was dead.

Neck's baby's mother smiled as she watched the acid eat

away at her baby's father little dick. Matrix and Bishop left her to clean up the mess, which she was glad to do because she got to keep all the shit Neck offered Matrix in exchange for his life.

"Karma is a bitch and she's showing her ass in Brooklyn," Neck's baby's mother said, while looking at the body of the man who had once been her only love, who had turned into her abuser. And now he was just a dead-ass nigga.

She shook her head, smiled, and began to clean up the mess.

*****

"Damn, bitch! Hurry up! We gotta go!"

"I'm coming," Juno said to Tammy, as she came in the room stuffing a few pieces of jewelry in her bag, including three diamond chains and a watch.

"Damn, bitch. Where you get that shit from?" Tammy asked Juno.

"Oh, that's my security," Juno stated, smiling at Tammy. "I took it out of Que's stash when they robbed Ball Till You Fall. He came to my house that night, and while his ass was drunk and knocked out, you know me, I sneak theft him. He never liked leaving shit at home because he was putting up a front for that bitch, Toki, acting like he was a drug dealer and not an infamous robber. So, most of the shit came here," Juno said, smirking.

She was being sarcastic because she knew Tammy had sucked her baby's father's dick, but she didn't care. What they were doing was all about business. That was her way of getting Qwan back for all the hospital trips she took because of his hits.

"Well, come on, bitch. We gotta go. I have to go pick my daughter up, so I'm gonna take you to your mother's first so you can get your daughter," Tammy told Juno.

They were in a state of bliss, thinking about what they were going to do with their share. Tammy was a snake, and she knew it. Tammy could live with setting her friends up, even if it cost them their life. Tammy knew the way she was living was foul, and she knew at any moment she could have been man down. She crossed everybody in her world, from her brother to her baby's father. She knew she had a casket waiting for her body. But living in the terror zone, better know as Brooklyn, you tend to grow a cold heart towards your feelings. Now Tammy was just living for the moment.

As Tammy pulled up in front of Juno's mother's building, she double-parked, not noticing the all-black Range Rover that pulled up behind her. As soon as Juno stepped out the truck, Tammy looked in her rearview mirror and saw what appeared to be a female hopping out with a hoodie on, creeping up on Juno. Tammy knew the heavy hitter was a girl, because she had a switch that would make a nigga's dick hard from a distance. Tammy watched as the girl reached behind her back and pulled her hammer, preparing to kill Juno. She squeezed, and Tammy watched Juno's body drop right in the walkway of her mother's building. Tammy pulled off slowly with the lights off, trying not to alarm the lady-killer who had flat-lined Juno. Without thinking, Tammy watched as she walked back to her truck and hopped in the driver's seat. That's when Tammy got a clear view of Lucy's face.

"Oh shit," Tammy said to herself, as she kept her eye on the black Range, trying to figure out an escape.

She knew it was a war going on in Brooklyn and that she was in the middle of it. She knew Lucy dropped Juno, but Tammy was confused as to why she didn't kill her, too. Tammy sped up, trying to lose Lucy, but Lucy was on her. They came to a red light. Tammy wasn't a shooter, so she was shitting in her pants.

Lucy rolled down her window, put her finger to her lips, and said, "Shhhhhh."

When the light turned green, Lucy turned left and Tammy

went straight, while letting out a sigh of relief that all Lucy did was warn her to keep her mouth shut.

*****

"A string of murders have been piling up on the streets of Brooklyn. There is said to be no known suspects at this time. The authorities say all the bodies that have fallen in the last two days have been sneak hits. The detective said the only way murders could occur by gunshot without anyone knowing is by using silencers. We're told the guns used for these strings of murders are straight off the army base."

Nice turned off his iPod after he finished listening to the late-night news. He lay on his bed in his private cell. He was the only nigga besides Junior that had a full-size bed in their jail cell. Nice smiled hard because he knew the family was out ripping Brooklyn apart looking for Toki. Now he could sleep.

*****

"You have the right to protect your life."

Toki kept playing back in her mind what her lawyer told her, contemplating on whether she should just end this nightmare by pushing Qwan's cap back while he was tied up in the chair. She sat on the floor of her basement across from Qwan, with her back leaned against the wall and one knee up with her arm resting on it. With Qwan's famous Glock in her hand, she looked at it, sizing it up.

So, this is the only thing this motherfucker is loyal to besides his pockets, Toki thought.

Toki knew she was in a life or death situation, but her heart had her on an emotional roller coaster, making her softhearted towards pulling the trigger on Qwan. Even though he had tied her up, beaten her, and even branded her body with no remorse, she still couldn't pull the trigger. For some reason, her feelings wouldn't bring her to that state she needed to be to pull the trigger on Qwan, even though she knew he would do it to her without a second thought. No doubt, Qwan would have pushed her shit back quick. Toki experienced a flashback of all the painful fights, sleepless nights, and verbal abuse she had endured while with Qwan.

Damn, why can't I just squeeze and let go? After all the shit, he's done to me, I still can't force myself to hate him.

As much as she wanted to and tried to pretend, she couldn't hate Qwan, and that shit had Toki vexed and confused. The reality of it was if she didn't smarten up, she was going to be the one getting carried out her house in a body bag.

They only thing Toki could do to reassure herself that she would win this war was to play it safe, go out the easy way, and pray the jury bought her testimony and found her not guilty.

Fuck, how did I get to this place? she thought. *If he was a rapist or a nigga in the street trying to hurt me, it would be so easy to just push his shit back. But, unfortunately, he is the man I once loved, and now the ball is in my court. I have to make this choice. Who will breathe when this day is over?*

Toki struggled with her thoughts, questioning what the smart move would be, and Qwan noticed. He peeped her getting weak for him, so he played on it.

"What happened, big-mouth Toki, the gangsta bitch? What, you just found out you wasn't built for this? You're a pretender. You was put together by a few street niggas, fronting like you grew up like I did. Fucking fraud. I hate bitches like you."

Qwan continued to verbally abuse Toki. Since he couldn't put his hands on her, he abused her emotions.

"Bitches like me? Really, Que? What about me? Do you hate my loyalty? No! Was it how much I loved you? Nah! It probably was my head game or pussy action. Or was it that I took care of you like you was my husband and the only thing you did for me was put your hands on me? You couldn't break me. That's why you hate me. You was jealous of my will to stand on my own two feet. I caught on to your shit, Que. I was just stuck in the denial state. So, who did you think you was fooling, Que?"

"Fooling you," he replied. "That's who I knew I was fooling. When I first met you, Toki, you thought you was all that, but look how I turned them tables. I wanted to show you that I'm a nigga that can break you, and I did, because you had no clue that I was lining you. Why I hate you?" Que repeated with a smirk, mocking Toki.

"Jealous is a disease Qwan it can even be life treating," Toki said with a giggle, curving his hate. "Yeah, that's it you a jealous bitch. I mean, how could you hate a bitch like me if it's not jealousy?

"Yeah, you right. I was fooled. I never thought a nigga like you would have some bitch in him. When a nigga hate on a bitch, that same nigga will bend over and let another man fuck him in the butt, fucking faggot," Toki shot back.

Qwan had her on ten thousand. After all the time, love, and energy she put into Qwan, he turned out to be a homo on top of him being a foul-ass grimy nigga. She began to taunt Qwan, reversing the abuse.

"With your disloyal ass. That's why Money took you down, 'cause that's all you loved. You never cared about no one, not even your mans. I should have treated you like a bitch and just fucked you in the ass with my .45. You hate me?" Toki repeated, making Qwan laugh.

"That's because me and you were cut from a different cloth. The difference between you and me is that no matter how much you hurt me, hit me, or disrespected me, I would have rather still been the one hurting than you. So, yeah, I would say I'm a fool…a fool for putting your life before mine."

Toki stood up. After popping shit, she felt more certain she could kill Que.

"Why you hate me, Que?" she asked. "Because I'm

getting money and doing what I gotta do? And I have more money than you, and I'm a bitch, not a nigga? You mad because from day one I was walking all over you? That's why you hate me Que, 'cause I'm balling and you crawling. Yeah, if I was you, I would hate me too. You hate me? Well, I hate you. I hate you for every kick, every hit, and every bruise I had to cover up for all my black eyes that at one point I couldn't hide. Come to think of it, I don't give a fuck if you hate me, because the hateful feeling I'm getting towards you I'm enjoying and the more I consume it the more I fall in love with it," Toki said with meaning behind it.

At that moment, her emotions allowed her to hate Qwan.

Qwan laughed like a sick-ass nigga. "Weak bitch, you don't have this life in you, because if it was the other way around, I would have been did it to you."

"Yeah, well, I think we can help Toki speed up the process," a familiar voice said from behind Toki.

When she turned to see her sisters from another mother standing there dressed in all black and gripping their hammers, Toki's heart started beating fast like that of a newborn. Her adrenaline began to rush, as she thanked God for sending her some support.

I love my muthafuckin' sisters, Toki said to herself. *I knew they would be back.*

What really fucked Toki up was seeing Ashley standing next to Sweets.

I love Nice. I knew he would send somebody to save me, she said to herself, then flashed her evil, sneaky, one eyebrow raised smile.

Looking at Ashley standing in the flesh in front of her hit Toki like a .45., and she shed a tear or two.

Ashley, who stood there void of any emotions, said to Toki, "Awww, where we do that at? No tears. I'm sorry for not being here for you sooner." Then she glared at Qwan with hate in her blue eyes.

Toki wiped her tears away. "No apologies needed. You was right on time." Toki smiled and looked at Sweets. "I'm sorry, Sweets, for not listening to you."

"No apology needed. We're sisters. We're supposed to have disagreements. Now the one who should be saying sorry is Que," Sweets said, pointing her gun at him. "I hate you," she said. "I want to set your ass on fire so bad that I'm fucking wet."

"Shut the fuck up, bitch! You pussy! You should have been pushed my shit, but you soft just like that bitch," Qwan said, referring to Toki. "You don't have the heart. You're a pretender," he shot back at Sweets.

Toki looked at Sweets, and Sweets looked at Toki.

"Go ahead. Take one for the team," Toki told Sweets, and without a thought, Sweets let her hammer ring, hitting Qwan in his left shoulder and again in his foot.

Sweets said, "I couldn't stop at a taste. I needed another bite. Sorry, but I had to, Toki."

Qwan's evil ass never screamed. He didn't cry or flinch. Toki started to think he actually liked the feeling.

"Say sorry, bitch, and that it will never happen again," Ashley told him.

"I would rather die before I fold!" Qwan shouted.

"Good, 'cause that's what's about to happen to you," Ashley informed him.

"I'm glad I treated you like shit, and every chance I got, I cheated on you, because I never trusted you. I was never in love with you. I knew who you was before you knew me. You was a hit, Toki. So, you was the fool, not me." Qwan laughed, trying to ignore the pain he was in. "You was so busy on my dick that you let it blind you to the point that you slept on this nigga. I thought you was a thinker. So how the fuck you didn't use that brain of yours to figure out you was a lick that could suck a mean dick? I played my cards wrong, though. I should have completed the job, but I got hooked on your lips and used my dick as my thinking tool."

"Yeah, and now look at you, nigga," Ashley said. "All tied up leaking popping hella shit right before your death."

Sweets cocked her hammer back again and said, "I got it, Toki. I'm just gonna put two right in between his eyes and finish him off 'cause he talks too much."

"Nah, Sweets. This is my fight. He beat me. If I let you kill him, it won't mean shit to me. I want to get the joy of hearing Que scream and the pleasure of watching him die like he's suffering from cancer. That would satisfy my soul, because it was me who he was killing slowly. Now it's my turn to return the favor. I got this, Sweets," Toki said, as she made her way towards Qwan's bloody ass as he sat there looking all crazy and smiling from ear-to-ear.

"Bitch, you don't have the heart!" Qwan yelled at Toki.

Holding his Glock, she raised her hand and aimed that bitch right at him as she walked toward him. She hit him in his chest twice. When he started gasping for air, Toki smiled viciously, as if putting those holes in Qwan's chest satisfied her. Toki shot him again, this time in his knee.

"That was for Shaunie," Toki said with a big smile on her face.

This time, Qwan screamed, but Toki acted like she couldn't hear him. She was in wonderland, watching Qwan hurt like she use to every time she took one of his hits.

The feeling Toki experienced after pulling the trigger was like a slow fuck for her brain. Killing Qwan was driving her insane, and she liked it. Just a minute ago, she couldn't bring herself to pull the trigger, but now that she had, she loved the feeling. It brought on a climax she never felt before.

Damn, I love this feeling, she thought to herself. *It feels like I'm getting my pussy eaten and squirting all in Que's face.* Toki smiled and licked her lips at her thought.

She hit him again in his right hand.

That's the hand he always used to backslap me, she said

to herself.

She hit him in his other knee, and Qwan screamed out like a bitch. The more she made him scream, the more Toki loved the feeling. She bit down on her bottom lip and hit Qwan in his other shoulder. Then she moved in as close as she could get to him and stared deep into his eyes to make sure she spoke to his lost soul.

"You said I wouldn't survive if I left, Que. You tried to use my family to keep me, by telling me if I left you, you would send your peeps to unleash like beast. What was it that you owed the EMF crew, Que? Four and a half of that raw?" Toki asked him, as she pushed his Glock into his stomach.

"I just thought you should know I took care of that for you a long time ago," she whispered to Qwan. "Too bad you was too busy hitting me and taking your greed out on me to see that my loyalty was always on a strong point with you. Que, the crazy shit is after I paid your debt, you stayed out and fucked, while I cried myself to sleep.

"What was it that you said to me, Que?" Toki continued. "The only way I could leave you is in a body bag? You said I was stuck until I stopped breathing. Remember that? So, let me read to you the vows that I wrote for us.

"Do I, Toki, take Qwan to be the fucked-up nigga he is, with all his flaws and evil ways? Will I stick by you through the abuse and your fucked-up cheating ways? Do I promise to let you walk all over me for the rest of our lives, for better and worse, till death do us part?" Toki stated and then kissed Qwan on his bloody lips while she emptied his clip right in his stomach.

He was at the end of his rope, but God let him hold on until Toki let him know he had hit on the wrong bitch. Toki stared Qwan directly in his eyes as she pumped each bullet in him, one after the other. She cried when his eyes closed and his soul left his body. Toki closed her eyes, and experiencing mixed emotions, the tears continued to fall down her face.

She had a satisfying feeling of watching Qwan die, while still having a little sympathy for him, even though he never had any for her.

She backed up off of Qwan's lifeless body and stood in front of him in a daze, realizing she had just killed the man she loved. Toki never knew her life would take a turn like this. She thought it would be a straight ride, but that day proved to her that she would never know the answer to everything. Toki realized that life planned her; she didn't plan it. The key to surviving was to make the plan work for you. Toki's plan was designed this way, and it was up to her to make this decision. Taking the hits wasn't as painful as killing Qwan, but what was she supposed to do? Sit around and let him kill her? Toki only had two options, and Qwan had made that very clear to her. It was either him or her, and she chose her life.

"Stupid motherfucker. Que never had a clue of who Toki really was."

That was the last thing Toki said before leaving Qwan's lifeless body tied to the chair in her basement.

1 Month Later

"Damn, bitch. Ride this dick like a nasty bitch."

"Yeah, nigga, you know I'm a nasty bitch. Give it to me."

"Whose pussy is this?" Numbers asked.

"It's your pussy!" she yelled out in lust.

"Damn, I missed this shit! My dick is throbbing in this nasty pussy. You like it?" Numbers asked Tammy before he was knocked out.

"Yeah," Tammy said, before getting knocked off her knees seconds later.

"Stink, bitch," Ashley said, slapping the shit out of Tammy's ass.

"Oh shit! What the fuck?" Tammy shouted, while trying to cover herself with the motel sheets when she noticed Toki, Lucy, and Ashley standing in front of her strapped up.

"Shhhh," Lucy said. "Don't scream. You'll just make it worse," she warned with a sadistic smile.

"Damn, bitch, it stinks in here. What ran up in your pussy and died?" Toki asked Tammy, screwing up her face to the horrible scent of spoiled fish.

"Yo, nigga, get the fuck up," Lucy said, as she slapped Numbers until he came to.

"Damn, son, you should have made this bitch douche or something before you fucked her, being that you knew we was coming in. Shit, I don't want to smell this stink bitch. It's making me sick. Yo, get this bitch some panties before I throw up," Toki told Numbers.

"Smelling like a dead rat," Ashley added, laughing.

"So what's up, bitch? Happy to see me?" Toki smirked. "Yeah, 'cause you thought I was pussy. You thought you could play fake with me. Fuck my man behind my back and then run off with my money. Nah, homegirl, I don't forget shit. I just wanted to have the pleasure of pushing your shit back."

Tammy tried to speak her peace, but Toki was running too short on time to listen. So, she said fuck it and pushed Tammy's shit. She knocked her head clean off her shoulders with one shot to the dome.

After Toki knocked Tammy off, Numbers passed over that cash and the extras Tammy had stolen from Qwan. Once Ashley checked the bag for the bread and bricks, she smiled at Toki and threw her a head nod, letting her know Numbers had kept his word. The shit was all there.

"So we even right, Toki?" Numbers asked.

"Yeah, homie, we good," Toki said, while she, Ashley, and Lucy attempted to make their way out the hotel room.

Just before Toki closed the door, she stopped, turned around, and aimed her .9mm at Numbers.

"Yo, Toki, what's up? I thought I was straight. I paid my debt, right?" he asked.

"Yeah, you right," Toki said with a smirk. "But, in the game and the way I was taught, right or wrong, you get left, nigga."

She squeezed and emptied the clip in Numbers.

"I heard he was a survivor, but I bet he ain't surviving this," Toki said with That evil smile of hers, before closing the hotel room door.

The End

A WORD FROM THE AUTHOR

Latoya McCoy is my name, but my last name just changed. I grew up in the Bronx in my younger years, lived a few of them years in Mount Vernon, New York, and then I was on my own. Not by force but by choice. Throughout the years of my life, I've been known to be the go getter. If we're rocking with loyalty, then I ride for you, whether friends or family. There's not too much I can say that you won't know when you meet me, so I'm gonna leave you on this note. I'm real to this, I never knew I had this gift, but now that I do, rock with me 'cause I'm about to take over the urban lit.

COMING SOON......

A
WAY OUT
ANIT PROMISE
BY CARLTON LUCK
C4

"SECRET DESIRES"
BY KEVIN FARRELL

www.ingramcontent.com/pod-product-compliance
Lightning Source LLC
Chambersburg PA
CBHW070312260626
47160CB00003B/812

* 9 7 8 0 6 1 5 5 1 9 7 1 5 *